LAST
REDEMPTION

Also By Matt Coyle

Yesterday's Echo

Night Tremors

Dark Fissures

Blood Truth

Wrong Light

Lost Tomorrows

Blind Vigil

LAST
REDEMPTION

A RICK CAHILL NOVEL

MATT COYLE

OCEANVIEW PUBLISHING
SARASOTA, FLORIDA

ISBN 978-1-60809-424-0

Published in the United States of America by Oceanview Publishing

Sarasota, Florida

www.oceanviewpub.com

10 9 8 7 6 5 4 3 2 1

PRINTED IN THE UNITED STATES OF AMERICA

This book is dedicated to Raymond Chandler and Ross Macdonald.

*If I hadn't read about Philip Marlowe and Lew Archer,
I never would have created Rick Cahill.*

ACKNOWLEDGMENTS

My sincerest thanks to the following people:

My agent, Kimberley Cameron, for pulling extra duty on this book at a moment's notice.

Bob and Pat Gussin, Lee Randall, Lisa Daily, and Kat Daue at Ocean-view Publishing for all the behind-the-scenes, and behind-the-glamour, work to get this book published and publicized.

Ken Wilson for continued marketing advice, Pam Stack for thoughtful audio/visual publicity, and Jane Ubell-Meyer for inspired marketing opportunities.

Kathy Krevat and Barrie Summy of the Thursday Writers Group for helping to polish the prose.

My family, Jan and Gene Wolfchief, Tim and Sue Coyle, Pam and Jorge Helmer, and Jennifer and Tom Cunningham for continued support and 24/7 word-of-mouth marketing.

Nancy Denton for an essential early paper clip read.

Bob Buckley for information on court-related legal issues.

David Putnam for information on law enforcement jurisdiction.

Kelly McLaurin for expertise on computer programming.

D.P. Lyle for medical information.

Tim Coyle for deep background on the machinations of Congress.

Bob and Pat Gussin for critical information on medical research.

Any errors regarding legal issues, law enforcement jurisdiction, computer programming, medical issues, Congress, and medical research are solely the author's.

LAST
REDEMPTION

CHAPTER ONE

PAIN IN MY head woke me. Again. I looked at the clock on my night-stand and had to squint way down to make out the red numbers. 4:17 a.m. Another night's sleep cratered by throbbing pain. I knew even if I downed 2,000 milligrams of Extra Strength Tylenol and stayed in bed for another two hours, that sleep wouldn't come and the head-ache wouldn't go away. It ran its course on its own timeline, not mine or painkillers'.

My neurologist's hypothesis: stage one CTE. Chronic Traumatic Encephalopathy. The pro football disease. Medical science hasn't caught up with the disease, yet. A determinative diagnosis can only be made after death. When they saw open your skull and examine the damage a life of violence has wrought. My three years as a Golden Gloves boxer, eleven years of Pop Warner, high school, and college football, plus the half a dozen or so concussions I incurred as a private investigator had caused enough brain trauma to make me a candidate. At least that's what my doctor thought.

Prognosis: dementia and early death.

I rolled over and looked at Leah's outline lying next to me. I hadn't told her about my condition. Not yet. Not now.

My eyes adjusted to the early morning darkness, but they couldn't adjust from their 20/200 vision without the aid of my glasses sitting on the nightstand. I let the glasses lie, snuggled up against Leah, and spooned her. She groaned. Closer to a purr. A drowsy reflex from sleep. I softly kissed her head, not wanting to wake her but to express a love I couldn't contain.

The throb in my head slipped into the background for an instant. Relief that no pain reliever could produce.

I moved my hand to Leah's naked belly and gently rubbed it, then let it rest there. Trying to feel the life growing inside. At eleven weeks, I knew it was way too early. Leah wasn't even showing, yet. But, still, I convinced myself I could sense the spark of life growing inside her. An innocent that'd I'd helped create. A blessing that had somehow come from my mangled life. A second chance.

Our child.

Leah had abandoned the dream of giving birth before we met, and I'd forsaken the possibility of being a father long ago after my wife, Colleen, was murdered.

Leah was forty-one. She'd hoped to become a mother while she was married. She and her husband tried everything, even artificial insemination. Nothing worked. The two times she did get pregnant, she had miscarriages. Both at eight weeks. Now, we were three weeks past that and just a week away of surpassing the three-month threshold when eighty percent of all miscarriages occur.

We hadn't even been trying to get pregnant. We'd talked about marriage over the last six months, but hadn't yet set a date. The day we got the official results back from Leah's OBGYN, we set one. We were getting married in three months.

A condensed engagement. We wanted to be married when the baby was born. I wanted to be fully cognitive. I was forty-one years old. The average life span of someone with CTE was fifty-one. There was no known treatment that could reverse the damage.

Time meant everything now.

The cleaving inside my head reawakened. Thoughts of Colleen wedged against my joy at getting married again. For many years, Colleen's memory had only brought me pain. Then, finally, warmth and gratefulness for the time we had together. Now Colleen was a reminder of my own mortality.

And the fleeting functional years I might have left.

CHAPTER TWO

THE NIGHT CLOSED in on me. I suddenly didn't know where I was. Or where I was going. Again.

I pulled over to the side of the road under a streetlight.

I did know that I was on Garnet Avenue in Pacific Beach and that I was headed to Moira MacFarlane's house in La Jolla. But this block of Garnet didn't look familiar even though I'd driven down it hundreds of times. And I couldn't remember how to get to Moira's despite having driven there twenty or thirty times over the past seven years. Not specifically how to get there, at least. I knew she lived on Fay Avenue in La Jolla. I pictured her house in my head and I knew Fay T-boned into Nautilus Street. I just didn't remember which streets I had to take to get to Nautilus.

The same thing had happened to me two other times over the past month. Not recognizing exactly where I was or how to get to where I was going. Each time, like tonight, I was alone and the incidents only lasted an instant, then I snapped right back on track. But this was the first time my mind remained muddled for five or six seconds afterwards.

Just a fraction of a minute, but an infinite vacuum of panic when you don't know where you are. Sweat edged my hairline. Panting breaths. I got a glimpse of myself in the rearview mirror. Mouth slack. Eyes blank.

I shook my head and blinked. The haze lifted from my brain, and I looked around. I recognized the Wienerschnitzel across the street. I'd eaten there many times as a kid with my dad. Soledad Mountain Road was only a couple hundred yards ahead. I pulled away from the curb and drove to Moira's. Up winding Soledad Mountain. The dog park on the left, houses on the right. The playground of the elementary school up ahead. On past the feeder that led to the street where I grew up. Everything in its proper place. The route now familiar. My breathing settled. A spark in my eyes in the rearview mirror.

Back to normal. Whatever it was passed. Again. But it's echo clung to me even as I drove by all the familiar sites. Something was happening to me, stealing small bites of my consciousness.

I hadn't talked to my neurologist about the fugue states yet. I wasn't ready for any more bad news. But I made my own diagnosis. The disease was worsening.

A miracle baby on the way. Finally, a healthy relationship with the woman I loved. Steady private investigative work where I didn't have to risk my life or the lives of others. The life I never thought I'd live was finally coming together.

But my mind was rebelling. Or fading away.

Five minutes later, I pulled in front of Moira's California Craftsman Bungalow home on Fay Avenue. I pushed worries about my health into the last empty compartment left in my head and walked up onto the covered porch and knocked on Moira's front door.

Moira MacFarlane opened the door and stood in the doorway. All one hundred pounds of her. Big brown eyes. Bob cut brown hair. Swollen lips. Everything about her face was oversized. Too big for her body. But her features meshed together to form unusual beauty. Moira was tiny in stature, but extra large in personality and presence.

Except for tonight.

She seemed shrunken. Even smaller than her five-foot frame.

"Thanks for coming over." She swung the door open for me to enter. Her normal machine-gun voice, lifeless. "I really appreciate this. I didn't want to talk about it over the phone."

It.

Moira had been cryptic on the phone call. She said she needed my help, but nothing else.

The weight of her voice concerned me enough to leave my house on the last night Leah and I would have together for two weeks.

Leah was driving up to Santa Barbara the next morning. Still her home until the wedding. Her interior design business was there. Income that would be missed for the next couple years until Leah felt comfortable handing our baby to a nanny a few hours a day while she started over again in San Diego.

Moira led me into the wood-beamed-ceiling living room over to the beige linen sofa I'd gotten to know well over the years. She sat down opposite me in a wingback chair, gazing down at the wool area rug between us. A large goblet, a quarter full of red wine, sat on a table next to her.

"What's going on?" I asked.

"It's Luke." Her twenty-four-year-old son. She didn't elaborate.

Despite knowing Moira for seven years, I'd only met Luke three or four times. Once had been at a dinner over Moira's home-cooked lasagna. The food was great. The conversation with Luke was nonexistent, unless grunts count.

Luke was a good-looking kid. On the short side and wiry like a rock climber. Brown hair and eyes like his mother, but less pronounced features. The few times I met him, he came off as a combination of shy, aloof, and arrogant. Sometimes all at once.

I'd kept my observations to myself. Moira was my best friend, but we didn't exactly socialize. I didn't socialize much with anyone. Our interactions were sporadic. Our friendship was born out of an irregular partnership built on long hours of surveillance boredom, simmering danger, and quick flashes of life and death violence.

"Is he okay?" I didn't think Luke had been injured. Moira's eyes weren't red with dried tears and she wasn't jumpy as a mother would be if her child was in the hospital.

"He's fine." She lifted her head, but still wouldn't look at me.

Shame?

"Then what's going on?"

"The San Diego Superior Court issued a temporary restraining order against Luke." Each word an effort.

"At who's request?"

"His girlfriend, Gabriela Dates." Moira frowned.

"What's the TRO say?"

"I don't know. It hasn't been made a public record, yet." She shifted in her chair. "All I know is that Luke can't contact Gabby or get within one hundred yards of her. The hearing to determine whether the restraining order should be extended is in two weeks."

"What did Luke say happened?"

"That he and Gabby got into an argument, said some nasty things to each other, and two days later, he was served with the TRO at work."

Had to be more to it than that. If Luke had been physical with Gabriela Dates, he'd probably be in jail or out on bond awaiting trial. That is, if she was willing to make a complaint of physical abuse to the police. Most domestic violence abuse victims won't. In the beginning.

"And Luke won't tell you what he did?"

"What do you mean, 'What he did'?" Moira snapped erect and rapid-fire energy filled her voice. "I just told you what happened."

"You can't get a restraining order on a whim. You know that as well as I do. There has to be a predicate for a judge to sign off on one." Moira had to see that even in full mama bear mode. "Did he touch her or threaten her?"

Moira was a parent defending her child. An instinct that would burn inside me in six more months. I could already feel its ignition. Something shifted inside me the moment Leah's doctor told us she was pregnant. A humbling and a resolve. My life was bigger than just me now.

"Luke would never hurt anyone. Especially a woman." Sharp, like the blade of a stiletto.

I'd heard that stated before by family members of their son or brother over the years while investigating domestic cases that turned ugly. So had Moira. Ninety percent of the time the family was wrong. I hoped Luke was in the other ten percent.

"I take it you've met her?" Moira referred to Luke's girlfriend as Gabby instead of Gabriela.

"Yes."

"And?"

"She's a lovely girl. Sweet, smart, pretty." Moira let go a wistful exhale. "I was elated when Luke started dating her. He hasn't had many girlfriends. This is the longest relationship he's ever been in."

"How long have they been dating?"

"About four months."

Twenty-four years old and four months was the longest Luke MacFarlane had been in a relationship. A little odd, but the dating world had changed since I was Luke's age. Now Gen Z'ers signed contracts before they started dating and conversed via texts across the table on their phones at dinner. Romance was dead.

And Luke must have broken the dating contract. Or worse.

"What do you need me to do?" Moira didn't call me just so I could be a shoulder for her to lean on. Much like me, she was a private fretter. Reaching out meant she had a task for me.

She grabbed the goblet of wine off the table next to her and took a large swig.

"I want to hire you." She wouldn't look at me again.

"I'll do whatever you need, but this seems like a run-of-the-mill TRO. Tell Luke to leave the girl alone and get on with his life." Blunt, but the kind of advice Moira had given me dozens of times over the years. It worked the few times I was smart enough to follow it.

"It's not that simple."

"It never is when the heart's involved, but I don't see any other options." I wished I'd let Moira's call go to voicemail at dinner. But I owed her. A debt I'd never be able to repay. "Where is Luke now? I'll need to talk to him. I need his address. Also need a list of all his friends. The name of the company he works for and their address. If you want me to talk to Gabby, I'll need her info, too. I'll be delicate. With everyone."

"I don't want you to do any of that."

"Then what *do* you want me to do?"

"I want you to surveil Luke." Dead voice. "I think he's breaking the restraining order."

"Why do you say that?"

"I drove by Gabby's condo an hour ago and Luke's car was parked a block down the street." Her eyes dark with worry.

Shit.

CHAPTER THREE

MIDNIGHT, MY BLACK Lab, greeted me at the door when I arrived home at 10:45 p.m. Leah didn't, but I hadn't expected her to. She had to get up at four the next morning to try to get ahead of the L.A. traffic on her drive to Santa Barbara.

I went upstairs to our room, but saw a light on in the guest bedroom that we were converting into a nursery.

Leah sat in a cushioned rocking chair across from the wall where a crib would be when we bought one. Her long blond hair was twisted over one shoulder. Radiant blue eyes that I thought about whenever I was away from her. The love in them, a warm blanket around my soul. She smiled, but not with the usual glow.

"What are you doing in here?" I walked into the nursery and stood next to Leah's chair, which would become a nursing chair when the baby arrived. We hadn't picked a color for the walls, yet. We didn't know if we were having a boy or a girl. "You should be in bed. Asleep."

"I can't sleep when you're not here." She took my right hand in both of hers. "I worry about you. This room calms me, just thinking about our future with our baby."

I'd given Leah plenty of reasons to worry. In the first year and a half we'd been together, I'd been shot in the face, stabbed in the throat, and nearly disemboweled. But that was in the past. Almost all of my detecting over the last year was done in my upstairs office, tapping on a keyboard or talking on the phone. Now I freelanced for major Southern California corporations conducting employee and executive background checks, among other innocuous tasks.

The work was steady and paid pretty well. Better than the process serving, infidelity, and workers' comp fraud cases that made up the bulk of my former income. But every once in a while, in that old life, I'd take a case that was about more than money, or cheating, or fraud. A case that mattered. Down deep. For the person who hired me and for my own soul. Some cases left scars. On the people who hired me and the people I investigated. And on me. But the work had meaning.

Now I'd settled into a quiet life with a regular income. I had a woman I loved and a miracle baby on the way. But I felt like I was driving with the parking brake on. That my skills weren't being directed at what they did best.

Becoming a private detective eight years ago had been a reawakening for me. It had given me a purpose. A quest. To help people who had nowhere else to go to find the truth. Their truth. My quest. My redemption.

Just the thought of something as mundane as surveilling Luke MacFarlane had sparked that feeling I'd missed over the last year. Moira needed my help to keep her son out of trouble. A case that mattered. One that couldn't simply be filled by the next San Diego private investigator listed on Google if I turned it down.

I was needed.

I had a mission.

I mattered.

Even with my worsening secret condition, I felt more alive on the drive back from Moira's house than I had in a year.

And it was a selfish feeling. My life had changed. I had other responsibilities than just myself and a home for Midnight. I had a
soon-to-be family to consider. To be responsible for. And I couldn't
abandon them.

I'd do my corporate work during the day and surveil Luke at night.
Keep an eye on him and straighten him out if it came to that. The tail
would probably only last a few nights. I'd be back at home full-time
when Leah returned from Santa Barbara.

"There's nothing to worry about." I squeezed her hand. "I went
over to Moira's like I told you. She's concerned about her son and
needs my help."

"But there's more." Leah stood up. "I can tell. Just by looking at
you. Something's changed."

Those eyes could read my soul. Hopefully, everything but the
darkness.

"I'm just helping a friend. It should only take a few days and I won't
miss any of my corporate work."

"I'm not worried about your corporate work. I'm worried about
you. I need you, Rick. I don't want you to get hurt. We have a baby to
think about." She traced the jagged scar along my neck with her hand.
"I know what can happen when you go all in to help a friend."

"I won't get hurt. I promise. There's nothing dangerous involved."
A simple case. Moira needed my help and I had a rare chance to get
out of the office.

"What does Moira want you to do?"

My practice was not to discuss cases with anyone, not even Leah.
Client confidentiality. I believed in it. But that was before Leah had
gotten pregnant. Now, my family came first. By surveilling Luke
MacFarlane, I was stepping back into the world I promised Leah I'd
left behind. She had a right to know what I was jumping back into, no
matter how shallow the water.

"Luke got into a fight with his girlfriend and she had a temporary restraining order put on him. Moira wants me to tail him and make sure he doesn't break the order."

"Was he violent with her?" Blue eyes round.

"I don't think so. He would have been arrested."

"Only if the girlfriend filed a complaint." Leah was from a cop family. She knew how domestic abuse worked.

"There's nothing to worry about." I kissed her on the lips and felt the surge any intimacy with Leah always gave me. "It will be a few nights of surveillance and that's it."

"I pray you're right." Leah turned off the light and led me out of the nursery. She stopped at our bedroom door. "But when you get involved with a case like this, there's always something else after the 'it.'"

CHAPTER FOUR

NIGHT THREE OF surveillance. Nights one and two had been uneventful, but I still maintained a spot in front of the cheese instead of staking out the mouse. If Luke MacFarlane was going to break the TRO again, as his mother feared, he'd end up at Gabriela Dates' home at some point. All I had to do was wait there.

I gripped the steering wheel of my black Honda Accord. Purchased to blend in with all the other ones on the road in Southern California. Luke MacFarlane didn't know my car. He knew his mother's, even though it blended in with the thousands of other white Honda Accords in San Diego. Moira was smart not to try to tail her son on her own or even tag team with me for a two car. Call it woo-woo or coincidence, but in my experience as a P.I. and a cop, some people can feel the presence of family nearby.

Maybe Moira had had the same experience.

My daily headache drifted away as soon as I got in my car to start my surveillance. Maybe activity was the key to staunch the pain in my head. Or maybe being forced to concentrate on old skills glossed over the pain that was still there.

My instincts were sharp. No more clouded brain. For the third night in a row, I knew where I was and what I was doing, and the adrenaline spike along my spine reminded me that even with a child on the way, a woman I loved sharing my bed, and a damaged brain, I was once again doing what life had molded me to do. Waiting for something to happen. Waiting to react as quickly as a reflex. No decisions to mull over. Find the truth no matter what by any means necessary and make justice be done.

Gabriela Dates lived in a condo on La Jolla Boulevard. Owned it. A 1.4 million-dollar unit with views of the ocean from a rooftop deck. She was twenty-five years old and the mortgage was soley in her name. I studied the wrong major in college. Hers had been computer science at Stanford. Graduated at twenty then got her PhD in genetics at Palo Alto, as well, by age twenty-three. A big brain. She worked for Sequence Corp, which dealt with DNA sequencing. Heady stuff, and, although Gabriela had only worked there for two years, she was a team leader for one of their research pods.

I learned through internet searches that Gabriela's mother's family were fourth-generation La Jollans and owned substantial developed parcels in town. Her father was a self-made millionaire restaurateur. He owned a chain of high-end, Californiafied pizza joints called Bernie's Brick Oven Pizza. I could speak for the quality of the pizza. Good stuff.

Hard work was in the Dates gene pool, and Gabriela had accomplished a lot at a very young age. She had good looks to match. Dark hair. Naturally beautiful. Tan without the all-day-at-the-beach look. Intelligent brown eyes that, despite her youthful beauty, made her seem, if not exactly look, a decade older than her twenty-five years.

I understood Luke's attraction.

A black 2019 Mazda 3 parked in front of Gabriela Dates' condo complex at 8:22 p.m. The same car and color that Luke MacFarlane drove. Well within the hundred-yard line of demarcation of the restraining order. I was on the other side of the boulevard and couldn't see the license plate to check it against Luke's. Didn't need to. Five seconds later, he stepped out of the car and walked toward the complex.

Violation.

A first-time offense is a misdemeanor with a.$1,000 fine and up to a year in the county jail. Normally, I'd take a picture of a target violating a restraining order. But nothing about this case was normal. Moira would take my word about what I saw. Neither of us wanted photographic evidence that could later be used in a court of law.

I hopped out of my car and ran across the divided road. Usually, I'd be working for the victim and keep my distance gathering information that would help put the harasser behind bars. But Moira, not Gabriela Dates, had hired me. She hadn't told me to intervene, only to report back to her on what I observed. I guess she hadn't considered that Luke would confront Gabby and not just spy on her. I couldn't take the chance to see what he might do. Not the son of my best friend.

The entrance to the complex was gated, surrounded by a black metal picket fence. I heard the gate click shut as I approached the sidewalk. Gabriela Dates' unit was to the left of the gate. I saw the back end of Luke enter through a door just as I hit the sidewalk.

But he hadn't entered Gabriela's unit. He'd gone inside the one across from hers.

CHAPTER FIVE

LUKE MACFARLANE LIVED in Solana Beach, fifteen miles up the coast from La Jolla. If he hadn't entered the complex to harass Gabriela Dates, what was he doing here?

A stone column next to the gate had an intercom and a keycard reader on it, along with a keypad full of numbers. Luke must have had his own keycard or knew the gate code. My instinct was to take action. I could press numbers on the keypad and hope someone answered who I'd tell I had an Amazon delivery and get buzzed into the complex. But what would I do once I was inside? Knock on a stranger's door and tell whomever answered that I wanted to talk to the young man who just entered their condo? With no badge or authority to do anything?

I went back to my car to continue the surveillance. Wisdom with my ever-advancing age? Growth? Maybe. I'd take it.

I pulled up a pay real estate website on my phone to try to find the owner of the unit across from Gabby Dates. Linda Rose Holland. She bought the condo four years ago. What did Linda Holland have to do with Luke MacFarlane?

I searched for Linda Rose Holland on a people finder website and got a hit. Her main residence was listed in Encinitas, which was only a few miles north of Solana Beach. Was geography the connection between her and Luke? Because nothing else made sense. Linda Holland was forty-four years old. The same age as Luke's mother. She was the founder of a charity called A Hand Up and married to Scot Sandstrom, a forty-eight-year-old venture capitalist.

I called Moira.

"What did you find out?" Her rapid-fire greeting.

"Luke just broke the restraining order, but he didn't interact with Gabby to do it. In fact, I doubt she even knows he's within a hundred yards of her."

"What?" More a command than a question.

I told her what I'd seen over the last five minutes and the little I'd learned about Linda Holland, the owner of the condo across from Gabriela Dates.

"You ever heard of Linda Holland?" I asked after I finished the recap.

"No." I could hear Moira's own question in her answer.

"How about Scot Sandstrom?"

"Nope, I've never heard of him either."

"Well, do you want to continue to pay me to track your son or do you think it's finally time for you to have a sit-down with him?"

Moira never had any trouble taking issues head-on, whether they had to do with me or cases we worked together. Her reluctance to confront Luke surprised me. But I'd kept that to myself until now.

"It's not that simple. We haven't talked since he told me about the restraining order." A long release of breath that sounded like a broken pressure valve. "I didn't take it well."

"That's understandable. There's no right way to handle something like that." I had no idea. Maybe raising a kid meant you winged it and hoped for the best. And sometimes winging it meant your own emotions got the better of you.

Though still Moira's firstborn and only born, Luke MacFarlane wasn't a child anymore. He was a twenty-four-year-old man who had broken a restraining order handed down by the Superior Court of San Diego.

"But he broke the TRO." My ignorance in child-rearing didn't mean I'd stay quiet when I thought my best friend was making a mistake. "Right now, nobody but me knows that. You need to talk to him before he does it again and someone else finds out and his life turns to shit."

"He's the only family I have left. Things are touchy between us right now."

"What you want me to do?" Moira had slashed a line in the sand. Her and her son on one side. Family. Me and the TRO on the other. I was done taking sides.

"Keep an eye on Luke tonight and tell me if he goes over to Gabby's and when he goes home." A burst of air. "If he goes home."

"Roger." I pulled the phone from my ear and moved my thumb to the *end call* button, but heard Moira say my name. I raised it back to my ear.

"... I really appreciate this."

"I'll find out everything I can."

"I know Luke can come off as aloof sometimes, but it's a coping mechanism. His whole life changed when his father died. I tried to fill the void, but ..."

I thought of Leah and my hand on her belly and could already understand Moira's pain.

*   *   *

I watched the front of the condo complex through binoculars from my car across the street. Switching views between unit one and unit four, pondering what the situation really meant. None of it made sense. Luke gets served with a temporary restraining order and breaks it to go inside a condo owned by a forty-four-year-old woman directly across from his girlfriend who requested the TRO?

Was he spying on Gabby Dates from across the way? With the approval of Linda Holland? Was the owner of the condo even there? She had a second home in Encinitas with Scot Sandstrom. A first home, really. As best I could tell, she was still married to Sandstrom. Had they separated? Or was Luke subletting the condo from her so he could stay creepy close to Gabby?

What the hell was going on?

At 9:33 p.m. a white Tesla swooshed into a parking spot a couple ahead of Luke's in front of the condo complex. A man in his late thirties got out of the car and walked toward the entrance. Thin, an inch or two over six feet. Dark hair. Blue jeans and a tweed sports coat. Looked like a college professor.

He stopped at the gate and punched the keypad, then waited. Someone must have buzzed him in because a couple seconds later he pushed open the gate and entered the complex. Unlike Luke MacFarlane, he didn't have a key or the code to open the gate on his own.

Once inside, the man went directly to the front door of Gabby Dates' home and knocked on it. A second later, the door opened and Gabby smiled at her visitor and let him in. A smile that could melt the heart of any twenty-four-year-old pining for his first girlfriend. Or anyone else. Gabby was attractive in her photos. Live, she was stunning. And apparently, she'd already moved on from Luke. Maybe that was the impetus for the temporary restraining order.

Did Luke know about Mr. Preppy? Had that been the reason for the argument and subsequent TRO on Luke? Had he seen the man enter Gabby's condo? What would he do if he did?

I targeted Linda Holland's condo, and movement in the upper part of the lenses caught my eye. On the rooftop deck. The back of a man's head and shoulders. The man's hair was dark and I guessed it was Luke. Two seconds later, a woman appeared. Blond and taller than the man. Again, just her back. Linda Holland? The woman's hair color matched that of the photo I'd seen of Holland online.

The two walked toward the back of the deck, and I lost sight of them. I swung the binos between the roof of Linda Holland's condo and Gabby Dates' front door. No movement from either for a solid ten minutes. Finally, the man and woman on top of Linda Holland's condo reappeared, walking back in my direction. Even in limited light, I could tell the man was Luke. The woman appeared to be at least fifteen to twenty years his elder and looked like the photo I'd seen of Holland.

They disappeared as they approached the edge of the roof. They must have gone back inside. Why had Luke broken his restraining order to visit a woman twenty years older than him?

My simple surveillance case had taken an odd twist.

CHAPTER SIX

TEN O'CLOCK CAME and went. Luke MacFarlane remained inside condo number 4. The woman I assumed was Linda Holland had to be in there with him. What were they doing? Talking? Not talking? Maybe this was a Spring/Fall romance.

The front door of Linda Holland's condo opened at 10:37 p.m. and Luke emerged. His face turned toward Gabby's front door.

I kept the binoculars up to my eyes but grabbed the car's door handle with my left hand. Ready to dash across the boulevard and stop whatever stupidity Luke was contemplating. Blown cover or not, I had to try to keep Moira's son out of jail one night at a time.

I pushed down the door handle, but Luke angled away from Gabby Dates' condo and toward the complex's entrance. He continued to look toward Gabby's front door as he carefully opened the gate and exited the complex. He didn't appear to notice the Tesla the professor type drove up in and went straight to his own car.

One crisis averted. Even though Luke did break the TRO, he looked to have escaped without anyone but me and the blond woman in condo number 4 knowing he'd been well within a hundred yards of Gabby Dates.

I watched Luke get into his Mazda 3 and make a U-turn in the roundabout a block behind me. I sunk down in my seat and watched his car lights drive past. On his way home? He was headed in the right direction to eventually catch I-5 North. I gave him a couple seconds, then started up my black blend-in Honda Accord and pulled onto the boulevard. I wanted to stay where I was and keep watching both condos 1 and 4. Linda Holland, if that was who was with Luke in condo number 4, needed further examination. So did Gabby Dates and her late-night visitor. Was it a booty call with a quick exit or an overnight stay? Or neither?

The vibe of the night and the surveillance of Luke MacFarlane changed when he went through the gate and turned right to unit 4 instead of left to see Gabby Dates. And changed again when the man in the Tesla entered Gabby's condo. But my directive was to follow Luke and report back to Moira.

I stayed well back of his car and followed at the speed limit. A speed Luke irritatingly adhered to. Another reason not to trust him. As expected, he got onto I-5 North and took it up to Lomas Santa Fe Drive. His next stop would be onto Solana Hills Drive, the street he lived on.

Except he drove right past it. I stayed ten to twelve car lengths back. Traffic was light at this time of night. I didn't want to give myself away. Not when things had suddenly gotten interesting.

Luke continued west on Lomas Santa Fe, past the mall on the left and the elementary school on the right. He proceeded for a few more blocks then turned left onto South Nardo Avenue at the stoplight. The light turned yellow, and I just made the turn as it changed to red. I caught sight of the back end of Luke's Mazda 3 as it completed a turn into the parking lot of a two-story commercial building. I drove past and saw him pull into a parking spot at the back of the building.

I whipped a three-point turn, shut off my lights, and crept toward the edge of the parking lot. Luke's car sat dark, five or so spaces away from the only other car in the lot. A white Lexus GS F. Somebody in that office building was making enough money to own or lease an $85,000 car.

I caught movement inside a glass-encased stairwell on the outside of the building. Possibly Luke. Too dark to get a clear image. I grabbed my binoculars, but was too late. A figure disappeared into the building on the second floor. I looked back at Luke's car through the binos. Empty. A lone light shone from the second story corner office. I presumed that was Luke's destination, as no other lights were on inside the building.

I noticed a sign above the office window and focused the binoculars on it. The sign read "ConnectTech." Luke's employer. I knew Connect-Tech was located in Solana Beach but hadn't remembered the address.

So, Luke breaks his TRO by hanging out in a condo across from his ex's, owned by a woman twenty years his senior, leaves the condo and drives up to his office at eleven o'clock at night.

There was something more going on than just a heartsick ex-boyfriend stalking the woman who dumped him. But I didn't have a clue what it was. Yet.

I targeted the binoculars on the license plate of the Lexus and wrote it down on a small notepad I kept in my bomber jacket pocket. The owner of the car may have no bearing on the suddenly confounding case, but I'd find out who it was anyway and look for connections. My guess now was that it belonged to the president of ConnectTech. Light on in the corner office. Who else could it be?

No sign of movement in the office. Fifteen minutes later, Luke MacFarlane emerged from the staircase and hurried to his car.

Why had he gone to work at 11:00 p.m. on a Friday night and left after only fifteen minutes?

CHAPTER SEVEN

I STAYED WELL back from Luke's car and followed him home to his apartment building on Solana Hills Drive. He parked and went upstairs to his second-story unit. I waited a half hour. The lights were still on in Luke's apartment, but he hadn't reemerged. My take: in for the night.

I called Moira on my twenty-five-minute drive home and ticked off everything I'd seen since I last talked to her. Luke with Linda Holland on the roof of her condo. The preppie in the Tesla going inside Gabby's condo. Luke driving up to his work where an $85,000 car was parked and a light was on in the corner office. I gave her the license plate number so she could check with her guy at the La Jolla Police Department to confirm my assumption that the car belonged to the ConnectTech president. Finally, Luke going inside the building for fifteen minutes then driving home.

When I was done, I asked her what she'd found out about Linda Holland.

The only new info she gave me was that the charity Holland founded, A Hand Up, helped low-income families get health insurance.

Not a lot of detail.

"I wonder what she wants with Luke," I said.

"Me, too." Angst in two words. "But you don't have to worry about her or following Luke anymore. I'm going to take your advice and talk to him in the morning. Thanks for the last three nights of work. You can keep the rest of the week's retainer."

"Let me dig a little deeper into Linda Holland and earn my keep." With a baby and who knows what kind of unforeseen expenses on the horizon, I needed the money but couldn't take it without earning it. Plus, this case was suddenly too interesting to walk away from. And, I needed the rush.

"You don't have to. Really." Weary. "I appreciate everything you've done, but I should have never hired you, or anyone, to spy on my son. I got worried that he broke the TRO and acted rashly. That was wrong. That's not how you treat your son. He needs my support, not someone spying on him. I'll touch base with you in a couple weeks. After the TRO hearing."

Click.

The parental handbook definitely didn't have a chapter on how to handle Luke's situation. Moira was doing the best she could. What she thought was right. The good news was that she would finally talk to Luke about what he was up to.

That left me to get back to my corporate work. Background checks from behind a computer. That meant I'd have to leave unanswered questions hanging. An itch I wasn't allowed to scratch. Like, why would Luke risk getting caught breaking his restraining order by going to Linda Holland's? If Luke needed to talk to her, why not just call?

Maybe they did more than talk. Maybe Moira thought the same thing and didn't want me to uncover the sordid details. We might have been brother and sister in the abstract, but we weren't blood. Luke was, and Moira didn't want me to learn family secrets she hadn't yet discovered.

That was fair. But what if it was something other than sex that made Luke break the TRO? It wasn't any of my business. But it had gotten me out from behind a keyboard and reawakened the man I used to be. And still really was.

All the good and the bad.

* * *

I got home at 12:15 a.m. Leah was still up in Santa Barbara keeping her interior design business afloat. She'd built a successful career before I came into her life and it hit warp speed right before someone tried to kill me and I ended up in the ICU at Scripps Memorial Hospital. Hovering over my recovery paused her career climb. She was still successful, but we were counting every dollar in anticipation of raising a child on one decent income for a couple years.

I told Leah I could be a stay-at-home dad since most of my work was done in my upstairs office sitting at a keyboard, but she was adamant about being with our child 24/7 for at least two years. Her maternal instincts and love were already in overdrive.

So, right now, Leah's time in Santa Barbara was important to our child's future. So was every side gig I could get as a P.I.

Midnight greeted me at the door. We'd been through a lot together. Graying along his jowls and eyebrows, he was still a fearsome guard dog and a sweet soul. But he'd slowed down just enough over the last year for me to notice. Still, his mind and his senses remained alert.

Just as when I was temporarily blinded two years ago, he now sensed I wasn't one hundred percent fit, either. He stayed close by my side when I was home and spent less time in the backyard alone. He'd pop his head through the doggie door I finally installed a few months ago and scan the kitchen and living room, then walk over and sit down next to my chair after he spotted me.

Some dogs are thought to be able to detect cancer growing inside humans. Maybe Midnight sensed the dysfunction growing inside my head. Whatever it was, I welcomed his vigil. And his love. I led Midnight up the stairs to the second floor. He moved ahead of my pace and went into the master bedroom, figuring we were down for the night. Not yet. I was tired, but wired. The way I used to feel back in Santa Barbara after my graveyard shift as a cop on the Santa Barbara Police Department almost twenty years ago.

My juices were flowing from being on the chase again. Even if most of it was done motionless sitting in a car. I went into my office and turned on the light, sat at the desk, and powered up my laptop computer. Midnight sauntered in and laid down under the desk at my feet.

I unlocked my laptop, opened a pay search engine, and looked up Linda Rose Holland. She deserved a deeper dive, on my own time. Something to do while the night's events wound out of me.

I skimmed over the information I'd found on her earlier that night and went all the way back to Holland's beginning. She was born and raised in Piedmont, California. A wealthy enclave in the San Francisco East Bay area, surrounded by the city of Oakland. Her parents were both alive and she had a brother four years her junior who taught environmental studies at the University of Oregon in Eugene.

Linda graduated with a BA in political science from UC Berkeley in 1998. She worked on a couple San Francisco City Councilperson's campaigns out of college then graduated to a successful congressional campaign for the U.S. House of Representatives. She moved to Washington D.C. and got on staff for the congresswoman she helped get elected. The congresswoman became a member of the Health, Education, Labor and Pensions Committee, which oversees the healthcare industry. After two years and another election of the now incumbent congresswoman, Holland worked her way up to chief of staff.

Holland quit the position in 2007, right after her boss became a member of the powerful Financial Services Committee. Strange time to quit the game. Congresspeople keep score by the importance of the committees they're on and their pecking order on them. I imagined their staff did the same. Holland moved on when her boss was moving on up. She started a nonprofit that advocated for low-income home ownership, but disbanded it after the subprime loan crisis and stock market crash of 2008.

She then went on to work for Sandstrom Capital, owned by her future husband, Scot Kendall Sandstrom. Sandstrom Capital was a venture capital firm that took minority positions in a lot of tech start-ups and medical research companies with mostly positive results. Its biggest success was an investment in Stemtech, a pharmaceutical company that had promising lab results in cancer fighting drugs. Sandstrom Capital gave Stemtech a much-needed injection of funds in 2016, then made $29,000,000 when it was bought by the German pharmaceutical giant Boehringer Ingelheim. Holland started her new charity and left Sandstrom Capital that same year.

Holland's position at Sandstrom Capital had been as an analyst. She became a board member in 2012 and married Scot Sandstrom a year later. It paid to sleep with the boss.

Multimillionaire Scot Sandstrom deserved a look of his own. He grew up here in San Diego and went to Stanford on an academic scholarship where he received a degree in economics. Straight out of college he got a job with the legendary venture capital firm Sequoia Capital. From the information I could glean online, Sandstrom appeared to learn the VC business at the elbow of Sequoia Capital founder Don Valentine. He worked at Sequoia for five years then left to work for three much less successful Silicon Valley VC firms over the next six years until he founded Sandstrom Capital in 2006.

An odd exit from one of the top venture capital firms in the country. Most people leave an established entity like Sequoia to start their own firm or to take a higher position with someone else. Sandstrom did neither. At least not right away. Maybe bad blood at Sequoia. And the other VCs he worked for before he started his own shop. Whatever the case, Sandstrom Capital somehow thrived during the 2008 financial crisis when some established VC firms were hurt badly during that time of tight cash.

A little deeper dive into Sandstrom's biography revealed that he'd been convicted of insider trading in 2012 and paid a $500,000 fine. Sandstrom's wardrobe off the rack to riches story had at least one dark chapter.

I leaned back in my chair and glanced at the lower right corner of the computer screen. The clock read 2:17 a.m. The last hour and a half of punching keys and staring at the screen had added more degrees of tired and erased all effects of wired. I was ready for bed, but now even more confused about Luke MacFarlane's connection with Linda Holland and, possibly by association, her rich, corner-cutting husband, Scot Sandstrom.

What could this twenty-four-year-old mid-level employee with a small, inconspicuous Solana Beach tech company have to do with the founder of a successful venture capital firm, whose personal wealth was in the tens of millions? A kid whose violation of a temporary restraining order seemed to be aided and abetted by Sandstrom's wife.

Technically, not my concern, but I was eager to try to find answers if Moira invited me back in.

I powered down the laptop and pushed back my roller executive chair from the desk. Midnight slipped out from under the desk and walked out of the office toward my bedroom.

I stared at the office doorway. Blank. The walls closed in on me. My mouth went slack. I knew I was in my office, but didn't know why or what time it was. I didn't know what day it was. My head sledgehammered. My heart shotgunned. Sweat pebbled up under my arms and along my hairline. My mouth stayed loose, but my breath double-pumped out of it.

Midnight peeked into the office. I knew he was my dog. I just couldn't remember from when. He walked over and laid his head on my lap and gazed up at me with big brown Lab eyes. But his tail didn't wag.

I looked down at him. Then finally put my right hand on his head and felt the warmth of his fur. Life's blood running through him. My eyelids spasmed in rapid fire blinks. I shook my head. Midnight lifted his head off my lap and stared me straight in the eyes. I stroked his fur behind his ears.

I was home. With Midnight. At 2:19 a.m. on Saturday, October 9, 2021. Leah was up in Santa Barbara for the third night in a row. I'd just finished doing research for a case Moira MacFarlane had hired me to do that I was now working alone.

I was vital. I was capable. And I wouldn't give in.

To anything.

CHAPTER EIGHT

I DEDICATED THE next day completely to running background checks for a new corporate client. Fulcrum Security was a defense contractor that needed airtight histories on potential new employees and they had a long list of people hoping to work for them. Hopefully, a constant source of income for me. With my life changing in so many ways, Fulcrum Security could become the most important client I'd ever have.

I finished up around 8:00 p.m. and considered calling Moira to see how her talk with Luke went, but thought better of it. Luke was her son, not a target of surveillance for me to follow up on. If there was anything she wanted me to know, she'd call me.

Sunday, I watched football and rooted against the Los Angeles Traitors, a team that used to have a home in San Diego. For five decades. But I was over it.

Moira didn't call and neither did I. But I still wanted to.

* * *

The next morning, I gave my Fulcrum Security background check report a final once-over and emailed it to the defense contractor a day early.

I had the rest of the day off to do whatever I wanted. Carefree wasn't in my DNA. Loose tendrils of adrenaline from surveilling Luke MacFarlane three nights ago still pulsed through my nervous system. The void between that case, the kind of work I felt called to do, and the Fulcrum Security job, the work I needed to do to support my family, made me fidgety.

Midnight chose that moment to stand at the office door and stare at me. Reading my mind? I didn't doubt his ability. He was my out for fidgety.

We went downstairs and I grabbed his leash harness off the hat rack by the door and he sat immediately and waited for me to hold it out in front of him so he could step into it. I cinched him up, grabbed a tennis ball, my Padres cap, a plastic bag for poop, and my sunglasses and went out the front door.

We walked three-quarters of a mile, mostly uphill to Cadman Recreation Center. The sun was bright, but the leftover air from the nighttime October marine layer made for a pleasantly brisk morning walk. I led Midnight on his leash all the way to the back Little League field. Baseball season was over and the field was empty. I found the gate that had enough play in the locked chain to be able to push it open so Midnight could slip through. I scanned the recreation area. No witnesses. I took off Midnight's leash and manipulated the gate for his illegal entry. I heaved the ball over the fence into right field and Midnight sprinted after it. I immediately regretted not warming up my arm before the first throw of the day. A twinge in the shoulder.

Nonetheless, I scaled the fence and plopped down on the other side. My arthritic left knee buckled at impact and my butt hit the ground, but I rolled out of it back up to my feet. All in all, a wash. I couldn't take the pounding I could five years ago, but my reflexes were still sharp enough to keep me from lying down.

I wiped the dirt off my pants as Midnight sped toward me, tennis ball wedged firmly between his teeth. He dropped the ball at my feet. This time, I slowly windmilled my right arm, before picking the ball up and throwing it again.

Midnight galloped after the ball. His gait, slightly shorter than I remembered it being a year ago. I closed the distance to him as he galloped back toward me. The remainder of my throws were shorter. More for Midnight's legs than my shoulder. Each sprint to the ball and jog back slightly slower than the last.

I cut the game short after fifteen minutes. Midnight barked at me when I put the slobbery tennis ball in my sweatshirt pocket. His mind and instincts always willing and now more able than his still muscular body. I had to be the regulator, the governor, over impulse and desire. Not my strongest suit. But Midnight's health was my responsibility.

The ravages of life had taken their toll on both Midnight and me. I sat down on the center field grass. Midnight sat next to me and I scratched him behind the ear. He looked into my eyes, long tongue hanging sideways out of his huffing mouth. Ten years bonded together. Midnight saved my life five years ago. Attacked a gunman before he could put a bullet in me. He'd also saved me from spiraling into deadly depression many times over the years.

My protector.

Now in the final years of his life, he would become the protector of my child. My blood. My salvation.

We each rose to our feet, Midnight quicker and more lithely than me, and began the walk back to our house. A little more slowly than during our trip to the rec center a half hour ago.

* * *

My cell phone buzzed in my pocket five minutes after Midnight and I arrived home. Moira.

"I can't find Luke." Her high-rattle voice a boiled-over teapot. "He won't return my calls or texts and he's not at his apartment. I've been trying him for three days. I even used the Family Find My iPhone. Nothing comes up. He must have his location services turned off."

There could be plenty of explanations why Luke couldn't be reached by Moira. Innocent explanations. And there could be some not so innocent.

I sat down at the butcherblock island in my kitchen and grabbed a notepad and pen from the drawer underneath.

"When did you talk to him last?"

"Tuesday."

"Before you called me?"

"Yes."

There were a couple possibilities that Moira had to have thought of that I didn't want to broach.

But had to.

"Have you called—"

"Yes." Almost relief. "I called every hospital in town and Luke hasn't been to any of them as of this morning."

"Good. And—"

"I talked to my contact at LJPD. He checked with every law enforcement agency in San Diego County. Luke hasn't been arrested."

A relief. No news was generally good news in those cases. Still, Luke could have met violence that hadn't been recorded yet.

Or discovered.

"Any activity on his social media?"

"Not that I could find. He doesn't use social media much. The last thing he posted was a photo of him and Clint on what would have been Clint's fiftieth birthday two months ago."

Clint, Moira's late husband and Luke's father. He died of a heart attack nine years ago and Moira found the body. With Luke at her side. Clint's birthday must have been a rough day for both of them. And I didn't even know about it.

"You home?" Moira needed my help again. Next to Leah, she was as close to family as I had. And I hadn't been the best sibling so far. "I'll head over and we can strategize when I get there."

"I'm at Luke's."

"I can be there in twenty-five minutes."

"There's one other thing you should know before you decide to help me." Moira's voice now slowed down; its volume low.

"What?" I grabbed my car keys off the hook in the kitchen and headed for my car in the driveway, concentrating on forward momentum. Moira's words only background music to the quest building inside me.

"Luke's boss, Jim Harkness, was found dead this morning at the ConnectTech office. Murdered."

Luke hurrying to his car after he left the ConnectTech building late Friday night flashed through my head.

Shit.

CHAPTER NINE

I PULLED INTO the Solana Mar Apartments parking lot at 9:50 a.m. I'd shaved a few minutes off the drive by averaging eighty-five miles an hour on the freeway. Moira's white Honda Accord was parked in Luke's spot in front of his unit.

I hustled upstairs to the front door and knocked. The door opened immediately. Dark circles hung below Moira's soda pop brown eyes as she let me inside.

I followed her into the apartment. Dirty dishes in the sink and on the counter in the kitchen. Moira stopped at a dinner table that separated the kitchen from the living area. I looked into the lone bedroom on the left. Small desk, no computer on it. An aluminum softball bat with neon green grip tape on the handle next to the bed. Clothes strewn all over the floor. The apartment looked disheveled, but not as though it had been ransacked. Just a messy inhabitant.

"How did you hear about Harkness? I had a local news channel on the radio during the drive up here. There was no mention of it while I was listening."

"I drove by Luke's work an hour ago to see if his car was in the parking lot. It wasn't but there were squad cars there and police tape up, so I called my contact at LJPD to find out if he knew anything."

"Solana Beach is in the San Diego Sheriff Department's jurisdiction."

"News of the murder of a business executive gets around local law enforcement quickly." Moira walked over to a faux leather sofa in the living area. Her usual crisp walk slowed to somnambulance. She eased down onto the sofa. The movements of someone much older than Moira's usually vital forty-four years. I sat down in a matching upright faux leather recliner across from the couch.

"Has anyone from SDSO called you looking for Luke yet?" Like many sheriff departments, San Diego's used the SO acronym for Sheriff's Office.

"No."

"Does anyone else know that Luke went by the ConnectTech office Friday night and met with Harkness?"

"Of course not." Moira stared at me without blinking.

"Did you ever have your guy run the plate on the white Lexus GS F?" I asked.

"Yes. It belonged to Jim Harkness and was in the parking lot this morning." Her big round eyes squinted horizontal.

She knew I was in a predicament. I had potential important evidence regarding Jim Harkness' murder. I'd followed Luke to the ConnectTech office late Friday night. Jim Harkness' car was in the parking lot. His office light was on when Luke entered the building. No other lights were on or subsequently turned on. Luke's destination had to be Harkness' office.

A question hit me that I should have asked the moment Moira told me that Harkness had been murdered. "How was Harkness killed?"

"That I don't know."

"I hope it was by gunshot," I said.

"Why?" Loud. Her tiny body recoiled.

"Because I didn't hear anything or see a muzzle flash while I was watching the building Friday night. If he was killed by a gun, the fact that I didn't see or hear anything could be exculpatory for Luke." Of course, the killer could have used a silencer, which also reduces muzzle flash.

I kept that to myself, but if the potential shooter was anyone but her son, Moira would have thought the same thing.

"Luke doesn't need exculpatory evidence. He didn't kill Jim Harkness, Rick." Her jaw rigid. "He couldn't kill anyone."

I didn't know whether or not Luke MacFarlane killed Jim Harkness. But I was certain of one thing. Under the right, or terribly wrong, circumstances, anyone was capable of murder. I was all the proof I needed.

But not the proper time to have a philosophical argument about man's capability for violence.

"You may know that, but the Sheriff's Department doesn't." I tried to sound optimistic. "At least, not yet. It would be helpful to find out how Harkness was killed. How comfortable would you be asking your guy at LJPD to find out?"

"I don't think that's a good idea. I've already made the connection between Luke and the ConnectTech building for him. My contact is a friend, but he's a cop first. I don't want him to start putting things together and contact SDSO."

"You're right." That still left me with my responsibility as a citizen and a former cop. If I weren't friends with the mother of someone I'd seen at a crime scene around the time a murder was probably committed, I'd contact SDSO on my own and tell them what I knew.

But Moira *was* a friend. The best one I had.

A triple knock on the front door broke the silence between us. We looked at each other without moving. I slowly stood up and crept over to the front door. Luckily, it had a peephole. I looked through it just in time to see a fist knock on the door three more times. The fist was connected to a sports coat. And an olive-complected man with a stern countenance. A fair-skinned woman with curly red hair pulled back into a thick ponytail stood next to him. Her attire similar to his.

Detectives. The woman looked familiar. I was pretty sure I'd met her when she was a uniformed Sheriff's Deputy a few years ago. She'd been promoted.

I felt Moira creep up behind me. I turned toward her and whispered, "Police."

She tightened and shook her head. She needn't worry. I wasn't going to answer the door. Moira had lawfully entered her son's domain with her own key. The detectives hadn't shouted "Police" and commanded we open the door. If they did, I'd have a decision to make. Or one to leave to Moira to make.

Three more knocks on the door, but no law enforcement command. They were looking for Luke, but there wasn't a warrant for his arrest out yet. The lone piece of good news this morning. Good that could turn to bad in the time it took to call a sympathetic judge.

I looked through the peephole again. The detectives backed away from the door and turned to the right and disappeared out of view. Good.

"We need to find Luke." Moira followed me back into the living room.

"Okay." But the cops already had a head start and way more resources than we did.

And badges. And the power of the state on their side.

CHAPTER TEN

I TURNED INTO John Hopkins Court at 1:05 p.m. It was just a driver and a three wood over Genesee Avenue to reach Torrey Pines Golf Course from the Sequence Corp headquarters. Okay, for me lately, driver, three wood, five iron.

Sequence Corp, where Gabby Dates worked, took up a big chunk of John Hopkins Court. The building was a rectangular two-story structure made of all glass with green shaded windows. It looked sterile and void of creativity. I guessed all the creativity was conserved for the work done inside. I'd staked out Sequence Corp one afternoon after I got my corporate work done early. Again, I stayed with the cheese and waited for the mouse to come. It never did. Luke didn't appear at Sequence Corp while I was watching it.

The day I staked out the company from a parking structure across the street, Gabby had exited the building at 1:00 p.m. carrying a sack lunch and a beach towel and walked across the street to eat under a pine tree next to a staircase alongside John Jay Hopkins Road. She was there again today.

I'd thought it was odd for her to eat alone in the public when she'd just filed a temporary restraining order against Luke. Wasn't she concerned that he might confront her when she had no protection? Or, was she baiting him? I hadn't come up with an answer the day I watched her and didn't have one now.

Today, I had other questions to ask Gabby Dates.

I exited the parking structure on foot and crossed John Hopkins Drive to the sidewalk on the other side. The sun had warmed up the afternoon, making it a perfect day to eat lunch outside. Low seventies, sunny, light breeze. The kind of weather tourists expect in San Diego all year round. The locals know that sometimes paradise turns gray.

I walked up a cement staircase that connected the sidewalk with a parking lot above it and stopped on the landing halfway up. Gabby sat on a blue and white beach towel under the shade of a pine tree. She wore gray slacks and a light blue blouse and a blue lab coat with her name embroidered on it. Buttoned-down beauty. A Sequence Corp keycard and name tag was clipped to her lab coat. Her short brown hair was pulled behind her ears and designer sunglasses were perched on her head. She took a bite of salad from a Tupperware container, then looked up at me. Dark eyes questioning.

Million-dollar condo in La Jolla, designer sunglasses, and a home-made salad in a Tupperware container from a brown paper bag. Gabby Dates had a lot of sides.

"Hi, Gabby." I decided to be direct instead of trying to work some kind of ploy. Gabby had limited time at lunch and was probably smart enough to smell out a ruse. "My name's Rick Cahill and I'm a friend of Moira MacFarlane, Luke's mom."

"Okay." Noncommittal. She set her fork down in the Tupperware container and raised her eyebrows.

"Luke's missing and Moira is worried about him." No change of expression from Gabby. Intelligent eyes, still probing mine. "Do you know where he is?"

"No. I'm sorry, I don't." Pleasantly matter-of-fact. No surprise or feigned surprise.

"When was the last time you talked to Luke?"

"As a friend of Mrs. MacFarlane, Mr. Cahill, I would think that you know that I filed a restraining order against Luke a week ago." A little patronizing, but I'd heard worse.

"Does that mean you don't care if something has happened to Luke? He must have done something really bad to you. What was it?"

She looked down at her salad and took another bite. In control. On her own schedule. Impressive. All of the wunderkinder I'd ever met didn't have the emotional IQ or poise to match their off-the-charts intelligence. Gabriela Dates was a rare breed.

I folded my arms, leaned my hip against the metal staircase railing, and waited. I'd dealt with exotic before.

Gabby finished chewing and swallowed.

"I still care about Luke. We just didn't work out. I'm sure he just wants to be off by himself for a while." She went back to her salad.

"Do all of your relationships that don't work out end up with you filing a restraining order?"

"No." She shook her head and put on an annoyed smile. "Only this one."

"When was the last time you talked to Luke?" I tried again.

"A week ago, Sunday."

"The night you two got into a fight?"

"Yes." Sibilant "S."

"What happened that made you go to court to get a restraining order against him?"

"That's between Luke and me." Another headshake.

And the Superior Court of San Diego, but I kept that to myself. Sarcasm hadn't worked so far.

"Moira and I aren't the only ones looking for Luke." A little shock to the system to see how she'd respond. "The police are, too."

"What?" Her cheeks squished up. "Why? Did he break the restraining order? If he did, he didn't harass me or anything."

"Someone killed his boss and now Luke's missing."

"Oh my God. That's horrible." Eyes wide, mouth open. She set down her salad on the beach towel. Legitimate surprise or a hell of an acting job. "They don't think Luke had anything to do with it, do they?"

"I don't know. Do you think he could do something like that?" She'd seen his anger up close. I needed to know.

"Of course not." A reflexive scowl. "Anything else, Mr. Cahill? I'd like to finish my lunch now. Alone."

Gabriela Dates filed a temporary restraining order against Luke for whatever he did to her during an argument, but she seemed certain he wasn't capable of murder. Good to know.

"One more thing." I gave her a neutral smile like I knew I was imposing, but I could live with it. "Did you know that Luke was seeing Linda Holland, your neighbor in La Jolla?"

"They were friends." Gabby neatly closed her Tupperware container, put it back in her brown paper sack. "Don't make it sound like something else."

"Just an observation. Do you think it's odd that he would hang out with a woman his mother's age?"

"Thank you for interrupting my lunch, Mr. Cahill. I hope you find Luke." Gabby grabbed her paper sack and stood up. She took her sunglasses off her head, put them on, and turned toward me. "Please tell Mrs. MacFarlane I only did what I thought was in Luke's best interests." Her voice softened when she mentioned Moira's name.

"Odd way of showing your affection." For Luke. She seemed to have genuine affection for his mother.

"Luke had an odd way of showing his affection, too." She walked across the street to the Sequence Corp building.

Moira thought Gabby Dates was sweet. I hadn't seen any of that, but maybe she just didn't like talking to private detectives. Not many people did. Whatever the case, I couldn't get a good read on her. I'd come at her head-on and she'd given me angles.

Gabby Dates had a lot of sides. I just didn't know if any of them had sharp edges.

CHAPTER ELEVEN

I DIDN'T SEE Moira's white Honda Accord when I pulled up in front of her house. She didn't have a garage or a driveway and her car wasn't on the street, but I knew she was home. She must have thought that the sheriff's deputies' next stop looking for Luke would be her house. I scanned the street. No slicked-top detective cars that I could see.

Moira opened her door before I could knock on it.

"No G rides out here," I said and slipped past her inside. Cop slang for government vehicles.

We sat down at her dinner table in the California Craftsman Bungalow modern open floorplan. The opposite of the outside façade's classic look. There were three neat rows of computer-printed records lined up next to each other on the table in front of Moira.

"What did Gabby tell you?" Moira asked. Her fingers pressed down hard on the tabletop.

"Not enough. I think maybe you should have talked to her. She genuinely seems to like you." I told her the little information I'd gotten out of Gabby Dates and about her cool demeanor. I left out that I'd asked her if she thought Luke was capable of murder. A plus for Luke that she didn't think so, but a minus for me in Moira's eyes if she knew I asked the question.

"She was always very nice to me."

"The court still hasn't posted the TRO." I'd gone on the San Diego Superior Court's website to buy a copy of the temporary restraining order complaint, but it wasn't available yet. I guess transcribing TROs and making them public was at the bottom of the court's to-do list. "What am I missing?"

You couldn't get a restraining order issued for just being a jerk. If you could, I'd have a paper trail from San Diego to Santa Barbara.

"What do you mean?" Machine-gunned rattle aimed at my head.

"Gabriela Dates is a pretty cool customer. She doesn't seem like someone who'd overreact to a loud argument. Something else must have happened."

"I only know what Luke told me." Moira looked off to the side. There was more. Something she hadn't told me. I could tell she was having a silent argument with herself whether or not to tell me now. But she knew I'd be able to find out once the TRO was finally transcribed and recorded. I stayed quiet for a change and waited for her to work it out.

She looked back at me. "He told me he broke a chair during the argument."

When I saw Gabby a half hour ago, she didn't have any visible bruises. Bruises fade over time, but most would still show after only a week. Her gait was even when I watched her walk from her picnic spot under the pine tree to Sequence Corp. Whatever Luke broke the chair over, I was pretty sure it wasn't Gabby Dates.

"Have you ever seen him do anything like that?" With each new hour I spent on this case, I realized how little I knew about Luke, my best friend's son, and about Moira's personal life.

During the seven years we'd known each other, almost all of our conversations had been about me. The trouble I'd gotten myself into, my recovery from violent attacks, my questionable ethics in relation to society's laws. My life had plenty of material to dominate conversations. Moira was tighter with her own life. I knew when she started dating someone new, but I'd never get a name. She only mentioned Luke when he'd notched a divot in life's fencepost, like getting the job at ConnectTech out of college. We never went much deeper than that, but we didn't have to. We were family. Even without shared blood.

Life had brought us together. Pain had pulled us close. We'd seen violence too many times and been forced to commit it more than once. And we'd seen death. We had an unbreakable bond forged in blood. Some of it mine.

But even with all that, I was worried about her answer to my question.

"None of this is relevant to finding Luke." Her tan skin turned adobe. "You're the one person I thought I could turn to with this. You know I can't go to the police. Not until we find Luke. There isn't anyone else I trust. You're all I have."

The last sentence hit me hard. I'd spent most of the second half of my life alone. Then I met Leah two years ago. I now had someone else. A backstop to keep me from falling into the abyss of my own nature. I'd always seen Moira as self-contained. A perfect, self-propelled entity. No additions needed. But she was human. Vulnerable. Something I too often overlooked.

And her son was missing. To find him, I needed to know everything. Especially the parts that hurt.

"I'm just trying to get to the truth so we can find Luke. Information is the key that unlocks the truth. Luke has secrets. The best-case scenario I can think of right now is that he's hiding somewhere because of one." I rested my hands on the table and lowered my voice. "Have you ever seen Luke get violent?"

Moira blew out a long painful breath.

"Never with people. When he was a teenager, he sometimes threw things when he got angry.

"What kind of things?"

"Goddammit, Rick. He lost his father. A man he adored." She bolted out of her chair and walked over to the peninsula in the kitchen, then turned back and looked at me. "He threw anything he could get his hands on. Books, flower vases, plates. And yes, even chairs. He was lost without his father and I wasn't enough for him. There's your fucking truth."

Tears ran down her face.

Shit.

I'd only seen Moira cry three times. Twice, really. I was blind the last time. All three times had been because of me. I didn't like it then. I didn't like it now. We had a bond that hadn't yet been broken, but I'd threatened it many times. Pulling, tugging, ripping. I had one gear when I worked a case. Go. I only hit stop when the truth was found. Then I noticed the damage the truth and I had wrought.

The truth and the damage were now in front of me. But not the final truth. Luke MacFarlane had a tough time as a teenager. Losing a parent at any age is tragic. Especially as a teen. Looking for guidance and love during the toughest stage of life. It affects everyone the same and differently. My father died when I was nineteen. The ache still pulses deep within me, even now. And sometimes breaks the surface like a dagger.

Luke's father's death stunted him as he was approaching adulthood. A delicate and potentially dangerous time. Hormones racing past maturity and reason. Luke's reaction had been anger and rage. And the toughest, most competent person I knew couldn't get a handle on him. Loving arms and firm boundaries couldn't rein him in.

And now Moira must have wondered if that anger, that out-of-control rage, had finally broken the most precious law of God and man.

"I'm sorry." I got up and walked over to Moira and put my arms out to hug her. She shoved me in the chest and I stumbled against the dinner table.

"I'm sure you are. You always are. You're always sorry afterwards." She crossed her arms in front of her.

I sat down at the table. Sincere or not, Moira had heard enough of my apologies. For a lifetime.

But I still had a case to figure out.

"Do you think it's possible Luke's gone somewhere to chill out and that he's embarrassed about the TRO? And that that's why he won't return your calls?"

"Probably not." She wiped her eyes, shook her head, and took a deep breath. Composed. Back to work. She sat down at the table and pushed one of the computer-printed stacks of paper at me. "He hasn't used his cell phone since Friday afternoon when he received a call from a number associated with A Hand Up charity."

"Linda Holland's charity. She was probably inviting him over for their meeting that night."

"Right."

"What are these?" I tapped one of the other two stacks of papers on the table with data on it. "Credit card transactions?"

"Yes, Luke's credit card charges this month. I printed them out while you were talking with Gabby. No new charges since he got gas at the Lomas Santa Fe Mobil last Wednesday." She pointed at the third short stack of paper. "And those are his banking transactions from the last two months."

"How did you get all of these?"

"He's been on my AT&T Family Plan since middle school and I had to cosign for his one credit card when he was eighteen." She leaned back in her chair and folded her arms. "And I did a favor for the manager at Luke's savings and loan last year. She got me access to

Luke's information. Nothing since a two-hundred-dollar withdrawal from an ATM two weeks ago after his paycheck was automatically deposited."

Favors for bank managers. P.I.s work cases and get paid. Usually a favor is something off the books. The kind of thing I do every once in a while. Get someone a little piece of information without a paper trail that can help keep them out of a jackpot or help them cash in on one. Not the kind of thing where you break the law, but maybe a rule or two. A shortcut to a preferred outcome. And sometimes, down the road, you ask for reciprocity. Maybe Moira wasn't that much different than me after all.

She looked at me and read my mind. "It's not what you think, Cahill." Using my last name to maintain a distance from me. And my actions. "Her daughter was being cyberbullied by the daughter of the CEO of one of her largest accounts. I resolved it quietly."

"Of course." Still a favor leveraged later. "Could Luke have more than one credit card or bank account?"

"No. I did a credit check on him. On my own son." She shook her head.

"Have you talked to Luke's friends?"

"Yes. The only two I know. They said they don't know where he is."

"Do you believe them?"

"Yes." A weak nod. The purple half circles under her eyes seemed to darken right in front of me. She looked like she hadn't slept since she hired me to tail her son last Tuesday night.

"So, we've got no use of Luke's phone since Friday." I walked Moira down the path she had to already be on. "It might be time to report him as a missing person to the police."

"I don't want to bring any more attention onto him."

If she were working the case for a client, she'd give them the same advice. Despite her protestations to the contrary, something must have whispered inside her that Luke could be capable of violence. Against another human being. But that should have been her secondary concern now. It was mine. There was one thing worse that could have happened.

"Moira, if Luke isn't staying with a friend or lying in a hospital bed, he has to be somewhere." I didn't want to have to say what must have already crossed her mind. Too many times. "The police can cast a much wider net than we can. What if he's injured somewhere?"

"He's not dead, Rick." She put her hand on my wrist. Moira rarely touched me. Too intimate for our strange relationship bound by hardship. "I'd know. I would have felt it. There'd be a void. Like the one I felt when Clint died. Luke's alive and we have to find him before the police do. He needs me now more than any time since he lost his father and I'm not going to let him down."

I put my free hand on Moira's and gently squeezed.

CHAPTER TWELVE

SCOT SANDSTROM AND Linda Holland's home in Encinitas sat on a cliff above the ocean. Modern with a little of that old *Miami Vice* vibe. The TV show that I watched with my older sister for its last season. I was ten and liked the flashy cars, boats, and homes. The Sandstrom house was white and it had a waterfall stone wall instead of a fence in the front yard. There was a glass half wall along the edge of the roof deck for safe ocean viewing. A *Miami Vice* helicopter camera pan with you as the star, gazing out at the ocean in your white linen suit and seafoam green t-shirt.

Now it would be a drone shot.

I knocked on the white oak front door. It looked and felt like it could hold off a horde of barbarians with battering rams.

Linda Holland had surprised me when she answered my call and agreed to talk to me. I'd found her phone number on a pay website that gets you more information than most people could even imagine was available. Legally. Privacy was so 20th century. I'd told her I was a private investigator working on a missing person's case involving Luke MacFarlane. My second surprise came when Linda invited me to her home to talk. The main home.

She opened the door at 4:00 p.m. Both of us were right on time.

Linda Holland could only be described with a term my mother sometimes used. Striking. Much more vibrant than the photos I'd seen online could translate. Tall and thin with short blond hair hung straight and bangs to her eyebrows. A dominant chin and prominent jaw. She was neither attractive nor unattractive. But her dark blue eyes seemed to shimmer. Like the afternoon wind riffling the water across Lake Tahoe. They were magnetic and cast a shadow over her other features, shrinking them and rounding off their edges. She looked her age at forty-four, but a well-lived honest forty-four.

Striking. Appealing, if not inviting.

She wore a light, flowing green and turquoise jumpsuit and gold sandals. Her feet were as tan as her face.

"Mr. Cahill?" Confident tenor voice.

"Yes." I focused. "Ms. Holland?"

She gave me a quick scan. I couldn't tell if she approved, but I'd dressed up for the occasion. You don't question a woman in her $10,000,000 home in jeans and a bomber jacket. I had on my blue, fine-checked sport coat to go with faded jeans and white t-shirt. A slumming Crockett or Tubbs.

"Please." She opened the door for me to enter. "Call me Linda."

She led me through a wide foyer decorated with driftwood and beach landscapes into a massive open floor plan living area with a white marble floor highlighted by black veins. You could park a fleet of limos in the living room. The back wall was all glass, partitioned by sliding pocket doors for indoor-outdoor flow. The ocean below massive and glistening blue in the afternoon sun like Linda Holland's eyes.

She walked to the glass wall, then stopped and turned toward me.

"Can I get you something to drink, Mr. Cahill?"

"Please, Linda, call me Rick." I smiled. "I'm fine. Thanks."

"Do you mind if we talk outside, Rick?" Friends. Until I started asking questions.

"Lead the way."

She slid back a section of the glass, stepped outside, and waited for me to follow before she swished the partition back in place. I stepped out onto a huge diamond-patterned brushed concrete deck that had the square footage of my house. Both stories combined.

An outdoor kitchen with a grill the size of my bed sat in one corner. Next to it was a marble slab table with ten space-age curved chairs. The other corner had a white cement fire ring that could keep the marble table party of ten toasty. While they looked over or through the glass handrail wall that extended the entire length of the patio. No whicker deck furniture or Weber kettle grills on Linda Holland's deck.

A wooden staircase, that probably cost $100,000 to construct, descended down a sloping bank to a strip of beach.

"Let's sit here." Linda walked over to two teak framed chaise lounges covered in white fabric, accented with blue pillows.

She slid down into one of them and kicked off her sandals. She grabbed a pair of Dolce Gabbana sunglasses off a small marble-top table between us and put them on to protect the sun from her eyes.

Relaxing on chaise lounges wasn't my top choice of furniture to use while questioning someone. Next, we'd be sipping salted rim margaritas.

I sat in the middle of the lounger and faced Linda Holland. I pulled my $80 Ray-Bans out of my blazer pocket and put them on.

Tied in the sunglass game in protection and concealment, if not cost.

Linda rested her arms above her head and angled her face toward me.

"Now, please tell me how I can help you, Rick." A little purr in the tenor. Margaritas just might be in our future.

"As I told you on the phone, I've been hired to find Luke MacFarlane." I edged forward. "When was the last time you saw him?"

"Hmm. Let me see." She ran an index finger along her bottom lip.

"I believe it was last Friday night."

"Where?" I knew where. The real question was, would she tell me?

"At my place in La Jolla."

"Your place in La Jolla?" I feigned ignorance.

"Yes. I have a condo in La Jolla I use as a remote office and to entertain donors from time to time."

"Was this a business meeting?"

Linda Holland turned onto her side, her whole body now facing me. She ran a tan foot along her other leg, pulling up the light pantsuit material with her big toe to reveal a tan ankle. Then a tan calf.

"No. He came over for some advice." No sexual purr that her languid body language suggested.

"What kind of advice?"

"He was having work and girlfriend problems."

"What kind of work problems?"

"He felt undervalued and was thinking of quitting his job."

His job. His office. His boss.

Dead.

Did Luke give his notice along with a chair over Jim Harkness' head Friday night?

"What about the girlfriend problems?"

"He said he and his girlfriend had gotten into a big fight and she broke up with him."

"Did he ever tell you he wanted to get away? Some favorite place where he'd like to go?"

"No. He never mentioned that." Her voice, settled. She slid her left foot onto the brushed cement patio and draped her other leg over her knee, then crooked an elbow on the headrest of the lounger and set her head in her hand.

"Did he tell you where he was going when he left?"

"Home." Her truth. Or not. But Luke hadn't gone straight home. He might be missing because he didn't. And a man might be dead for the same reason.

"How do you know Luke?" I took off my sunglasses and furrowed my brow. "You two seem like an odd couple."

"We're not a couple." Disdain. She lifted her head off her hand. "Luke did some computer work for my charity. He wrote a program that made it much easier for us to identify low income families in need of health care. Searches that used to take all day now are completed in a matter of minutes. He's really quite brilliant."

"Did he do this work for you recently?"

"Five or six months ago." She shrugged.

"So, your relationship with Luke has been going on for five or six months?"

"It isn't a relationship. It's a mentoring friendship."

"Do you mentor all the young men who do work for your charity?" I couldn't help myself. My gut told me Linda Holland was hiding the truth about her relationship with Luke. My instinct was to push until the truth or deception revealed themselves.

"Luke's a troubled soul. I try to help those in need, not ignore them."

"Does your husband know about your consiglieri role with Luke?" My annoyance got the best of me. Not for the first time. Not for the hundredth. "Or whatever it is."

Linda Holland took off her sunglasses and rolled into a sitting position matching mine. I had two inches on her and she was more long-legged than long-waisted, but her electric blue eyes were even with mine. Must have been good posture.

"Is that some sort of threat, Mr. Cahill? Is this the way a one-man private detective agency that uses a restaurant in La Jolla for an office and still owes $328,000 on his mortgage operates?" This time the smile showed teeth below ice cold eyes. Predator teeth.

Linda Holland was striking. And she looked ready to pounce.

She had gotten a lot of information about me in the two hours since I called her. The mortgage was easy. There were many online property search websites where she or someone she hired could get that information. That's how I originally found her the night Luke went to her condo. The fact that I'd used a booth at Muldoon's Steak House to meet clients took human intel, not just some web search. Only clients, a handful of friends, a few other private investigators, and the staff at Muldoon's knew I used the restaurant to meet clients because I didn't have an office. That meant that Linda Holland had instant access to someone who does what I do, but with much greater reach.

Why did she need that kind of on call access?

"No threat. Just trying to find the truth." I stared into the blue shimmer of Linda Holland's eyes and held steady. I could take the heat. And the ice. "You don't seem to be concerned that a young man you had enough interest in to invite over to your crash pad in La Jolla and, ah, mentor, is missing. Why is that?"

"Why don't you ask him?" Holland gave me the toothless smile and lolled her head toward the glass wall behind me that separated inside from outside at the Sandstrom mansion.

I turned and saw a man about my height standing next to an open section of the glass wall that I hadn't heard open. He had styled blond hair, gelled back on top, cut tight on the sides. He wore slacks, and a sports coat and loafers. No socks. His clothes were Italian and probably worth the Blue Book value of my Honda Accord.

Scot Sandstrom sauntered toward me. A toothier predatory smile. His ankles were as tan as Linda's. Men without socks.

"Why don't you ask me what?" Friendly. A tenor, like his wife, but without the growl.

Linda Holland and I stood at the same instant and faced Scot Sandstrom.

"This is Rick Cahill. He's a . . . private eye." She made it sound like something you tried to avoid at a dog park. "And he wants to know if I'm sleeping with Luke MacFarlane."

"Who?" Sandstrom stopped a couple feet in front of me. His smile stayed toothy.

"The twenty-four-year-old son of a friend of mine who's been missing since Friday night after he left your wife's condo in La Jolla." I studied Sandstrom's eyes. They gave away nothing. "But I didn't ask her if they'd slept together. I just want to know where Luke is and I think your wife knows more than she's telling me."

"My wife has nothing to hide, Mr. Cahill. And who she does or doesn't sleep with is no mystery to me. We have no secrets." Easy, but the smile was gone. "I sure hope you find this young man. Let us know if there's anything we can do to help. You can see the front door from here. I'm sure you don't need any help getting out."

I turned toward Linda Holland instead of the glass door. Time to show my hole cards. Although, I had the feeling they'd shrunk from aces down to a deuce-seven. "You knew that Luke was dating Gabriela Dates, your neighbor across the condo quad in La Jolla, right?"

"Yes, of course." Knitted eyebrows. "I introduced them."

Another layer to the Luke/Linda Holland relationship. A relationship that Moira, Luke's mother, knew nothing about.

"Then why did you let Luke come to your condo last Friday night?" I tried to drill my eyes into her skull but was blocked by her blue force-field. "You must have known about the restraining order that Gabby had the court put on him. He broke the law when he met you in La

Jolla. You could have met here, which is much closer to Luke's apartment. Especially since you and Scot have no secrets."

"I didn't learn about the restraining order until he told me that night." Matter of fact. She was good. And dangerous. "When he did, I told him he needed to leave."

"You seemed really concerned about Luke's welfare up until he went missing. Now it seems like you don't care at all. Kind of strange."

"I am concerned, Rick." The purr returned to her voice. "But with someone as competent as you searching for him, I'm sure you'll find Luke soon."

"Again, let us know if there's anything we can do to help." Scot Sandstrom's hand squeezed my shoulder. "I'll walk you out. Now."

"I'll find my way." I sloughed off his hand. "Thanks for the help. I'm sure we'll talk again."

I walked through the living room of the $10,000,000 home and out the front door. Linda Holland and Scot Sandstrom may not have secrets between each other, but they did from the rest of the world.

And I was afraid of what they might do, or already had done, to keep them hidden.

CHAPTER THIRTEEN

An hour later, I sat on Moira's sofa. I'd parked in front of her house when I arrived. I not only wasn't hiding from law enforcement, I wanted them to find me at Moira's and hope they'd come knocking. Her car was still parked a block away.

"You'd never heard of Linda Holland before I told you Luke was at her condo last Friday night, right?"

"Right." Moira sat up in her chair across from me. "Why?"

"Because she seemed to have quite an influence on Luke's life. She's the one who introduced him to Gabby Dates."

"What?" Her voice pitched high.

I told her everything that happened with the Sandstroms. Blow by blow. I wanted her to understand who Luke had spent time with the night before he went missing.

Then I told her what I'd learned about the Sandstroms online. About Scot Sandstrom's conviction for insider trading. And that Linda Holland was a former chief of staff for a congresswoman who sat on the Financial Services Committee in the U.S. House of Representatives, which oversees the Securities and Exchange Commission, before she quit the position and started working for Sandstrom.

"The congresswoman Holland worked for was also on the Health, Education, Labor and Pensions Committee, which oversees health care. Now Holland runs a charity that connects low-income families with health insurance companies." I was connecting dots for Moira as they connected in my head.

"There's nothing wrong with that. It's a noble cause." Reflexive, like she had to stand up for anyone in Luke's orbit.

"And it just so happens to be the same industry that Holland's husband invests in. There are probably some health industry executives on the charity's board. That makes for all sorts of opportunities for crony capitalism machinations."

"And you think Luke's involved in this?" Simmering anger.

"No." A half lie. I wasn't sure. "But now you can understand Holland's interest in him and why she set him up with Gabby Dates. Sequence Corp is the kind of company Sandstrom, Mr. Insider Trading, has made a lot of money investing in. Holland and Sandstrom must have been pumping Luke for whatever inside information he could get on Sequence Corp from Gabby."

Moira folded her arms and sat quietly for at least a minute. She had to be wondering about the same things I was.

How deep were Holland's hooks into Luke? Why did he go to his office at ConnectTech and, ostensibly, meet with the owner of the company after he left Holland's condo? Had Holland commanded Luke to kill Jim Harkness? Why?

I didn't have Moira's confidence in Luke's inability to cause harm to another human being. The rage she'd admitted that sometimes took posession of Luke is a hard thing to control. Maybe he graduated from breaking furniture to breaking heads. But I hadn't seen any of that rage Friday night. Not a buildup to it. Not an aftermath. And no violent shadows racing across Jim Harkness' office window. If Luke didn't kill Harkness, why do he go to the office? And if he didn't kill him, who did?

But my biggest concern wasn't that Luke could be a killer. It was that he might no longer be alive.

He had a strange connection to the wife who was one-half of a uber-rich and powerful couple. I hadn't found a violent rap sheet on either Scot Sandstrom or Linda Holland, but they certainly had the kind of money to have someone far removed from them do their killing. But if so, why?

"I think we should contact the police." My voice low and suddenly hoarse. I felt Moira's pain without ever having experienced it myself. The pain of a parent with uncertainty about a child's health. "There's more to this than just Luke and Gabby Dates and Luke and Jim Harkness. There's something not right with the Sandstroms. And they have the kind of wealth to do wrong and get away with it. The police are already looking for Luke. They need to know as much as we do so they can find him before things get worse."

"He needs me, Rick. I can't call the police on my son. I need to find him." A hollow rasp in her voice. Empty desperation. "Let's work the case a couple more days, then we can talk to SDSO if we don't find him before then."

"What if he's lying injured somewhere?" My voice rose in frustration. "Or locked in some room in the Sandstrom mansion? Who knows what those people are capable of? We need to go to the cops now. We can still work the case after we talk to them."

"He's my son." A tremor in her voice.

"I know. That's why you have to call the police."

Moira sat quietly without moving for a full minute. Finally, she slipped her hand into the back pocket of her jeans and pulled out a cell phone.

"Please put me through to the detective in charge of the Jim Harkness murder investigation. I have some information pertinent to the case."

CHAPTER FOURTEEN

AN HOUR LATER, the San Diego Sheriff's Department detectives who'd knocked on Luke MacFarlane's apartment door, while Moira and I hid inside, sat on Moira's couch. I'd just finished telling them everything I'd told Moira before she called SDSO, including what I witnessed Friday on top of Linda Holland's condo and at the ConnectTech office.

Detective Stan Hartunian ran lead and asked most of the questions while Detective Darcy Shane took notes and tossed out an intermittent intelligent question.

"And what was Luke's demeanor when he left ConnectTech that night?" Hartunian was conversational, not threatening. No gotchas. He had short black hair that grew forward. The kind of hair that looks the same when you get up in the morning as it did when you went to bed the night before.

"He already told you," Moira jumped in before I could answer.

"We're double-checking everything, Mrs. MacFarlane. We need to get everything correct so we can best utilize our resources." Hartunian, calm. He looked to be about forty-five. Compact. Solid.

"You should be out looking for him now instead of double-checking everything we tell you." Moira's arms, rubber bands pulled right around her chest. "Did you run a BOLO on Luke's car?"

"We're doing everything we can to locate your son, Mrs. Mac-Farlane." He didn't mention they were looking for him for a different reason than we were. "Now, Mr. Cahill, what was Luke's demeanor when he left the ConnectTech office Friday night?"

"Like I said, it was dark and I didn't get a good look at his face, but he didn't seem frantic or crazed." I looked over at Moira from my perch on a chair I'd carried over from the dinner table, then back at Detective Hartunian. I understood her anger, but I knew how detectives work. So did she. Until her son was the target of their questions.

"But you said he ran to his car, correct?"

"I said he hurried. He definitely wasn't running. It was late. It seemed like he'd had a long day. I'm sure he was eager to get home."

"And he went straight home?"

"Yes."

"And you left the Solana Hills Apartments parking lot at what time?" Hartunian.

"Around midnight."

"And where did you go to then?"

He hadn't asked that question the first time around.

"Home. Why?"

"Like I said, we just want to get everything right."

Now he'd flipped my switch. I could only play on the cops' terms for so long. Even when they didn't have me in a square room under the white lights.

"Well, the way I see it, Detective, is that getting it right would be to talk to Linda Holland and Scot Sandstrom as soon as you can, because they seem to be the catalyst in all of this. Linda Holland claimed to be some sort of mentor to Luke, but she's completely unconcerned that he's missing. Does that bother you at all?"

"Rick." This from Moira, as we'd finally morphed back to our normal positions. Me the hothead and her the cool reasonable one.

"We only have a few more questions." Hartunian. Calm as ever. Ignoring my question and jab. "Mrs. MacFarlane, have you ever known your son to have violent outbursts?"

Took them a while to get there, but they'd finally reached their destination. The question that had to be asked. Moira had already volunteered everything she'd learned since Luke's disappearance on their first round of questioning. His phone, credit card, and bank records. All unchanged since before he disappeared. She told the detectives what she'd learned from Luke's friends, which was nothing. They'd asked her if she had a family vacation home or cabin somewhere. She didn't. If she did, the two of us would already be on a plane or on the road to wherever it was.

All that had been the preliminary to the main event. Was Luke capable of murder? I didn't know the answer to that question. Moira thought she did. No, Luke wouldn't hurt anyone. At least she'd tried to convince herself of that.

I had the feeling Detective Hartunian had asked the question because he had already made up his mind and wanted to find a crack in Moira's defense of her son that would solidify his conclusion. And force her to wonder.

"No. Luke's a kind, caring person." Confidant, not defensive.

"I'm sure you know about the restraining order that the court enforced at Gabriela Dates' request, right?" Hartunian. Again, not in a gotcha voice. Matter of fact.

"Of course. He had an argument with his girlfriend, which she overreacted to. It happens all the time in relationships."

"But I'm sure you'll agree with me, Mrs. MacFarlane, that lifting up a heavy wooden chair and slamming it into pieces on the floor right at the feet of a girlfriend doesn't happen all the time. Shrapnel from the chair cut Ms. Dates' shin."

Moira hadn't told me about the injury to Gabby's leg. Neither had Gabby, for that matter. But I wondered if Luke had told his mother.

"Luke didn't intend for the piece of the chair to hit Gabby." Moira gave away nothing. I couldn't tell if she'd already known about Gabby's leg. "It was an accident."

"Like the accident with the chemistry professor and the glass beaker at Cal Poly San Luis Obispo?" This from Detective Shane.

Detectives Hartunian and Shane had been busy. They'd gone all the way back into Luke's college life. And found gold. For them.

"I don't know what you're talking about." Alarm in Moira's voice that she couldn't hide.

"What does all this have to do with finding Luke, Detectives?" I jumped in on reflex. And to give Moira a chance to breathe and regain her composure. "You're wasting time while Luke is out there missing somewhere and I've given you a lead with the Sandstroms you should be following up on right now instead of pestering a mother who's worried about her son."

"What about the chemistry professor and the beaker, Detective Shane?" Moira, concern in her voice and etched on her ashen face.

Shit. Whatever came out of Shane's mouth next was certain to cause more uncertainty in Moira. And anxiety. As planned. A crack in her total belief in her son. A crack that might open wide enough for her to think Luke was capable of violence against another human being so that she might call the police if he contacted her.

My allegiance to Moira led me to deflect and defend. My allegiance to the truth and justice was to listen to whatever Shane had to say and process it with an open mind.

But I feared none of it mattered because Luke might already be dead.

"Luke's chemistry professor accused Luke of throwing a glass beaker at his head after class one day in the fall of 2016 and Luke was suspended for the Spring quarter." Shane.

Moira's whole body slumped. She didn't know.

"I guess he didn't tell you." Hartunian in a low voice.

"Wait a second." I went back for more. "You telling us Luke threw a glass beaker at the head of a professor and was only suspended? That certainly seems like an expellable offense to me."

Hartunian and Shane looked at each other. Hartunian gave a slight nod.

"There was a witness who backed Luke's contention that he gestured with the beaker and it slipped out of his hand." Shane's words seemed forced. Not calm and conversational as they'd been before. They hadn't taken the reason for the suspension at face value either. They dug deeper, just as I would have.

"An accident." Moira, more desperate than certain.

My heartbeat spiked, but couldn't send blood to the hollow of my stomach. They'd chipped a fissure into Moira's resolve. Mission accomplished. But their emphasis on broken chairs and glass beakers told me something else. Something I feared.

"Why are you going back five years to a college mishap that a witness confirmed was an accident?" I raised my voice to a sharpened edge. I was looking for a crack now. In the detectives. Confrontation to cause them to misspeak. Tell the truth. "Who gives a shit about broken furniture and chemistry lab equipment? Jim Harkness was shot, not bludgeoned to death."

I hoped I was right, but feared I was wrong.

Shane threw a side glance at Hartunian. He gave her a micro headshake. A crack. Body language as loud as spoken words.

"The manner of death hasn't been made official, yet." Detective Shane made an effort to stare me in the eyes and not blink. The truth, but a lie of intention.

There are five legal definitions for manner of death as determined by a medical examiner, or sometimes, a coroner. Natural, accident, suicide, homicide, and undetermined. Theoretically, the medical examiner will conclusively rule the manner of death after an autopsy, which may not occur for days due to backlogs. There's a reason a true crime TV show about real-life homicide detectives working cases is called *The First 48*. Homicide detectives can't wait a day or even an hour to learn the official manner of death before they begin the work to track down murderers. They get a quick determination and start working right away.

And they don't ask the mother of a missing employee whose boss has died if the son had violent tendencies if they don't consider him a suspect in a murder.

Shane had said the manner of death hadn't been made official to protect information, but she might as well have said the method of murder hadn't yet been decided, which also would have been a lie.

The detective's deflection made me think that Jim Harkness had been bludgeoned to death. Probably with an object in his office. A fit of rage rather than a premeditated act. Murder two. Maybe Luke could even plead down to manslaughter.

If he was still alive.

But there was still the issue of what I saw and didn't see at Connect-Tech Friday night. No violent movements cast in shadows across Harkness' window. A hurrying, but not frantic, Luke driving home after he left the office.

"Detective." I looked at Shane. No more feints. I went straight at her. "It's clear by your and Detective Hartunian's line of questioning that Harkness was murdered. I was sitting in a car with my window down about ninety feet from the building when Luke was inside it. I didn't hear a gunshot on a quiet night. Unless you're going to tell me Harkness was shot with a silenced weapon and you think Luke is a

contract killer, Harkness was beaten or strangled to death. I had my
binoculars on his open-curtained office window the whole time Luke
was inside. There weren't any quick, violent shadow movements. No
muzzle flashes. I'll testify to that in court with my hand on a bible."

Detective Shane's chin rose a hair and her eyelids closed the same
amount. "Did you see any shadows at all, Mr. Cahill?"

Shit.

"No, but I'm sure that if anything violent had happened while I was
watching the window, I would have seen moving shadows." I wasn't
sure. I hadn't thought about the fact that I didn't see any shadows at
all while Luke was inside the ConnectTech building and possibly in
Jim Harkness's office. But I wouldn't give in. "The fact that I didn't
tells me that Luke and Harkness had a calm conversation with
Harkness seated behind his desk or that Luke never even talked to
him. Did anyone bother to check Luke's work computer? Maybe he
went to the office to get some work done."

A late-night drive to the office to get fifteen minutes of work done?
Not likely, but I was swimming against the tide for my best friend.

"As a matter of fact, we did." A bit of "gotcha" in Detective Shane's
voice. The first from either of the detectives so far. I was wearing on
them. And it wasn't going well for team Luke. Any lawyer worth their
fee knows not to ask a question of a witness the lawyer doesn't already
know the answer to. I wasn't a lawyer, we weren't in court, and
Detective Shane wasn't a witness, but I knew I wasn't going to like
what she said next. "The last time Luke used his office computer was
at 3:37 p.m. Friday afternoon."

No, things weren't going well for team Luke at all.

The detectives left a couple minutes later after asking Moira to call
them if Luke tried to contact her.

"I'll talk to some of Luke's fellow employees at ConnectTech tomorrow." I tried to sound upbeat as if the information we'd learned

from the detectives hadn't been devastating. "Maybe he's got a friend there that he never told you about who may know where he is."

"What?" Moira hadn't comprehended my words. She was staring at the door the detectives exited through. The thousand-yard stare of a soldier who'd seen too much in war. Or the stare of a mother who just learned the best-case scenario for her missing son might be life in prison. The stare was worse than the tears I'd seen earlier. Capitulation. A look and attitude I'd never seen from Moira. One I didn't think was possible. "Oh, okay."

"I'll call you with whatever I learn."

"Sure." The word came out on a breath that could have been Luke MacFarlane's death rattle.

CHAPTER FIFTEEN

I'D FINALLY GOTTEN a hold of Luke MacFarlane's college transcripts by 10:30 the next morning. It took a lot of phone calls and internet searches, but I found the name of his chemistry professor for his 2016 Spring quarter class at Cal Poly San Luis Obispo. Mathias Charles, age forty-nine, married, no children. His wife was twenty-eight.

I found Mathias Charles' personal phone number a minute later on a people finder website.

I checked the professor's schedule on the Cal Poly San Luis Obispo website. No classes until 11:30 p.m. today. Good. I called his number.

"Mathias Charles." Charles answered his personal cell phone by stating his full name. Maybe he liked the sound of it.

"Hello, Professor Charles." I used his title to show respect. "My name is Rick Cahill and I'm a private investigator doing a background check on a student you taught back in 2016. I'm hoping you can help me."

I didn't even have to lie about this one. I was doing a background check. On my own. I didn't tell Moira what I'd planned to do before I left her house last night. That would have added injury to insult. A dagger to the heart from the man who considered her his best friend.

I prayed that Luke was still alive, even though with each new day missing, the chances of that were less and less. However, dead or alive, I needed to know just how violent he'd been in the past. Was he capable of murder? He'd smashed a chair in an argument with his girlfriend. Was there a rage within him that he couldn't control? That burst out while he was in Jim Harkness' office Friday night? If he was a murderer, I'd turn him into the police. No matter how much Moira meant to me.

"2016? That was five years ago." Dismissive. "As much as every student likes to think they're unforgettable and have left their imprint on my career, the truth is, for the vast majority of them, I wouldn't be able to put a name to a face five weeks after they left my class, much less five years."

A mentor.

"His name is Luke MacFarlane."

"Ooooh." Uh-oh "That one I'd remember even if the police hadn't called me asking about him yesterday. They wouldn't tell me what kind of trouble he'd gotten himself into. What did he do now?"

"I don't know that he's done anything. I just need to ask you a few questions about him, then I'll let you get back to your day. What can you tell me about your recollections of Luke?"

"My recollections?" High pitched at the end. "Recollections sound like things I have to dig through my memory to find. Something that's more of an impression than a fact. I have memories of Luke MacFarlane, Mr. Cahill, not recollections."

"Okay. Tell me about the glass beaker incident."

"Ha!" More of a stab than a laugh. "Is that what people are calling it?"

"People aren't calling it anything. I just heard about an incident. What happened?"

"How did you hear about it?"

"That's confidential."

"What if I consider it confidential myself and don't tell you a damn thing?" Somehow, I'd gotten under Charles' skin. Must be paper thin. I usually have to at least work a little to piss someone off. A conscious effort. This one, I hadn't earned.

Time for a gamble that could either shut me out and cause me a hell of a lot more web searching or get Charles to tell me something he'd think I already knew.

"You were the wronged party. I'd really like to hear your side, but I can always talk to the witness if you don't want to tell me your truth."

I figured the "your truth" would appeal to a college professor. More on the humanities side than the sciences, though.

"Witness?" Another stab. "You mean that Perino kid? He's a liar." I could almost feel the venom spitting through the phone.

Perino. Not a common name. Shouldn't be too hard to track him down, whatever his first name was. Undergrad at Cal Poly SLO in 2016. I'd try to talk to him after I was done with the professor.

"I called you first, Professor Charles. Your version is the most important."

"There are no versions. There's only the truth."

"How about you tell it to me?"

"Okay. I'll tell you what happened." Animated. Good. I stayed silent in hopes that he'd spew in anger for a while. His version of the truth. "That MacFarlane kid had a bad temper. Hair trigger that could go off at any time. If he didn't like a grade you gave him or you called him out in class, he'd go from equilibrium to combustion in a fraction of a second."

"So, what happened that day with the beaker?"

"He got mad after class and threw a beaker at my head. I had to duck not to be decapitated."

There was something he'd either forgotten or didn't want to tell me. My money was on the latter.

"Why was he so mad?"

"I just told you it didn't take much of anything for him to go off."

"Actually, you told me he'd quickly lose his temper when he felt he'd been wronged."

"I don't remember what set him off." Defensiveness hidden in anger. I was right. He did know. "All I know is that he tried to put me in the hospital. He should have been expelled, not suspended. I should have pressed charges. Then that damn Perino kid would have been forced to perjure himself in a courtroom and not some faux disciplinary board. They should have both gone to jail."

For some reason, Charles didn't want to tell me what instigated Luke MacFarlane's beaker inside fastball. Maybe he'd tell me something else.

"You mentioned that Mr. MacFarlane would get angry if you gave him a bad grade or called him out in class. Why did you have to call him out in class?"

"He was in my class five years ago." Frazzled. "How the hell am I supposed to remember why I had to dress him down in class?"

Interesting choice of words for someone who couldn't remember why he had to call out a student.

"Only a couple more questions and then I'll let you get back to class prep."

"I give lectures. I don't prep for classes."

"My mistake. I apologize." Hopefully, sufficiently cowed for Lecturer Charles to deign his continued participation in our conversation. "But I'm confused about something that I hope you can clear up for me."

"Very well." Lord of the manor. "What is it?"

"You said Luke got upset when he received a bad grade." No gotcha in my voice, just a confused investigator. Which I was. "But according to his transcripts, he received an A minus in your class. How did he complete your class and how could he have received an A minus if you gave him bad grades?"

No sound on the other end of the phone for at least five seconds. Finally, "I can't remember what his grade was when he was suspended. I guess he was allowed to take the final in a summer session. Must have scored high. Anything else? I have other things to do."

One of them being not prepping for class.

"He was suspended during the seventh week of the quarter, correct?"

"Again, I don't remember." Snippy.

"According to the research I've done, it was the seventh week, which would mean that he took his midterm in your class, right?"

"I suppose." But he had to know where I was going.

"I know finals are usually weighted more than midterms, but to receive an A minus for the class, and clearly, acing the final, he couldn't have gotten anything lower than a B plus, B at the worst, from you on his midterm, correct?"

"What's your point?"

"Luke is a bright kid, but he got all Bs, B pluses, and A minuses on all courses outside of his computer sciences major. So, it doesn't make sense that he'd have a volcanic eruption if he got a B on a midterm in chemistry."

"Students these days think they deserve As just for showing up. I'm a chem professor, Mr. Cahill, not a psychologist."

"What was the beaker eruption really about, Mathias? Now's your chance to give me the straight story before I talk to Mr. Perino." I thought of Charles' twenty-eight-year-old wife and wished I could be in front of him to read his reaction to the next question. "Were you hitting on a coed Luke had a crush on? Flirting with his girlfriend in front of him in class?"

"Fuck you!" His voice echoed in my ears. "Don't ever fucking call me again!" Professor Mathias Charles hung up.

Turned out I didn't have to see him to read the truth in his answer. The glass beaker incident had something to do with a female student that Luke was either dating or interested in, not some bad grade or dressing down in class. Nothing gets the blood running hotter in a nineteen-year-old male than a crush on a coed.

Firing a glass beaker at an arrogant lothario professor is out of bounds, but any kid in Luke's situation would get angry. And Professor Charles' inability to come up with any details about Luke's supposed blow-ups for bad grades or calling-outs in class made me think that they never happened and that the professor was covering for his part in the beaker affair.

Luke MacFarlane had trouble controlling his anger. As a teenager, in college five years ago, and last week with his girlfriend. But how dark that anger could push him was still unknown to me.

CHAPTER SIXTEEN

I DID A couple hours of internet searching after I got off the phone with Mathias Charles, then called Moira. I didn't tell her about my talk with the professor. Not yet. That had been solely for my edification. And it hadn't convinced me that Luke wasn't the hot-headed killer the SDSO detectives hinted he might be.

Moira sounded as wrung out as she had last night.

"I found a list of employees who worked for ConnectTech in 2020." Again, I tried to sound upbeat and optimistic. A stretch for me under any circumstance. "Couldn't find anything more current than that, but hopefully most of the employees still work there and know Luke. I'll start contacting them today."

"Okay." Hollow.

"There's a total of twenty-seven employees on the list. How about I send you half?"

"You seem to be on top of things. You handle it." A dull edge to her voice, but an edge nonetheless. Good. A hint of the Moira I'd known for seven years. There was still hope.

"No. I'm sending you half of the list. Have it done by this evening. I'll touch base tonight and we can share what we found out." I hung up. She never accepted my shoulder to cry on, so I gave her a hand.

Two, in fact. And a good shove in the back. Hopefully it made her angry and started her mental juices flowing. Moira was the best private investigator I knew. And Luke needed that Moira MacFarlane now, not the one who was his mother.

* * *

The two hours I spent on the internet after my call with Mathias Charles hadn't all been spent discovering who worked for Connect-Tech in 2020 and collecting their contact info. I'd spent the first hour tracking down unknown first name Perino, Cal Poly San Luis Obispo student circa 2016 and witness for Luke in front of the college's disciplinary board.

I found him. Vincent Raines Perino. Twenty-six. Single. Born in Bakersfield. He'd gone to law school at the University of San Diego after he graduated from Cal Poly San Luis Obispo. USD was one of the top law schools in the country. Professor Charles had called Perino a liar, but he hadn't called him stupid.

Perino was now a second-year associate for the Stack, Ubell and Meyer law firm in San Diego. Lived downtown in Little Italy.

I left a message with the receptionist at Perino's work and on his cell phone's voicemail to call me. He returned my call a half hour later.

"Not every day that I get a private dick calling me. Twice. What's so urgent?" At twenty-six, Vincent Perino already had a courtroom baritone that made him sound older. So did using the term "private dick." Sounded like something out of a Mickey Spillane novel.

"I just want to ask you a few questions about Luke MacFarlane."

"What about him?"

"When was the last time you saw him?"

"It's been years. Why?"

"He's missing and I'm trying to find him." Sometimes you just tell the truth.

"Whoa." He sounded genuinely surprised.

"I have a few questions I hope you can help me with."

"What's this all about? I haven't talked to the guy in years and I'm on my way to a meeting right now. I don't know how I can help you."

A private investigator's toughest decision. Try to talk to someone who claims to be busy and risk incomplete answers and a ready excuse to end the interview or let them off the hook and request to talk at a later time knowing you may never get to talk to them again. I didn't have a badge and the power of the state to compel people to talk to me. Just my charm.

"How about we talk later? It won't take very long." I took the chance. Something about Perino's directness told me he'd either tell me to F off or give me a chance to talk to him later.

"Yeah, that'll work." His tone matched his words. "I'm jammed up all day with meetings and ass-kissing, but I can meet you tonight."

"I'm pretty sure we can cover everything in a ten-minute phone conversation."

"You said this is about Luke MacFarlane, right?"

"Yes."

"Then it's going to take longer than ten minutes." A throaty laugh. Not a reassuring one. Whatever he wanted to tell me wouldn't improve my opinion of Luke. "Let's meet for beers at Dirty Birds in Rolando at 6:30 p.m.? It's out by San Diego State. Your treat?"

"Sure."

"I'll be the only guy in there wearing a skinny cut dark blue pin-striped suit." Another chuckle in his voice. "I'll put on a red tie to make it easy. Gotta run. See you tonight."

He hung up.

I'd expected another teeth-pulling affair with Vincent Perino like I'd had with Luke's former Chem 101 professor, but I'd gotten the opposite. A smiling face over the phone who was looking forward to telling me more than I might want to know about Luke MacFarlane.

But would any of it help me find him?

CHAPTER SEVENTEEN

ACCORDING TO THE ConnectTech switchboard voicemail, the company was closed today and would reopen tomorrow. Not promising. I decided to try a different tack to connect with the ConnectTech employees. Like any savvy Millennial (the time period, not the generation) tech company, ConnectTech had a social media presence. I pulled up their Facebook page. It took a lot of scrolling, but I finally found photos and posts from a company party. There were three pictures of Luke MacFarlane looking dour in jeans and a black long-sleeve shirt and sunglasses at a beach party in Crown Point.

The Facebook posts all had names attached to the employees who were forced to have fun, fun, fun times at the beach party.

Most of the company party photos were action shots of volleyball, badminton, and general drinking and frolicking. Luke took part in none of it. He was sitting at the same picnic table in his three photos. He didn't appear to be interacting or talking with anyone, but there was one woman who sat across from him in all three pictures. The woman was looking at him in each photo and she seemed to finally catch his eye in the last one.

A one-way crush? That's what it looked like in still life. Someone who would be concerned that Luke was missing and would be willing to talk. I hoped.

The woman wore shorts and a bare midriff blouse and sunglasses. She had dark spikey hair and both arms were tattooed with blue and yellow tulips on pale skin.

According to the posts attached to the photos, the woman's name was Sheila Perkins. I found her name on my 2020 ConnectTech list of employees. The beach party was from last year and I hoped Sheila still worked at the tech firm.

I'd already called the two numbers I found for her and left a voice-mail message earlier in the day. The message was banal, just my name, occupation, and phone number. The same message I left of the other thirteen employees on my half of the list. So far, no one had been curious enough about a message from a private detective to return my call. ConnectTech management must have really clamped down about discussing what had transpired at the office.

I found Perkins' address online on my computer and checked the time. One twenty-seven. The back end of lunchtime. I hoped Sheila Perkins was home.

*   *   *

My drive to Sheila Perkins' home from my house took all of eight minutes. She lived on Bannock Avenue in North Clairemont right across from the North Clairemont Recreation Center. About a mile from the duplex I lived in seven years ago. I used to walk Midnight over to the rec center and throw a tennis ball with him on the grassy back field.

Perkins lived in the front unit of a well-kept ground-level duplex. North Clairemont was the duplex capital of San Diego. More private than apartment buildings and you got your own backyard. I never had any complaints when I lived in one. Except for the year a persistent whistler lived behind me. He moved out before there was bloodshed.

I knocked on the white door that had intertwining blue and yellow tulips painted on it. The flowers and pattern looked familiar. The door opened a few seconds later and I remembered why. Sheila Perkins stood in the doorway wearing a white halter top that showed off her tulip tattoos on both her arms that matched the ones on the door. I sensed a trend. She had on khaki shorts and was barefoot.

"Can I help you?" The sunglasses she'd worn in the Facebook photos had been replaced by black horn-rimmed prescription glasses that only added to the intellect coming from her dark brown eyes. Her brown hair, no longer spiked like in the Facebook photos, was cut short.

"I hope so." I smiled. "My name is Rick Cahill. I'm a private investigator. Luke MacFarlane's mother hired me to try to find him."

"You mean Luke's missing?" Her voice cracked high. Her eyes widened behind thick lenses.

"Yes. I'm hoping you can help me find him."

She studied me for a couple seconds before she spoke again.

"You have a badge or something?" Her voice apologetic, but her grasp on the door remained firm. Smart. Practical. Good. Hopefully she lived by the motto "verify, then trust."

"Just a paper one." I pulled out my wallet and flipped to the clear backside of my driver's license compartment and showed her the license given to me by the California Bureau of Security and Investigative Services. She looked at it and nodded. I pulled a business card out of the wallet and handed it to her.

"Thanks." More of a question than a statement.

"Can you give me a few minutes to talk about Luke?" I asked.

"Of course." She still stood sentry at the door. I didn't say anything. If we talked on her porch, it would be much easier for her to end the conversation quickly. I wanted to sit inside her home and talk. I needed time to pick her brain. We looked at each other in awkward silence. Well, not awkward for me. I specialized in uncomfortable silences. Finally, she put out an open hand. "Can I look at that license again?"

Her caution again made me happy. Cautious people think and observe. That's who I needed to talk to.

"Sure." I took out my wallet, removed the P.I. license, and handed it to her.

Sheila Perkins studied the license carefully, seeming to pay particular attention to the seal of California printed on it. She handed it back to me.

"Sorry." She smiled a pleasant, disarming smile. "You can't be too careful. Would you like to come in?"

"Sure." I made it sound like it had been her idea.

Sheila opened the door and led me into a small, but neat living room with mismatched furniture and lots of plants. The smell of peppermint permeated the air. Strong, but pleasant. Made me think of Christmas. A small polished bark coffee table sat between a love seat and a wooden rocking chair. The table had a vase with tulips in it. These were white. And real.

"Have a seat." Sheila stood behind me.

I looked at the rocking chair, then chose the love seat. Hard to pass up a rocking chair, but figured it was her favorite spot. A knit shawl hung off the back of it. Plus, the gravity of the situation called for my continued equilibrium.

"Can I get you some peppermint tea? I just poured myself a cup when you knocked."

Ah, the pleasant scent.

"I'm good. Thanks."

"Excuse me while I grab mine." She walked around a wall, presumably, into the kitchen, then came out holding a coffee mug with steam wafting from it. She sat down on the rocker and held the mug in front of her in both hands, as tea drinkers often do. She didn't rock. "Are you sure I can't get you anything? Guava juice? Almond milk? Some filtered water?"

"I'm sure. Thanks." Sheila Perkins was a nice young woman and a very polite host, but I hadn't come for tea. I came for clues to find Luke. "I don't want to take up too much of your time, so I'll get right down to business."

"Okay." She nodded; her eyes again big behind the glasses.

"Do you have any idea where Luke MacFarlane could be?"

"No." Defensive, but I didn't think she was lying. The question had been purposely direct to get a quick read on her. I read her as honest, but unsettled. As most people in her situation would be. She'd found out the president of her company was dead and that the guy she had a crush on was missing.

"Do you still work at ConnectTech?"

"Yes."

"Are you and Luke MacFarlane still friends?" I took a stab at what the Facebook photos implied. At least on her part.

"Yes. I mean, like, we don't really socialize much, but I'd consider us friends."

"Great." I gave her a smile to reassure her that she was being helpful. "When was the last time you saw him?"

"Last Friday at work. He left around three thirty."

"Is that when the workday normally ends on a Friday?"

I had the impression tech companies were go, go, go all the time, but maybe that was only in Silicon Valley. The ConnectTech office building was on the small side and there were other businesses also occupying it. Probably too small for a rumpus room and a safe space retreat. Maybe they had a Ping-Pong table in a hallway.

"Not really. You can leave after two on Fridays, but Luke almost always stays late."

"Has he left early on any other days in the last couple weeks?"

"Just last Thursday and Friday." She took a sip of her tea.

Sheila Perkins kept track of the comings and goings of Luke MacFarlane. Was that because she had a crush on him or for some other reason?

"How many employees does ConnectTech have?"

"Thirty-three." She didn't roll her eyes up to think. Perkins was tuned in to ConnectTech. And Luke MacFarlane.

And the company had six more employees than last year. Business must have been good.

"Did you work near Luke?" I had to tread carefully here. Sheila was free and easy with information so far. If I embarrassed her about her interest in Luke, she might clam up.

"Yes. I'm in the cube right on the other side of him."

"What do you do for the company?" From their website, I knew that ConnectTech had something to do with outsourcing computer programmers and matching small tech companies with companies of similar size that had synergistic, but not overlapping platforms. Whatever that meant.

"I'm a team leader and startup liaison."

"Was Luke a member of your team?" Whatever that team did.

"Well, he was." Her eyes drifted off to the right. She didn't say anything else, but there was more to say.

"Until when?"

"About a month ago." Quiet again.

"Sheila." I sterned my voice a degree. "Luke has been missing for four days now. His mother is worried. I'm worried. And I think you're worried. If not, you should be. I need to know everything you do. I can't guess at what you should tell me. Any little bit of information that you might think is insignificant may not be. What happened a month ago?"

"He started working directly for Jim." Her eyes teared up when she mentioned the name Jim.

"Jim Harkness?" The dead boss Luke met late last Friday night at ConnectTech.

Her face fell and her mouth quivered. "Yes."

CHAPTER EIGHTEEN

THE FACT THAT Luke had been working directly under Jim Harkness made it unlikely that he *didn't* go into Harkness' office when he went to ConnectTech last Friday night. But why did he go there? That was the key to his disappearance. It had to be.

Maybe Sheila Perkins knew enough to give me a clue. Even if she didn't know what she knew. But right now, she was reliving the memory of learning that the man who founded the company she worked for was dead. A boss she referred to by his first name.

"I'm sorry for your loss." I was. I forced myself to take a step back from my quest and see the pain the death of someone I didn't know caused to someone I just met. The pain that may have been caused by the man I was trying to find.

"Thank you. Jim was a good person." A breathless hitch in her voice.

"How long did you work with Jim?" This wasn't background to set a foundation for finding the truth. This was being human in a moment that demanded it.

"Six years." Wistful. "I started right out of college. Jim had just started ConnectTech the summer before my senior year at San Diego State. I worked there as an intern that summer."

"Jim must have been a mentor to you."

"Yes. Very much so. I learned a lot from him." A deep, rasping breath. "I don't know what the company will do now."

"I'm sure with people like you, they'll continue to move forward."

She wiped a tear from her eye and took a deep breath. "Thank you. I know we got a little bit off track. What else would you like to know about Luke?"

I leaned forward toward her on the love seat. "For starters, what kind of work was Luke doing for Jim?"

"It was some special project that Luke told me he wasn't allowed to talk about." Sheila was back in control. Wanting to help.

"Was that unusual? For Luke to keep a secret from you and for Jim to have a special project that the other employees weren't privy to? Especially, you?"

Sheila had worked for ConnectTech for almost the entirety of its existence. She was a team leader and Luke worked under her. I didn't know anything about the company, but it seemed to me that she would have been the logical choice to help out on a special project instead of a twenty-four-year-old kid who'd been with the company less than two years.

"Well . . . yes." All in. Concentration in her eyes. "Of course, as the founder and CEO of the company, I'm sure Jim had projects that the other employees and I weren't privy to, but he never pulled someone from a team to work on something and told them not to talk to anyone else about it."

"Were you surprised that he chose Luke to help him on this kind of unusual project?"

"Yes and no." Her brow furrowed. "To be honest with you, I should have been the logical choice. Jim had me work with him on special projects before along with Jack, another team leader. But those weren't secret."

Her eyes rolled up looking at nothing while she concentrated on something inside her head.

"What's the no part? You said yes and no."

"Luke is a genius. A rock star programmer." Shelia started slowly rocking in her rocking chair. He's written some kickass programs that have really helped us curate new clients. So, if Jim wanted a new program, it made sense for him to pull Luke from my team to work on it. But . . ."

"But what?"

"I'll admit, I was kind of jealous that Luke got the assignment and not me . . ."

"A-huh."

"I snuck up behind him a couple times while he was at his desk after Jim chose him and I never saw him working on anything new."

"What did you see him working on?"

"Nothing, really." She bobbed her shoulders and raised her eyebrows. "He just seemed to be mindlessly searching the internet."

"Searching the internet for what?"

"I only got a good look at his screen once. I didn't want him to think I was spying on him." A long exhale. "Which, of course, I was. Anyway, he was reading about Elizabeth Holmes."

"Who?" I'd heard the name sometime in the last couple years, but I couldn't remember why.

"She was the founder of Theranos, a Silicon Valley startup that was supposed to have a new way to test blood for diseases but crashed and burned. She was arrested for fraud, but the trial was delayed because of the pandemic."

"Did ConnectTech do any business with Theranos?"

"No, but a lot of tech nerds followed her rise and fall. Kind of our version of reading *People* magazine."

"Could this Elizabeth Holmes have had anything to do with Luke's project?"

"No." She laughed and shook her head. "Strictly nerd candy."

"Had Jim assigned Luke to a special project before? One that wasn't secret?"

"No. He'd had me pick a couple people from my team to work some projects three or four times and I chose Luke each time. But I was on the team, too. Everything went through me." She bit her lower lip. "This was unusual."

*　*　*

I called Moira at 3:00 p.m. after I got home from Sheila Perkins' house and told her what the team leader from ConnectTech told me about Luke, Jim Harkness, and the special project.

"Did Luke tell you what he was working on? What the special project was?"

"No. He only talked about his job in the most general terms when I could get him to talk to me about it." Moira sounded worse than yesterday. Her voice a flat monotone at normal speed.

The way she talked about Luke now made me realize that the difficulty in their relationship brought on by her husband's death was ongoing and not just a teenage phase. I suddenly felt sorry for Moira. Not just because of what she was going through now, but because of all she'd gone through and kept hidden the whole time I knew her. She'd quietly and privately dealt with the pain of her life while I'd worn mine in front of her like a face tattoo.

I was on unfamiliar turf. I'd never felt sorry for Moira before. I didn't like it.

If I tried to comfort her, she'd see my sympathy as a sign of her own weakness and feel worse about herself. Better to concentrate on the now.

"Did Detectives Hartunian and Shane contact you again?"

"No." Soft, almost a whisper. "I can't imagine if they do, it will be with good news."

Of course, she was right, but I'd continue to play the fool instead of giving into Moira's darkness. And my own.

"You never know. In the meantime, we'll keep investigating on our own." I chose a faintly upbeat tone over a saccharine one that neither one of us would buy. "Any luck with the list of employees I gave you?"

A couple seconds of silence. I was about to repeat the question when she finally answered it.

"Not yet."

"Not yet, as in no one has returned your call or not yet because you haven't made any calls?"

"Fuck you, Rick." Anger. Finally. And the anger told me she was mad at herself for being paralyzed by her depression and mad at me for reminding her. Good.

"I have no idea what you're going through, but right now that doesn't matter. And neither does the self-pity you're feeling." I started calmly then rode my own momentum. "You can't afford that right now. Luke is missing and we need to find him. So grab that list and start making some calls!"

I hung up before she could react. I felt badly about yelling at a woman who was alone and afraid for her missing son, but I'd do it again. Moira would either turn her anger at me into action and start calling ConnectTech employees or she'd cocoon further into her own anguish.

I was betting on the former. That was the Moira I knew. And admired. And tough loved.

CHAPTER NINETEEN

I ARRIVED AT the Dirty Birds Bar and Grill at 6:25 p.m. and grabbed an open two-top in the back. I ordered a water from the t-shirt and shorts waitress. The bar was known for its multitudes of craft beers on tap and variety of hot wings. There were flat-screens featuring live sports wedged in every possible line of sight vantage point. The crowd was made up mostly of shorts and flip-flops and tight jeans and halter tops. The bar hummed with energy.

I spotted Vincent Perino strutting through the front entrance at 6:37 p.m. Tall and blond, he was the only person in the bar wearing a blue skinny-legged suit and red tie, as advertised. Conventionally good looking, but not a pretty boy

He spotted me and walked over to my table in the back.

"Rick Cahill?" He smiled and stuck out his hand. "Vincent Perino."

"How'd you know it was me?" I shook his hand

"Google."

I'd made enough news over the years, good and bad, to have my own cascading Google pages.

The waitress arrived. Perino ordered wings with Diablo sauce and a Bay City IPA.

I stuck with water.

"Not drinking?" Perino tilted his head.

"On the clock, but I'm still buying."

"Good." Bigger smile. "So, what do you want to know about Kook MacFarlane?"

"Why don't we start with that nickname, Kook?" While I found Luke to be somewhat unpleasant, nothing about him read kook to me. But maybe the definition had changed since I was young. Growing up in San Diego, I remember it as a derogative surfing term.

"Kook? That's just what we always called him."

"We?"

"The guys at the fraternity."

"Fraternity?" I hadn't found any record of Luke belonging to a fraternity online. I'd read even less frat bro than kook in Luke. But I hardly knew him.

"Yeah. Phi Sigma Kappa."

He could have said any combination of Greek letters and I wouldn't have been able to tell the difference. I found enough to drink in college on my own without having to join an organization to do it.

"There's usually a story with a nickname like Kook. Did your frat surf?"

"Huh? No." The waitress returned with Perino's beer and he took a sip. "Ah, nice. Anyway, Luke was just a kook. A little weird and an out-of-control drunk."

"What do you mean? What did he do when he got drunk?" An itch ran down the back of my neck.

"One incident that I remember happened the night of the crossing ceremony—"

"The what?" A hellish image of burning crosses invaded my mind.

"The crossing ceremony." Perino looked puzzled by my question. "It means crossing the burning sands and it signifies a pledge becoming a full member."

"Oh." Thank God. "Please continue."

"Anyway, MacFarlane got all wasted and climbed on top of the roof of the frat shack, stripped down to his tighty whities, and started screaming, 'I'm a fucking MacFarlane! I'm a fucking MacFarlane!' He was crazed and wouldn't come down. We had to borrow a ladder from the Sigma Chi house to climb up and get him. Still don't know how he got up there. Anyway, we stuck him in an empty bedroom to sleep it off and he puked all over himself and the bed about an hour later. So, we put him in a shower and he locked himself in the bathroom and spent the next two hours crying to someone on his phone. Every time somebody tried to use the bathroom, they'd hear him in there balling his ass off."

"Do you know who he was talking to on the phone?"

"No, but someone thought it was his mom."

"Must have been rough for him for a while." Hard thing to live down in college. Especially in a fraternity.

"Yeah. A bunch of us wanted to kick him out of the frat. He could have been a liability and endangered our existence. A lot has changed since you went to school. Frats . . . "

"Yeah, I hear they have color TVs now."

"What? Color TVs . . . Oh. That's funny, bro." He thrust out a fist for me to bump. I did. "But really, frats are looked down upon, not only by the college administration, but by much of the student population. Hell, Cal Poly suspended a frat a couple years ago for forcing pledges who answered frat history questions wrong to do push-ups. Push-ups!"

"Push-ups is cruel and unusual punishment for kids who spend their lives with a joystick in their hands." No fist bump for that. "I take it the fraternity didn't kick him out."

"No. The Greek geeks talked us into keeping him. MacFarlane was some kind of computer genius. Some of the rest of us saw the benefit of having him as, ah, a tutor to help with computer science requirements." Perino smiled. "And he did end up helping a lot of guys get passing grades."

"Did that make him popular?"

"Not exactly popular." His face pinched up. "More like he was accepted."

"But he was still called Kook."

"Yeah." Smile with a head nod. "I think he grew to like it."

Doubted that.

Perino's food arrived and he stripped two wings bare before the waitress left. I let him finish the plate before I got down to the real reason I'd called him.

"Tell me about the beaker incident." I wanted to see if that sentence was enough to jolt his memory about Luke's altercation with Mathias Charles. The professor made it sound like Perino was the reason Luke wasn't expelled from Cal Poly. Was he?

"That was fucking crazy." Memory jolted.

"What happened?" Fucking crazy was not the kind of summary I was hoping for.

"Like I said, Luke tutored some of the guys in the frat." He looked over both shoulders, then leaned toward me like he had a secret. "I was one of them, and the day Luke wigged out on Professor Charles, he was supposed to give me a thumb drive with a coding assignment that he had, ah, tutored me on. It was a Monday and I'd spent the weekend with my girlfriend, so I didn't get a chance to get the drive from him at the frat house. I knew his schedule so I went over to the chemistry department to grab the drive from him after class. Got there early and waited out in the hall. Saw every kid in that class leave after it was over except for Luke."

Another scan of the bar, then he continued.

"So, I stuck my head in the door to see if Luke was still in there. He and Professor Charles were arguing in front of the professor's desk.

Charles screamed at Luke to leave his class and to only come back if he could behave like an adult. Then he turned and walked over to the chalkboard and Luke grabbed a glass beaker off Charles' desk and heaved it at him! Missed his head by about six inches. It was crazy! The thing shattered against the blackboard and a piece of glass must have nicked Charles because when he turned around, he had a little cut on his cheek. I'll never forget the expression on the professor's face. Sheer terror. I grabbed Luke and hustled him out of the classroom."

Shit. Pretty much as Professor Charles recounted the story. And another incident where Luke lost his temper and violently broke something. And another time someone caught shrapnel from that broken something.

"Charles said he had to duck or the beaker would have hit him in the head."

"That's bullshit." A chuckle. "He didn't even see it."

"Do you think Luke was aiming at him?" The act in itself inexcusable, but the intent was crucial. Did Luke hurt people accidentally when he lost control, the shrapnel to Mathias Charles' cheek and Gabby Dates' leg, or did he deliberately try to inflict damage?

"I've always wondered about that." Perino bit his lower lip. "Luke wasn't a jock, but he was kind of a natural athlete. We had a coed softball game one time with our sister sorority. Luke said he'd only played a couple years of Little League baseball so we stuck him out in right field where you put the losers. He fricken hit a home run and threw a dude out at home who tried to tag up on a fly ball. So, I'm guessing that if he wanted to hit Professor Charles in the head with a glass beaker from fifteen feet away, he probably could have."

"Did Luke tell you why he was so upset with Charles?"

"He said Charles was harassing a girl in his class and Luke told him to stop and Charles mocked him."

"Did you believe him?"

"Yeah, but I had the feeling this was more about the professor hitting on a girl Luke liked." A smirk.

"Did the student report Professor Charles to university officials for sexual harassment?"

"I don't know. The rumor around campus was that he had a lot of little hottie coed girlfriends. In fact, his wife was an ex–Cal Poly student who was twenty years younger than him. I don't think that stopped him from his locked door office hours meetings with pretty girls. But, as far as I know, no one ever complained about him."

"What happened at the disciplinary board hearing?"

"Luke got off with a suspension."

"How did he get off so lightly after firing a potential lethal weapon at the professor?"

"Potential lethal weapon?" He leaned back in his chair. "Did you used to be a lawyer in your earlier life?"

I now had an earlier life like I was a senior citizen, although AARP was still eight years away.

"No. Worked for plenty, though."

"Well, you think like one."

"My burden." I turned the corners of my mouth up. "The disciplinary hearing?"

"I backed up Luke's testimony and he got a suspension."

"What was his testimony?"

"He said he was gesturing with the beaker and it slipped out of his hand."

"Did Luke tell the truth at the hearing about why he was arguing with the professor?"

"He said he was arguing over a grade on a paper."

That more or less matched what Charles told me.

"What did Professor Charles say?"

"I have no idea. Witnesses are interviewed one at a time and the testimony is not made public."

"I understand Luke lying about throwing the beaker at Charles, but why didn't he tell the board what he told you about Charles coming on to the girl in class? That could have changed the tenor of the whole thing. Luke standing up for a student who was being sexually harassed." That would have been my lawyerly counsel.

"I can't be a hundred percent sure, but I think the girl who the professor was hitting on asked Luke not to go that route." He raised his shoulders and eyebrows at the same time. "He got suspended for the rest of the quarter, which was only three more weeks. I think he was able to take all his finals in the summer and nailed them."

"Thanks for your help, Vincent. I have one last question for you, but feel free to order another beer if you like."

"I'll take you up on the beer. And all my friends call me Vinny." He shot up his hand to get the waitress's attention. "What's your question?"

"Do you know of any other time Luke got violent at school?" Maybe the beaker incident was a one-off. Being mocked by a professor who hit on a girl you liked in front of the whole class could set anyone off. But not to that degree.

"Not firsthand, but I heard about something he did that got him kicked out of the frat after I graduated."

"What did he do?"

"Like I said, this is thirdhand, but I heard that he got into a fight with the frat president at the time. Supposedly, sucker punched him and knocked him out cold."

More flash violence from my best friend's son—who was a person of interest in a murder investigation.

"Let me guess, the punch had something to do with a girl?"

"Bingo."

"Why wasn't he expelled after two violent incidents?"

"Phi Sigma Kappa never reported it to the Cal Poly administration. Remember, I told you colleges hold frats in low esteem. Reporting the incident could have been a black mark against the whole fraternity, not just against Luke. Having a Phi Sigma Kappa member expelled wasn't good for their reputation. They handled it internally."

The waitress appeared with Perino's third beer.

"Thanks, Vinny." I pushed forward a fist and he bumped it. When in Rome . . .

My takeaway from the last half hour was that Luke MacFarlane was a fuse waiting to be lit when it came to someone infringing upon his crush on a woman.

"No problem. Now let me ask you a question."

"Okay."

"I heard about Luke's boss getting murdered." He did the over the shoulders look again. "Do you think Luke had something to do with it?"

"How'd you hear about that?" He told me that he hadn't talked to Luke in years.

"I asked around about Luke after you called. It's not every day that a private eye asks about an old fraternity brother." Perino leaned across the table a little too eagerly. "Well, what do you think? Did he do it?"

"No." That was more for Moira than me. "Do you think he's capable of something like that?"

Perino tilted his head and raised his hands. "Maybe."

I paid the bill and left.

CHAPTER TWENTY

I KNOCKED ON Moira's front door at 8:10 p.m. that night. With two bags of Chinese food and a six-pack of Tsingtao beer dangling from my hands. Had to drive all the way to Ocean Beach for the Tsingtao. Worth it.

I mostly drank to soften the end of sharp-edged days. I liked some beers over others. Same with liquor, colored and clear. But I hadn't ever been able to do the food pairing thing with beer. Probably should turn in my San Diego residence card for that. After all, we are the craft beer capital of America. Hell, the world. I drank alcohol to get happy or drunk and sometimes both, not to enhance the flavor of food. With one exception. No beverage goes better with any food than Tsingtao beer goes with Chinese food. At least, American Chinese food.

Moira ignored my first two rounds of knocks. Her car was parked right out front. I didn't care if she didn't want to see me. Well, I did care, but my need to update her on what I'd learned today took precedence. Plus, I wanted to know how she was doing with the Connect-Tech employee list.

She finally opened the door after round three of knocks. Which were really hard pounds.

"What?" The only color left on Moira's year-round-tan face were the deep purple circles under her eyes. A t-shirt hung off her like a muumuu and her jeans sagged below her waist. She looked like she'd been locked in a crypt for a month without any food or sleep.

"I brought dinner." I held up the bags and the beer.

"You weren't invited and I already ate."

"Last week doesn't count." I forearmed the door open and walked inside to a surprisingly spic and span home that smelled faintly of Pine-Sol.

When my life hit the skids, more than once, I'd let my health and soul go to hell and my home go to seed. Moira had only lost the handle on her health. Her house was immaculate and her soul was between her and God.

"I'm not hungry and I don't need cheering up." She still held the door open as I set the food and beer down on her dinner table.

"This is a working dinner and I'm not here to cheer you up." I emptied the bags of to-go cartons full of moo shu pork, cashew chicken, steamed rice, pot stickers, and fried wontons. "I met someone today and learned a couple interesting things."

"Did this person tell you where Luke is?" A tiny shudder in her voice when she said her son's name.

"Unfortunately, no. But have a seat and I'll tell you what I learned." I went into the kitchen and grabbed a couple dinner plates from a cabinet. I put the plates on the table with the complimentary chopsticks that came with the food.

Moira slammed the front door and walked over to the table. Not the kind of slam that rattled the walls of her house. Less angry. She slumped down into the chair to the left of the head of the table. I took the head and started spooning moo shu pork onto a pancake. She folded her arms and stared at me.

"I appreciate you trying to look after me in your obnoxious way, but I don't need it or want it. Just tell me who you met and what he or she said."

"Has Luke ever mentioned Vincent Perino?"

"No. Who's he?"

"He was Luke's witness at his Cal Poly SLO disciplinary hearing. He lied on Luke's behalf to keep him from getting expelled."

"What do you mean, he lied at the disciplinary hearing?"

I told her about my conversation with Professor Charles this morning and my talk with Vincent Perino at Dirty Birds. I left out the part about Luke cold-cocking the fraternity president and Perino's opinion on what Luke might be capable of. Moira needed food, not more doubt. Even if that's what I'd come away with after my talk with Perino.

Moira didn't say anything for at least a minute. Neither did I.

Finally, she spoke in a cool tone. "Why did you do that? What could something that happened five years ago have to do with Luke missing right now?"

"I don't think it does." I shoveled out some steamed rice on Moira's plate with my chopsticks and grabbed the cashew chicken carton. "But I wanted to know what Detectives Hartunian and Shane knew. And now we both do. And we also know that Luke probably didn't aim the beaker at the professor's head when he threw it."

"I could have told you that."

A mother's point of view. She was entitled to it.

I grabbed the six-pack of Tsingtao, went into the kitchen, found a bottle opener in a drawer, opened two bottles of beer, and put the rest in the refrigerator. I sat down at the dinner table and placed a beer next to Moira's plate. She took a sip and we spent the next fifteen minutes eating Chinese food and drinking Chinese beer in silence.

Moira started slowly but picked up speed and ate like a castaway on the TV show *Survivor*. She finally took the last bite of cashew chicken, chewed, swallowed, and looked at me. I took that as the sign to start talking again.

"Were you able to talk to any of the ConnectTech employees?" I asked about the list of employees I'd found on the internet.

"Only one. A gentleman named Steve Renker. He doesn't know Luke very well, but something happened last Thursday that he thought was odd." Moira was back to her professional staccato delivery. Maybe the food had done her some good. "He rode his bike to work and locked it behind the building and entered the office from the back entrance. Luke was already there, which Renker said was normal because he was always the first person in. But he said Luke was talking to someone on Sheila Perkins' phone, at her desk, not his own."

"What was Luke saying?" I took the last bite of my second mu shoo pork pancake.

"Renker said Luke was talking quietly and hung up when he realized Renker was in the office."

"Any idea who he could have been talking to?" I asked. He didn't have many friends. The call pool must have been pretty shallow.

"No."

"Did Renker tell all of this to the Sheriff's deputies? They'd be able to track the call from Sheila Perkins's work phone to whoever was on the other end." Not that it would do us any good right now. Unless it led to the police finding Luke. Alive.

"Yes. He said Detective Shane questioned him this morning and he said he told her everything."

"Have you talked to either detective today?"

"No." She avoided my eyes. I tried to put myself in Moira's shoes. Worried about her missing son and anxious to find out who Luke had talked to the week before he went missing. But on the flip side, worried about her son, the murder suspect, and whether the police were closing in on him. And battling the fear that he might be capable of murder.

I grabbed up the empty food cartons and went into the kitchen to dump them in the trash. Something popped into my head when I opened the cabinet under the sink and tossed the cartons into the trashcan. I walked back to the dinner table.

"Did you go through Luke's trash at his apartment?" The thought should have come to me instantaneously at the time. Had CTE slowed my cognitive capabilities? Did each fugue state reduce my ability to think, to reason, incrementally?

"Yes." Her eyes looked up to the left and she shook her head. "Damn. I looked through the trash in the little trashcan next to his desk in his bedroom, but not in the one under his sink. I was going to, then you arrived and the police knocked on the door and I focused on what to do about them and forgot to check the trashcan."

"That's understandable." I wondered if the detectives had already beaten her to it. If they were able to find the right judge, they may have already been able to get a warrant to search Luke's apartment. A fifty/fifty proposition. "If you give me his key, I'll swing by his apartment on my way home and grab what's in that trashcan."

"That's okay. I'll do it. I should have done it on Monday."

I took the plates into the kitchen and put them in the sink. "I'll go with you."

"You don't have to."

"I want to. Let's go now before we get hungry again."

"Clever." No humor in her voice.

I rinsed the plates and put them in the dishwasher. Moira disappeared down the hallway and I went around the house and checked to make sure all the windows were closed and locked. Habit. I didn't want any evil entering Moira's life next to the desperation that was already there.

CHAPTER TWENTY-ONE

I ENTERED THE parking lot of Luke's apartment complex at 9:25 p.m. There were a few open parking spots scattered throughout the lot. I parked the car a good fifty yards from Luke's unit.

"What are you doing?" Moira one-eightied the parking lot. "There's plenty of spaces right in front of Luke's apartment."

"I'm looking for surveillance teams." I reached across her and pulled out the vintage folding opera glasses I kept in my glove compartment for situations like this when I wanted a closer look at something without having to grab my binoculars from the trunk.

"I doubt SDSO would put plain-clothed deputies to work overtime staking out Luke's apartment with budget cuts going on everywhere."

"You may be right, but there are two people sitting in a white BMW X6 a row back from the curb with a great view of Luke's apartment. Males. I can't get the plate number because there's a car parked behind them."

"A BMW isn't exactly a sheriff department G-ride. Not even in Solana Beach." The dismissive tone Moira used with me so often in the past. Some normalcy. "I think this is just your inborn paranoia speaking."

"Possible, but I still don't think it's a good idea to go sauntering into Luke's apartment with eyes on us. Why take a chance if it's sheriff's deputies or someone else?"

"Maybe you're right." Moira peered at the BMW. "What do you suggest?"

"I have something in mind. I'll be right back." I handed her the opera glasses.

I opened the door and slipped out of the car, leaving the door open. The inside dome light didn't go on because I'd unscrewed the bulb as soon as I bought the car years ago. The same thing with the interior light of the trunk, which I opened with the lid only halfway up. No signal flares to give up my location when I didn't want to be located.

I found the canvas duffle bag I kept in the trunk that contained various articles of clothing for when I was on all-day surveillance and had to change up my look. Plus a few devices that helped in role-playing.

There was a smaller duffle bag hidden in the spare tire wheel well. It contained a different set of tools. Ones I'd never shown Moira or anyone else. Moira knew about the bag, but not everything that was in it. Things that would be hard to explain to law enforcement if they ever found them.

I grabbed the larger duffle and quietly closed the trunk, then crept back to the driver's seat and got in. Still leaving the door open.

Moira lowered the opera glasses from her eyes.

"Oh, not the damn duffle bag." She shook her head and her voice sounded like an index finger waving in my face.

"It's either the bag or I accidentally ram the rear end of their car. I'd rather not have to use my auto insurance. I've got a good streak going." I opened the duffle bag. After some rummaging, I found what I needed.

I took off my shirt and replaced it with a khaki button-down Dickies work shirt that had a sewn-on patch over the left pocket with the name "Dave" embroidered on it. Next, a light brown baseball hat with the word "SECURITY" printed on it in black bold lettering.

"All right, no peeking."

"Please." She raised the opera glasses back up to her eyes.

I slid sideways putting my feet out the car door and slipped off my black Galls' duty boots, then slid out of my jeans and wiggled into a pair of khaki Dickies work pants. Once I got my boots back on, I turned to Moira.

"Okay, now you." I handed her a pair of black men's running shorts, a gray sweatshirt, and my Padres ball cap.

"What do you expect me to do with these?" She held up the running shorts.

"They have an inside string belt so, hopefully, you'll be able to get them tight enough to stay on." I suddenly wished I had a stapler. "The sweatshirt is way too big, but that will hide your figure."

"Are you sure we have to do this?"

"Yes." I gently pulled the opera glasses out of her hand. "You know the drill. I'm security and you're the exhausted jogger. Your cross trainers are close enough to pass for running shoes. Now get undressed and dressed."

I watched the profiles of the men in the BMW from a back left angle while Moira got into costume. They faced forward the whole time. The parking lot had a couple tall streetlights, but the men were shaded by an SUV parked next to them. The driver had a buzz cut that gave off a military vibe. Or law enforcement. The passenger's hair was longer, but still short. The driver looked to be Caucasian and the passenger Latin. Either could have had a bit of both. Hard to tell just staring at the back left sides of their heads in shadowed light.

A couple minutes in, Moira tapped me on the arm.

"Let's get the show on the sidewalk."

I grabbed an ever-present water bottle out of the console and was glad I'd only drank half of it. "Okay, face me."

Moira turned in her seat and I pressed the open mouth of the bottle against the sweatshirt directly under her chin and squeezed. Water inundated the cotton sweatshirt. I moved the bottle around until

Moira had a nice wet V below her neck. I did the same to the back of the sweatshirt but made the faux sweat spot rounder and not as long as in the front.

She opened the glove compartment, stuck her hand in, and came out with a rubber band and put her hair into a ponytail, then put on the Padre hat and pulled her hair through the opening in the back where the size adjustment was.

"How did you know I had rubber bands? I didn't even know I had rubber bands."

"Chipotle. I had a lot of wardrobe changes in that case. I left some in here."

Always prepared.

I reached across her and grabbed a Maglite flashlight from the glove compartment. One last look through the opera glasses at the back of the heads of the BMW inhabitants. No change. Still faces forward. Good.

"Showtime," I said and slipped out of the car, this time quietly closing the door.

Moira got out on the other side. She made an adjustment on her Apple watch.

"Set your silent phone alarm for ninety seconds on my go." Moira's command, a confidant low staccato. The sound of purpose in her voice. Getting out of the house to go to Luke's apartment to search for clues had forced her to quit wallowing in despair over Luke's situation and forced her to try to solve it. Action. Solve the problem. Be a private investigator. Rely on her skills and instincts.

"You sure ninety is enough?" I asked.

"Yes. I'll need cover at thirty seconds and ninety."

"Roger."

"Ninety. On my go." Stern. She held a keychain with Luke's spare key in her right hand.

I set a silent vibration alarm for ninety seconds on my phone and placed my thumb above the start button. "Ready."

"Go." Moira tapped her watch at the same time I tapped my phone. I started a silent count to thirty and Moira jogged back toward the entrance of the parking lot, away from me and the BMW. Once she hit the sidewalk, she followed it toward the front of the complex and increased her pace.

I walked toward the BMW, using parked cars for cover. My angle to the car was at forty-five degrees from the left. A blind spot for the rearview and side mirrors and the driver's peripheral vision unless, by chance, he turned his head toward me.

I lost sight of Moira but trusted her skill and timing. The count in my head was at twenty seconds. In another five, she'd pull up in front of Luke's apartment, nestled in between two others, bend over and put her hands on her knees, breathing heavily. A jogger done with her run.

The BMW was now only two yards away. When the count in my head hit twenty-five, I turned on my Maglite, took two long strides to the driver side, knocked on the window, and shined the flashlight into the car. The driver turned toward me, calm. Like a flashlight and tap on the car window were everyday occurrences. Dead brown eyes, ears shaped like devil's horns.

I shifted my eyes to his hands in his lap. Nothing in them. The driver tapped the ignition button and rolled down his window. As he did, I crouched down a few inches and pointed the flashlight at the passenger. I had his attention, too. Latino with dark eyes. His hands visible and empty. Squarer built than his partner. Both mid to late thirties. Both had the steely calm of experienced operators. Military. Possibly ex special forces. My heartbeat shifted up a gear.

Shit. What had Luke gotten himself into?

"How are you gentlemen doing tonight?" I gave them a friendly, but not too friendly smile.

"Just fine." The driver gave me back my smile and twisted his head exaggeratedly to get a look at my name tag, which he could read without moving his head. "Dave. What can we do for you?"

Moira would already be inside Luke's apartment by now. Phase one of our mission complete. Phase two was getting her out.

"I'm just wondering what you boys are doing sitting here in the dark." I was pretty sure neither one of them liked being called boys, but age and irritants have their privileges. "I don't believe I've seen you before and I've met all the tenants."

"That's probably because we don't live here." The driver. Patronizing with a smile. "We're waiting on a friend."

"Terrific. What's your friend's name?"

"All due respect." He did the twisted head thing again and looked at my name tag. "Dave, that's none of your damn business. So why don't you take your flashlight and go see if you can find a couple getting busy in a car."

The passenger turned his head back toward Luke's apartment. I pointed the light at the side of his face. "I'm going to have to ask you two to move along or give me the name of the tenant you're waiting for."

The passenger turned back toward me. Good. Eyes off Luke's apartment.

"Get that light out of my eyes, *pendejo*." He gave the last word a full Latin accent that wasn't present before. I kept the light on the passenger's face. His hand shot to his door handle, but his partner grabbed his leg. The passenger put his hand back in his lap and the driver turned toward me.

My silent phone alarm in my pocket buzzed my leg. Moira should have exited Luke's apartment by now.

"We're not breaking any laws, Dave." More of a show of teeth than a smile. "So why don't you head on back to your car or truck with the magnet security signs on the doors and go bother somebody else?"

"So, are you gentlemen refusing to comply?" I eyeballed the driver. "I'm going to have to speak to my supervisor about this."

The driver snorted a laugh and his partner did the same. I backed away from the driver, took a picture of the rear license plate with my phone, and walked back to my car. Moira was already inside, breathing heavily and holding a bulging white trash bag. Good. The trash showed that the police hadn't gotten a search warrant for Luke's apartment. Meaning they hadn't accumulated enough evidence for a judge to sign off on a warrant or they hadn't even tried to get one. Some good news in a night where there'd only been bad.

"How did it go?" Moira asked.

"Pretty sure you were clear." I started the car and pulled out of Luke MacFarlane's parking lot where the BMW was parked with two dangerous men inside. "But we have a problem."

CHAPTER TWENTY-TWO

I TURNED ONTO Solana Hills Drive and unlocked my phone and handed it to Moira.

"That's the license plate of the Beemer. Think your guy at LJPD will run it for you?"

"Probably." She took a picture of the screen with her own phone. "If you don't know who owns the car, how do you know there's a problem? What did they say? You don't think they're cops, do you?"

"They're not cops. Maybe ex-cops, but I read them as ex-military." I took the exit onto I-5 South. "They gave me some lip and tried to intimidate me, but they didn't do anything out of line. They were just irritated. The good news is I'm pretty sure they bought the ruse. The bad news is that they looked like they were on a mission. I think they're surveilling Luke's apartment."

"Why would they be watching Luke's apartment?" Shrill. I caught the fear in her eyes out of the corner of my own.

"I think someone hired them to find Luke, but I could be wrong." I kept my voice calm, but my concern matched Moira's. "They could just be two dudes waiting for someone other than Luke who didn't like being hassled by a security guard. I probably would have reacted the same way."

"But you think they're pros?" More a statement than a question.

"Yeah, I do." Moira was the best P.I. I knew. Smarter and, usually, more emotionally stable than me. I needed her help to unravel the mystery of her missing son. The only way she could do that was if she knew all the facts that I did. And if I gave her my honest, unfiltered impressions. I couldn't hold things back because I was worried how she'd react to them. She'd either compartmentalize them or be pulled deeper into the void. An internal battle that I couldn't reach. "But I don't think they're P.I.s or ex-cops. Two dudes in a high-end vehicle that gets noticed, more or less sitting out in the open, doesn't read professional investigators to me. I think they're muscle."

"Muscle?" A shriek. "You think they want to hurt Luke?"

"I don't know what they were hired to do, just that they're not very good at surveillance." I patted Moira's thigh. Not reassuring enough to take the edge off my honest impression. "But there's a silver lining to all of this. Whoever hired those guys thinks Luke is alive."

"Do you think he's dead?" Alarmed and angry. She'd read me as having given up faith. Faith had shown mixed results in my life. In Luke's disappearance, I'd been operating on experience. But it looked like, hopefully, faith had won this time. For now.

Men who I was pretty certain had killed in their lives were looking for Luke. Faith wouldn't win out in the end if they found him.

"I thought it had been a possibility, but I think he's in hiding now. From the men in the Beemer and whoever hired them." I glanced at Moira. "We need to tell the police about them and whatever we find in Luke's trash. We still investigate on our own, but it can't be us against the police anymore. I'd rather have Luke questioned by Detectives Hartunian and Shane than by the two dudes in the BMW."

Moira sat silent for three or four minutes as we passed freeway exits that led to areas of Southern California paradise. Peaceful beauty without. Some dark secrets within.

"Okay. I'll call Detective Hartunian." She finally spoke as I took the La Jolla Village exit. "But we need to go through Luke's trash before we hand it over to the detectives. If there's a lead in there, I want to see it first. Otherwise, we'll have no way of following it. SDSO is not going to share anything with us on their own. We'll give them everything we find, but we still have to investigate as if we're the only ones trying to find Luke."

"Agreed. Let's go through the trash tonight so Hartunian and Shane can get going on the Beemer Boys as soon as possible. How much pull do you still have with your contact at LJPD?"

"I wouldn't really say I have pull with Ja—" She stopped herself. She'd never told me who her inside man was at LJPD. It didn't matter to me. Even if I knew who her contact was, he'd never help me on a case. I was forever a pariah to the La Jolla Police Department. "He gives me information when he can." The rustle of trash and clink of bottles as she turned toward me. "Why?"

"The Beemer could be a rental." I sometimes used rentals on surveillance. We passed La Jolla Shores Drive on Torrey Pines Road, just a few minutes from Moira's house. "If it is, do you think he'll go the extra mile with the car rental agency and find out who's name is on the rental agreement?"

"I'll try. He knows that Luke's missing and I'm desperate. I think he'll want to help, but won't stick his neck out too far."

"Roger." Someone needed to stick their neck out or Luke Mac-Farlane might end up dead.

If he wasn't already.

CHAPTER TWENTY-THREE

MOIRA CHANGED OUT of my running gear when we got back to her place. She went into her kitchen and came out with two black outdoor trash bags, a pair of kitchen shears, duct tape, and a woven straw Easter basket she kept on top of her refrigerator.

She cut down the sides of the trash bags, so that they were each one long rectangular strip of plastic, and taped them together length-wise, then taped them to her hardwood floor next to the dinner table. I carefully emptied Luke's garbage bag onto the middle of the taped plastic sheets. The stink of rotting food filled up Moira's living room. Brown liquid bled from the pile, creating a small puddle in front. The good news was that there were a lot of potential clues to go through. The bad news was that the potential clues were garbage.

I set the empty white trash bag down flat on the floor.

Moira put the Easter basket just outside the taped plastic, halfway between both ends. The basket was for anything that might hold a clue to Luke's whereabouts or explain what was going on in his life that would make him want to hide out.

"Hold on." Moira hustled down the hall.

I went into her kitchen and gabbed the trashcan under the sink. I pulled out the trash bag and put it in her garbage can in the backyard.

By the time I got back, Moira was sitting on the floor at one end of our indoor dump wearing blue nitrile gloves. I picked up the empty trash bag from Luke's apartment and used it to line Moira's trashcan.

All the garbage we examined was going back into Luke's trash bag. If we found anything to give clues to where he was, we'd document and separate them and give them to Detectives Hartunian and Shane along with the bag of trash.

If they wanted them.

"Here." Moira held up a pair of gloves, saving me a trip to the trunk of my car to grab a pair from my hidden black ops duffle bag. The gloves I kept there were black and the least sinister items in the bag.

I put on the gloves and sat down on the opposite end of the landfill from Moira. We each spent a couple minutes transferring perishables that had perished from the trash pile into the trashcan liner from Luke's apartment now lining Moira's trashcan. Banana peels, apple cores, orange skins all went into the trashcan. The remnants of Luke's diet explained why he'd looked fit the few times I met him. There were a few empty beer bottles, but many more empty energy drink cans. A couple Mountain Dews. Apparently, Luke didn't recycle. A cancel culture offense among his peers. His secret was safe with me. Not a single empty Starbucks cup. Luke was definitely an outcast from his generation.

Five minutes in, and half the trash pile gone, neither Moira nor I had placed a single item in the Easter basket. Even if we didn't find anything worthy of the basket, the trip to Luke's apartment had already proved valuable. Not in finding Luke, but in learning that Moira and I and the police weren't the only ones looking for him. And either we, or the cops, had better find him first.

A minute later, I picked up a to-go Pannikin coffee cup. The Pannikin was a tiny San Diego coastal chain of coffee shops that was founded a couple years before Starbucks. The La Jolla shop was less than a mile from Moira's house. I started to toss the cup into the trashcan, but changed my mind. It was the only coffee cup I'd seen in the trash, so far.

"Is this yours?" I asked Moira.

"No. And I doubt it's Luke's, either. He doesn't drink coffee."

I looked at the rim and smelled the cup and noticed two things. The cup didn't smell like coffee and it had a faint half circle pink lipstick stain on the rim. I tried to remember if Gabby Dates had worn lipstick when I talked to her. I didn't think so. I googled her on my phone and couldn't find her wearing lipstick in any of the photos I found.

"This has lipstick on it and I think there was tea and not coffee in it." My left knee, the one I'd injured playing college football, cracked when I got up and handed the cup to Moira. At least no headaches or fugue states today.

Moira sniffed the cup. I never drank tea, but thought I'd smelled a hint of something floral. I'd seen Moira drink tea a few times over the years.

"I agree that this cup didn't have coffee in it." She stuck her nose in it again and took another long sniff. "It may have had black tea in it. Hard to tell with all the other trash smells."

"Did you ever see Gabby wearing pink lipstick?" I reached for the cup and Moira handed it back to me.

I tried to remember if Linda Holland wore lipstick, but her electric blue eyes made it hard to remember anything else.

"No. I don't think she wore lipstick." She smirked at me like old times. "But that's not pink. It's coral."

"Noted." I pulled my phone from my pocket and took a picture of the cup and the lipstick, then put it in the Easter basket. Our first egg.

"What does the cup prove?" Moira asked. "How does it help us find Luke?"

"I don't know how it helps us find Luke at this point, but I think it proves that a woman other than Gabby was in Luke's apartment fairly recently. Maybe I'm wrong, but I don't think Luke had a lot of female friends." I said it as delicately as I could even as I was thinking that Luke didn't have a lot of friends, period. "It will probably have DNA on it that might help the police track down someone who knows where Luke is."

Moira frowned and shook her head. "You're right about female friends. I've never seen him with anyone other than Gabby since he's been home from college. I've never even heard him talk about other women."

*　*　*

About three-quarters of the way through the trash pile, I found a Walmart receipt. The total was $88.30. The receipt had soaked up some of the garbage juice. There appeared to be two items on it, but the liquid funk had stained a blob over the name of the items. The word "card" was visible for one of the two line items, but nothing else but "Walma . . .," the date, and the total were legible. Moira had found a couple Von's receipts and I found one for Target earlier during our trash dive and we'd tossed them into the trashcan with Luke's garbage bag in it.

I was about to toss this one, too, but then the listed date of the purchase struck me. Saturday, October 9. The day after I tailed Luke from Linda Holland's condo to his office, then home. I looked at the receipt again to check the date. I had it right. The time of the purchase was 8:23 a.m.

"What do you have?"

I looked up from the slip and saw Moira with a hand outstretched toward me.

"Walmart receipt." I leaned across the remainder of our pile of garbage and handed Moira the slip of paper.

"Walmart?" Moira took the receipt from me. "He never shops there. He's a bit of a snob that way."

"Check the date of purchase."

"What?" She shot a glance at me, eyes wide. "Last Saturday morning at 8:23 a.m.? He had to pay with cash because this purchase wasn't on his debit or credit card records."

I pulled out my phone and googled Walmarts near Solana Beach. The nearest one was on Leucadia Boulevard in Encinitas. Opened at 7:00 a.m. seven days a week.

"So, Luke drove to Walmart early Saturday morning and bought a few things for eighty-eighty bucks, then went home, threw the receipt in the trash, and disappeared." I almost said "forever" but caught myself.

"This doesn't make any sense." Moira shook her head.

"I know, but we have to make it make sense." I stood up to get circulation back into my legs and walked over to Moira. "I think it should go in the basket. Maybe the police can use it to check Walmart's security cameras and see what Luke bought or if anyone was with him at the time of the purchase. Or even if Luke made the purchase?"

Moira handed me the receipt. I took a picture of it with my cell phone and placed it in the Easter basket of possibilities.

A few minutes later, Moira picked up a white letter-sized envelope. It was damp and slightly browned on one corner where it had come in contact with the liquid in the trash pile. It looked empty and didn't have anything written on the front of it. The top had been ripped open like it had once been sealed and someone removed its contents.

Moira opened the envelope and looked inside.

"Empty," she said and flipped it over to look on the other side. "No writing on either side, but something was definitely inside it."

She held it by a dry corner with her thumb and index finger and lifted it up to the light. Then she sniffed inside it. Her face dropped.

I took the envelope from her hand and held it up to the light, then looked at the other side. And saw what had shaken Moira. Slight rectangular protrusions in the middle of the envelope, front and back. I took a dollar bill out of my wallet and held it against the rectangle just to leave no doubt to what Moira and I already knew. It fit perfectly.

The empty envelope that Luke or someone else had thrown in his trash had once had a lot of money in the form of bills stuffed inside it. Enough to bulge the envelope and leave its mark.

CHAPTER TWENTY-FOUR

"AT LEAST WE know he has cash to sustain himself on the run," I said. That was the best spin I could come up with. I took a picture of the envelope and put it into the basket. Our most telling Easter egg.

"Are you out of your mind?" Moira bolted up off the floor with surprising quickness. "I don't want him on the run. We need to find him and now we know he's untraceable. The impression in the envelope was probably about an inch thick. That's two-hundred-fifty bills. If they were a hundred each, that's $25,000. Luke could live for a year off the grid on that kind of money."

She paced back and forth across the living room.

She was right. As private investigators, Moira and I had had our hands on plenty of envelopes full of cash. We could do the geometry and the times tables. But her frantic need to locate Luke had caused her to miss the big picture.

I had misshaped facts fitting together to form a nasty little puzzle. I needed to get Moira looking at the same puzzle I was.

"Where do you think the money came from? Could Luke have a bank account you don't know about?"

Moira stopped and scowled at me. "That was the first thing I looked for. No phantom accounts under his social security number. I have all his bank records for the last six months. No large withdrawals."

She had to be thinking what I was, but just didn't want to verbalize it and make it real.

"Then where do you think that money came from?"

"I wish I knew." She started pacing again.

"Even if you're wrong about the denomination and they were fifties or twenties, that's a lot of money for Luke to borrow from a friend. Most twenty-four-year-olds don't have an extra five or ten grand lying around." I stepped in front of Moira and stopped her pacing. "But Luke knows one who could. Gabby."

"You think Luke borrowed the money from Gabby? She just put out a restraining order on him."

"I'm just checking all the possibilities off the list."

"Well, that one isn't on the list." Moira put her hands on her hips. "What other dumb possibilities do you have?"

"Somebody paid him for services rendered or paid him to keep quiet about something and he got scared and rabbited."

I didn't see the slap coming quickly enough to get a hand up to block it, but I twisted my head with the blow. It caught me high on the cheekbone and knocked my glasses off. The living room turned gray. Not from the force of the blow, although my face stung, but from my uncorrected vision. Moira was a barely recognizable fuzzy form in front of me. She didn't say anything or hit me again.

I looked on the floor to the right, the direction I'd twisted my head, for my glasses. A gray fog. I bent down for a closer look.

"I'll get them." Embarrassment hung off her words, even if she didn't apologize. She walked a few feet away, grabbed something off the floor, came back, and handed me my glasses.

I put them on. My left cheek was on fire. My left ear ringing. Injured, but not bowed.

"You have to face the facts or get out of the way and let me do my job." My own anger caught me by surprise. Not all from the slap.

Moira had hit me once before. She apologized that time. But I didn't need an apology. I needed the old Moira back. I pointed a finger at her face. "Your son is involved in something. Probably something illegal. Someone gave him a large amount of money for a reason. In cash, not a check. Untraceable cash. The sooner you accept that and get back to being the smartest P.I. I know, the quicker we'll be able to figure out what's going on and find Luke. If he goes to jail, he goes to jail. But at least he won't be dead."

Moira scowled, but she didn't say anything.

I filled the void. "Here's the good news. The cash payment makes it less probable, not more, that Luke killed Jim Harkness. Luke's violence happens because he can't control his emotions." I fought off the urge to say, "Like you." "He's not a stone-cold assassin. He's an emotionally stunted twenty-four-year-old who's still grieving his father's death nine years later. If anyone was paid to kill Harkness, it was the two operators we saw looking for Luke tonight. But he's in worse danger than if he had killed Harkness and only the police were after him. We have to find him or he has to come in from the cold, because whoever's paying the men in the BMW likely has access to more resources than just those two."

Gasps exploded from Moira and tears poured down her cheeks. I pulled her into a hug. She pushed me, but I held her close. Her strength ebbed and she curled her arms into her chest and melted into me. Her sobs hyperventilated and the tears kept running. I held her until she was spent. The sleeve of my Dickies shirt, soaked with her emotion.

I walked her over to the couch and we sat down. She slowly untangled herself from me and pulled her feet up and curled into a ball. I went into the kitchen and found a box of gallon Ziplock plastic bags in a drawer. I removed three, went over to the Easter basket, and transferred the Pannikin coffee cup, the Walmart receipt, and the envelope no longer full of cash into separate plastic bags. When Moira gave Luke's last remaining trash from his apartment to the sheriff's detectives, we'd make it easy for them to look at the only items of importance that we'd found.

I set the plastic bags on the dinner table and walked back to Moira on the couch.

"The basket items are in Ziplock bags on the table. Do you want me to be with you tomorrow when you talk to the detectives?"

"No. Thanks. I'll be fine. I need to try to get some sleep now." She got off the couch and patted me on the chest, then softly touched the cheek she'd slapped five minutes ago. "I'm sorry I hit you."

"Karma for past sins. I already forgot about it."

Moira squeezed my arm and walked toward the dining room. I headed for the front door. When I opened it, I looked back at Moira. I saw a flash of white in her right hand, which disappeared behind her like she put something in her back pocket.

The envelope.

She wasn't willing to risk that the sheriff's detectives would read the envelope the way I did. She knew they might see it as payment for murder.

CHAPTER TWENTY-FIVE

MOIRA CALLED ME at 10:17 a.m. the next morning. My cheek was still sore, but I answered anyway.

"Hartunian and Shane are coming over at noon today. I called Angus about Luke's trash before I called the detectives." Angus Buttis was a lawyer Moira sometimes investigated for and who let her use his offices when she met with clients. "He said if the police found anything inculpatory toward Luke, should there be a trial, it likely wouldn't be admitted due to chain of custody issues. SDSO wouldn't be able to have definitive proof that the trash had been Luke's."

If they found Luke's DNA on the trash, a prosecutor might work really hard to get it admitted. I kept that speculation to myself, too. There was only one thing that could be considered even remotely prejudicial to Luke in the trash, anyway. The envelope. But its implications could go two ways. Both would give the sheriff's deputies new urgency. The envelope could have been full of money as payment for Luke killing Jim Harkness or a blackmail payment for Luke to keep quiet about something. Something dangerous.

"But you're still not going to give them, or tell them about, the empty envelope?"

"Nope." The word landed like last night's slap to my face. No point in arguing. I'd let Moira weigh the risks of Luke's freedom versus his safety.

"You sure you don't want me to be there when you talk to them?" I asked.

"I'll handle it on my own." A rough edge of dismissiveness. Moira didn't want to risk me telling Hartunian and Shane more than she'd determined what was safe for Luke. To me, anything less than everything wasn't safe for Luke. But he wasn't my son.

"Okay. Let me know how it goes. Anything on the BMW from your guy at LJPD?"

"Yes. I'll text it to you in a couple minutes. Gotta go."

I went downstairs and took Midnight into the backyard. Time for some ball toss. I grabbed the tennis ball off the grass and Midnight sat stock still in front of me, eyeing my hand holding the ball. He might not have the speed and endurance he had a couple years ago, but he still had the want. I hoped that he'd still have that want when my child was old enough to be the one throwing the ball.

I tossed the ball and he sped after it and made a deft snag of a carom off the back fence. Still got it. My phone pinged with a text ten minutes in. I wiped Midnight's saliva off my hands with a towel I kept on the table on the deck for just that reason, pulled out my phone, and sat down. Midnight panted in front of me, wanting more.

I opened the text. Moira's contact at LJPD came through. Twice. The BMW X6 that the two tough guys were in last night watching Luke MacFarlane's apartment was indeed a rental car. The name on the rental agreement and California driver's license was Dan Williams. No middle name or the formal Daniel. Thirty-eight years old from San Jose. A common name. Too common. Not as ubiquitous as John Smith, but common enough not to be memorable. And from the third largest city in California.

Ninety percent that this Dan Williams from San Jose was a fake identity.

I went back in the house and upstairs to my office. Midnight followed me inside, slopped up some water from his bowl in the kitchen, then found his favorite spot under my desk by the time I'd pulled up information on Dan Williams on a paid people search website.

I found a copy of his CDL. The photo matched that of the driver in the Beemer last night. The photo looked to be fairly recent, even though the expiration of his driver's license was in just two years. The information I was able to find for this Dan Williams was that he went to high school in San Jose, college at the University of Southern California, and was now a computer consultant. No record of military service or work in law enforcement.

I blocked my phone number and called the number listed with his consulting business, Williams Computer Consultants. An automated voicemail answered.

San Jose, a big enough city for the name to blend in with other Dan Williamses, but far enough from Southern California to make it difficult for law enforcement or a private investigator to visit his residence, if needed.

College at USC, the college with the biggest enrollment in California. Another chance for his transcripts to be lost in the maze of other Dan Williamses.

Computer consulting business. He used his last name, innocuous and, again, not memorable in a Silicon Valley city with dozens of computer consultants with catchy names fighting for business. I doubted Williams Computer Consultants had too many voicemails requesting its service.

Hiding in plain sight.

No military or law enforcement experience. The "Dan Williams" I saw in the BMW X6 last night spent time in the armed forces. I was sure of it. Possibly as a special operator. A killer. He and his partner had been in the parking lot waiting for Luke MacFarlane. I'd bet my life on it, but hoped I wouldn't have to. Or Luke's.

Dan Williams was a fake identity, but the man in the Beemer was real. Why were he and his partner looking for Luke? Who hired them? What had Luke done or what did he know that forced people to hire potential killers to track him down? Who in his, mostly insular, world would know how to contact professional killers?

I knew of three who could easily afford it. Gabriela Dates, Linda Holland, and her husband, Scot Sandstrom.

Why would Gabby hire a hit team to kill Luke a week after she put a temporary restraining order on him? Had Luke gone from furniture destroyer to a real threat to Gabby in a week? He'd broken the TRO the night I saw him at Linda Holland's, within one hundred yards of Gabby's condo. Had she seen him that night? Was that enough to mark him for death or had he done something else? Threatened her? The Gabby I met on Monday was cool and intelligent. I doubted she'd make a rash decision on something as consequential as murder. When Luke's body was found, she'd have to know that, because of the restraining order and being his ex-girlfriend, she'd be suspect number one on the cops' hit list.

Gabby Dates was a long shot.

But I was leaving out another Dates who may want to see Luke dead. Two in fact. Gabby's parents, Bernie and Elizabeth. Luke's act of smashing a chair was implied violence. Maybe there were more incidents of Luke's intimidating behavior toward Gabby that Moira didn't know about. Maybe Gabby's parents decided on their own that Luke was too dangerous to their daughter to live.

I'd eaten at a couple of the Bernie's Brick Oven Pizzas in San Diego. Each of the restaurants had a portion of a wall dedicated to local San Diegans who lost their lives in service to our nation. Bernie's bio didn't mention that he'd been in the military, but he probably had a lot of friends and customers who were. It wouldn't be too hard for him to find someone to connect with the men in the BMW.

Bernie and Elizabeth Dates might have a motive to want Luke dead and the means to get it done. Linda Holland and Scot Sandstrom certainly had the financial means. A thousand times over. A couple decades as a venture capitalist, no doubt, enabled Sandstrom to meet a wide variety of people with a wide variety of skill sets. And contacts.

The motive was murky. But so was Luke's relationship with Linda Holland. And by extension, her husband. Linda's claim to be some kind of mentor to Luke didn't play for me. Thus, neither did her story about why Luke was at her condo last Friday night. Could their relationship be as simple as sex? It made more sense to me than the mentor story. So what if she and Luke were having sex? She wouldn't have to hide it. She and Sandstrom seemed to have an open marriage. Scot had intimated as much to me Monday night.

But maybe Scot only liked it open on his end. Maybe there was jealousy hiding in his openness.

Or, maybe it was something else. My mind kept rolling over blackmail.

Luke had been paid in cash. Somewhere around two-hundred-fifty bills of unknown denominations. My guess was the total amount was between $15,000–$25,000. But if whoever he was blackmailing paid him off, why were two potential hit men waiting for him outside his apartment? Had he demanded more money after he collected the first envelope and the blackmailers decided it was time for option two? The definitive one?

If Luke was blackmailing someone, the logical choices were Holland and Sandstrom. Couldn't be Gabby Dates. Would she really put a restraining order on someone she paid blackmail money to? Now she'd pissed him off after he collected the ransom. What would keep him from giving up what she just paid him to keep quiet about to an entity that could hurt her?

Gabby was out for blackmail.

That left Linda Holland and Scot Sandstrom. What could Luke, a twenty-four-year-old computer nerd, possibly have on a multi-multimillionaire and his philanthropic wife? Completely different social set and yet, they had one overlapping circle in the Venn diagram. Luke and Linda's relationship.

None of it made sense. But neither did Luke MacFarlane on the run as a murder suspect. There was still too much I didn't know.

What I did know was that the last time Luke was visible on the grid was when he bought something at a Walmart last Saturday at 8:23 a.m.

CHAPTER TWENTY-SIX

THE WALMART ON Leucadia Boulevard was a supercenter. I thought they were all supercenters. The store was about the size of two football fields. A cheerful senior citizen greeted me when I entered the store. He had a gray mustache that would have made Geraldo Rivera proud.

I went to the help desk and asked a less cheerful young female employee with brown hair and dark eye shadow if I could speak with the manager. Her name tag read: Shylby. She picked up a phone receiver and told someone named Jeff that somebody wanted to talk to him. She remained on the phone for about another ten seconds before she hung up.

"He'll be right here." Shylby's tone and posture had improved after the phone call. Maybe she got a talking-to for referring to me as "somebody" as opposed to a guest or customer. New to the job or disillusioned by the royal blue façade. Or both.

Ninety seconds later, a thin man with short curly black hair and a blue Walmart vest approached from the inner store. He appeared to be in his early thirties. His name placard read: Jeff M, Manager.

"How can I help you, sir?" His cheer matched the senior citizen's greeting "guests" at the entrance.

"Is there somewhere we can speak privately?" I flipped open my wallet to reveal my private investigator's license as if it had some cache.

Jeff looked at the P.I. license, then back at me, his eyes slightly rounder underneath raised eyebrows. Even Shylby seemed impressed. The badge had a little more cache to polish today.

"Sure. Let's go back into my office." Jeff invited me behind the service desk counter and into a modest, but not tiny, office off to the right. He closed the door behind me and sat behind a stripped-down industrial office desk. I took one of the two metal chairs opposite him. "Now, what can I do for you, Mr. Cahill?"

The desk had a computer with two large monitors on it. The computer and what it could reveal on those monitors was my pot of gold. I took out my phone and pulled up the photo I'd taken of the Walmart receipt from Luke MacFarlane's trash.

"I've been hired by a mother to find her missing son, Luke MacFarlane." I slid the phone across the table. "His last established whereabouts was in a Walmart last Saturday morning at 8:23 a.m. when he bought whatever that receipt was for. He's now been missing for five days and his mother is extremely worried. Is there a numerical code on that receipt that denotes that the items were purchased at this Walmart?"

Jeff looked at the image on my phone without picking it up. "Some of the numbers are covered up, but I'm pretty sure the receipt is from this store."

"Great." I bobbed my head. "Thanks, Jeff. I need your help with something else."

"What would you like me to do?" His tone was neither helpful nor dismissive.

"Just two things." One I was sure he wouldn't do. The other was a reach, but he might be more inclined to do the second after having to reject the first. He'd already been helpful. "Show me your security cam footage of Luke making the purchase and tell me what he bought."

"Are the police looking for this missing person?" He sat stock still in his chair.

"Yes, they are, but Luke's mother is a friend of mine and she wants as many people trying to find her son as possible." I remained bent forward. A sprinter in the blocks waiting for the starter's pistol. That Jeff M. held.

"I'm afraid I can't show the tape to anyone but law enforcement." He slid my phone back at me and leaned back in his seat and folded his arms. One false start, edging on disqualification.

I left the phone on the desk.

"I understand. That's the by-the-book way to do things." I leaned back and matched his posture. "But if Luke was with someone when he made those purchases in your store, that person might be able to lead us to him. Has anyone from law enforcement come into the store to ask you or any other manager to look at the security cam footage?"

"Not that I know of, but they could have spoken with one of the other managers."

"Possibly, but I think you'd agree that kind of event would get around the water cooler." I leaned forward again and dropped my right hand on the desk. "By the book isn't working, Jeff. The police are focusing on other things. The clock is ticking on Luke. His mother deserves answers and the police don't have any. I want to give her some."

"There's nothing I can do, Mr. Cahill." Sincere. He released his own arms. "It's company policy. We have to maintain the privacy of our guests."

The guests again, like Walmart was a mom-and-pop shop instead of the most powerful retail establishment the world has ever seen.

I picked up my phone and looked at the photo of the receipt, then slid it back across the desk.

"Would you happen to know what the items are on that receipt? Someone I know bought them and I'm looking for something similar."

Walmart manager Jeff M. looked at my phone but didn't pick it up.

"It would be very helpful to my friend's mother to know." I gave one more push.

Jeff looked at the phone again, then back at me. I could almost hear the synapses firing inside his brain. Could he square my question, taken on its own, with company policy? Telling a guest what products were attached to certain item codes didn't have to pertain to another guest's privacy. Even when it did. Jeff picked up my phone for a closer look, then pushed it back across his desk to me.

I waited.

"He bought something in electronics. I can't be one hundred percent sure, but it looks like it was two Tracfones and two memory cards."

Bingo. Two Tracfones. Burners. Two untraceable phones that Luke bought the day he disappeared. With cash. He bought untraceable phones in an untraceable manner. Well, mostly untraceable. Walmart would have security footage of the purchase. The only question besides where the hell was he, was who was the second phone for?

CHAPTER TWENTY-SEVEN

THE OCTOBER MORNING haze still hung in the afternoon air. I ran what I'd learned at Walmart through my brain, looking for a pathway to track down Luke MacFarlane.

The cash and the burner phones spelled a planned disappearance with a possible accomplice. Good news and bad. Luke was probably alive, but he did something that forced him to run and there was someone other than the police chasing him. Someone more dangerous. Like the men in the BMW.

Whether a Walmart security video showed Luke was alone or not, he'd bought the phones for a reason. He needed them to call someone while he was on the run. He'd been gone five days and hadn't called his mother. The one person in this world who loved him. He had very few friends. But he bought two phones. He had to be calling someone. I needed to find out who that someone was.

As the freeway traffic slowed at the Manchester Avenue exit, the Lomas Santa Fe Drive sign caught my eye. ConnectTech was supposed to be back up and running today. I thought of Luke's friend, Sheila Perkins. It was lunchtime, although I figured most techies lived on delivery pizza and Red Bull. Even while at the office.

I took the Lomas Santa Fe exit and headed west toward the beach. About a mile later, I pulled into the parking lot of ConnectTech, which was full of cars. No more yellow crime scene tape. No white Lexus owned by Jim Harkness. I parked and scanned the outside of the building for security cameras. Businesses and private citizens put up cameras to see and to have them be seen. They're more for discouraging people from committing crimes than to catch them in the act.

No cameras that I could see.

I called the company's main number and asked for Sheila. The receptionist put me on hold and twenty seconds later Sheila Perkins said hello.

"Sheila, it's Rick Cahill. Can I buy you lunch?"

"Well . . ." I'd stunned her. "I guess so. When?"

"Right now."

"I . . . I . . . I have to finish up something. I can leave here in about ten minutes. Where should I meet you?"

"Your parking lot. I'm already here."

"Okay. I'll make it five."

A few minutes later, Sheila Perkins came down the stairs from the ConnectTech office. I stuck my hand out the window when she hit the parking lot and she came over and got into my car.

"Thanks for meeting me," I said. "Today must be a tough day."

"Yeah. It's hard for everybody. We're all walking around like zombies." Sheila half smiled under her horn-rimmed glasses. She wore jeans and a blouse with a bright yellow and purple tulip print. The girl loved her tulips. "It's nice of you to ask and get me out of the office, but I'm guessing you came by for some other reason than just lunch."

"Yeah, you're right, but I'm still buying. Where to?"

"How about Chief's Burgers and Brew? It's down a block toward the beach on the north side of Loma Santa Fe."

I made the one-minute drive while Sheila eyed me from the passenger seat. She looked to be trying to figure out why I showed up at work. She'd learn soon enough.

I pulled into a strip mall that had a faux Scandinavian look to it. The sign for Chief's Burgers and Brew had a distinct franchise feel. I opened the door for Sheila and the interior was slightly more inviting, despite the drop ceiling. The smell of burgers and fries hung in the air. A welcome smell for any red-meated American. We grabbed a four top in the corner away from the sparse lunch crowd.

"I'm sure this is about Luke. What do you want to know?" Sheila asked.

"It's mostly about Luke. Did the police ever get around to questioning you about your boss's death?" No time or patience for a preamble.

"Yes. They came by my house after you left yesterday."

"Detectives Hartunian and Shane?" I unrolled my silverware from the paper napkin in front of me.

"Yes. That was them."

"What did they want to know?"

"They asked what time I left work on Friday and if I went to the office over the weekend. Which I didn't. And they wanted to know if I noticed anything different about Jim the last few weeks he was alive." The last few words were garbled with emotion. You don't get over losing your mentor in a couple days.

I let her regain her composure before I started up again.

"When they asked if you'd noticed anything different about Jim, did you tell them about the special project he had Luke working on?"

"No." She stared down at the table for a full five seconds before she spoke again. "Maybe I should have, but to mention it might give it greater significance than it deserves. If they would have asked me a direct question about it, I would have answered it."

"Did they ask you about Luke?"

"Yes. They wanted to know if he'd contacted me since last Friday and if I thought he had a problem with Jim. I answered no, of course."

"And you didn't volunteer anything else?"

"No."

Sheila was definitely on team Luke. I studied her for a second. Something about her was wrong. Then it hit me. No lanyard with a keycard that most high-tech companies or security-conscious businesses issue to their employees.

"Doesn't ConnectTech use keycards to get in and out of the building?"

"No. We're sort of like a temp company. We don't really have any intellectual property to safeguard."

If they did, Jim Harkness might still be alive. Whoever killed him would have been automatically locked out of the building. Unless the killer was Luke MacFarlane.

"Anything else of consequence with the detectives?"

"No, that was about it."

I looked at Sheila and thought of Luke's garbage and the Pannikin cardboard cup. The one that Moira said had tea in it. Sheila drank tea when I talked to her on Monday. Even offered me some. But Sheila didn't wear lipstick. Pink, coral, or otherwise. Maybe she wore it when she went out on a date. "Have you ever been to Luke MacFarlane's apartment?"

"Why?" She squinted at me from across the table. Neither, "yes, why," or "no, why." Just "why."

"Because I'm trying to find out where he is and anything I learn can help. Were you ever in his apartment?"

The waitress showed up before Sheila could reply or choose not to. Sheila ordered without looking at a menu. The Super Chief. Double meat. Double cheese. Double everything. She added bacon and substituted sweet potato fries, which were extra. And a pint of ale. I figured Sheila weighed around one hundred thirty pounds and she was about to consume two percent of her body weight. Maybe she hadn't eaten since breakfast Monday. Before she went to work and found out her boss was dead.

I ordered the hamburger, listed as Hamburger on the menu. And a water. Less than half of one percent of my body weight.

Sheila didn't volunteer anything, so I took up the space. But with a different tack.

"No tea with the burger?"

Sheila eyed me through half-closed eyes again. I somehow pissed away all the goodwill I'd gained in her home yesterday with my question about being in Luke's apartment.

"I don't think they serve tea here." Defensive. Still wary. "Do you have a problem with me having a beer at lunch?"

"I do not." I smiled and shook my head. "I just remembered you were drinking tea at your house when we met. I have a friend who likes tea and I'm wondering if you know of any good places to drink it in La Jolla."

"That's why you took me to lunch? To ask about tea?"

The waitress stopped by with Sheila's mug of pale ale.

"No. Just thought of it, but I could use the expertise. It's someone I want to impress. I've heard the Pannikin serves a decent variety of tea. Ever been there?"

"Not the one in La Jolla, but I've been to the one in Encinitas many times." Her shoulders dropped and she loosened up a little. "They have a nice variety. I like their fair-trade Green Sencha."

I nodded like I knew what that was.

"Ever go there with Luke?" I threw it off nonchalantly.

"We met there once." Her eyes probed, once again. "Why?"

"His mother and I found a cup from the Pannikin in Luke's trash that had had tea in it." Time to plow ahead instead of feinting and moving. "The last trash in his house before he disappeared. Was the cup yours?"

"No." Her eyes looked to the left. A look some body language experts ascribe to someone trying to recollect past experiences. If true about Sheila, it told me that she'd been in Luke's apartment and was trying to remember when she was last there.

"Sheila." I leaned forward. "I've learned some things since we talked yesterday. Luke's in danger. And not from the police. I need to find him before people who want to hurt him do. Has he called you in the last week?"

"What do you mean people who want to hurt him?" Her eyes went round.

Sheila Perkins had been the only person who worked with Luke willing to talk to me. She'd given me information that I felt was important but couldn't figure out why, yet. Maybe she could learn more and connect the dots. I needed her on my team. She deserved to hear the truth. At least, some of it.

"There are people looking for him, staking out his apartment, who will either kidnap or kill him if they get the chance."

"Oh my God!" Her body tensed into a fist. "Are you sure?"

"Yes." Maybe not one hundred percent sure, but close enough not to take any chances on Luke's safety. I took my phone out of my pocket, pulled up the driver's license screenshot of Dan Williams I grabbed off the internet, and held it up for Sheila to see. "You ever see this man before?"

She leaned across the table and looked at my phone. She studied it hard, then finally spoke. "I don't think so. Who is he?"

"He's one of two men I saw staking out Luke's apartment last night."

"Why do you think he wants to find Luke?"

"I don't know, but I'm pretty sure someone hired him and the other man to do it. Hold on a second." I pulled back my phone and googled

Linda Holland. Her photo came up connected to her charity. I enlarged it so Holland's face filled up the entire screen and showed it to Sheila. "Have you ever seen this woman before?"

"Yes. That's Linda Holland. She contracted with ConnectTech to do some programming for her charity about six months ago and Luke handled the contract."

"She also became some kind of mentor to Luke."

"I know."

"Did Luke ever talk about her?"

"A little bit, but not much. He never went into the specifics." Her eyes drifted to the left again. "It was weird. About two weeks ago at lunch, I could tell he wanted to tell me more about her, but then he cut the whole discussion off like he wished he'd never talked about it in the first place."

What secrets was Luke keeping about Linda Holland? His own or ones he shared with her?

"It sounds like you and Luke were close."

"We used to be closer." Wistfulness in her voice.

"You mean lovers?" No point in being cute now. I'd drafted Sheila onto the team.

"Yes." Sad.

"When did that end?"

"Pretty soon after it started. We both got drunk at a company team bonding event earlier this year and hooked up at his apartment that night. We went out for about a month and a half and then he broke up with me."

"Sorry about that." I liked Sheila Perkins. She was smart and earnest. And probably too nice for the Luke MacFarlane I knew. But love, and lust, don't listen to reason. "I hope you don't mind me asking this question, but I think it might be important. Do you know when—"

"Luke started dating Gabriela Dates?" Sheila cut me off. "Only a couple weeks after he dumped me."

"But you two remained friends the whole time?"

"Mostly. I'm not going to lie—my feelings were hurt when he broke up with me and then started seeing the Ice Queen, but I wasn't going to lose a friend over it. I mean, have you seen Gabriela? What red-blooded computer geek wouldn't rather date her than me?"

"Sometimes it takes a while, but most men prefer flesh and blood to ice." I thought of someone else with an icy exterior. "Did Luke ever tell you he didn't like his job and was thinking of quitting?"

"No. He loved his job." Surprise on her face. "Did someone tell you that?"

"Yes. Linda Holland."

"Hmm. I've never heard him say anything like that."

A lie from Holland? Why lie about something like that? To give me a fake reason why Luke came to her condo last Friday night?

A wisp of adrenaline swept through my body. A feeling I'd gotten before when I found the linchpins to solving cases. Luke and Linda. Luke and Jim Harkness. Luke and Gabby Dates. Something was bent about all the relationships in this case, except maybe the one Luke had with Sheila. The relationships were the key to finding Luke. I was sure of it.

The thing I wasn't sure of, yet, but felt there had to be a connection, was how all of Luke's relationships overlapped with his work and the death of Jim Harkness. But I was sitting across from the one person I knew who might be able to help me figure that out.

"Did Luke talk to you about the temporary restraining order that Gabby Dates filed against him?"

"Not right away." She put down the burger she'd just picked up and leaned forward. "But I was there when he got it. I was leading a meeting with my team in the glass conference room, which is right off the lobby. The receptionist called in and said there was someone waiting to see Luke. He went into the lobby and some hot chick handed him an envelope. She said something to him, then left the office. Luke opened the envelope and immediately went into Jim's office, shut the door, and pulled down the blinds."

"Did Harkness call him into his office or did Luke go there on his own?"

"On his own."

Why would Luke go into his boss's office after receiving the TRO? It's not the kind of document that you show your boss to climb the company ladder. Just the opposite.

"How long was he in Jim's office?"

"At least twenty minutes."

"Why do you think that the first thing he did after receiving the Temporary Restraining Order was talk to his boss?"

"I don't know." She shook her head. "The whole thing freaked me out and Luke got all closed off when I asked him about it."

I needed Sheila Perkins. Moira needed her, and more importantly, Luke needed her. But was it fair to ask her for help.? I'd asked a lot of people to help me over the years during my quest for the truth. Some of them had gotten hurt because of it. But Luke MacFarlane might get killed if I didn't ask.

"I need your help, Sheila."

"Okay." She nodded. "Whatever I can do."

The answer I'd hoped for and the one I didn't want to hear at the same time. I pushed my burger plate to the side. I'd lost my appetite. I didn't have these dilemmas sitting behind a computer running background checks. I didn't want them anymore. But Moira's son was in danger.

"If you help me, you become my responsibility." My throat tightened and I thought of all the people I'd become responsible for

working cases over the years and all the ones who were worse off because of it. "That's a dangerous position to be in. If you feel anyone
getting onto what you're doing or if you just have a bad feeling that
you can't explain, quit what you're doing immediately."

"Quit what?"

"You have to promise me, Sheila, if you get any bad vibes at all, you
quit." I clenched my fists under the table. "Do you understand?"

"Yes. I promise." Her eyes went big again. I'd gotten through. Half
the battle. "Tell me how I can help."

"See if you can find out what Jim Harkness had Luke working on.
That special project." My fists clenched tighter. "But be subtle about
it. I know it won't be easy because I'm sure sheriff's deputies took all
of Jim Harkness' computers and digital devices. Maybe even his hard
copy files. What about Luke's computer? Is it still at his desk?"

"Yes."

"Do you think you could stay late some night and get a look at it?
Get into his files? His emails?"

"Everything is probably password protected."

"Yeah, that's a problem."

"Don't worry. It may take me a while, but I'll get in." She tilted her
head down and looked at me over her glasses. "This won't be my first
email hack."

"Really?" Another layer to Sheila Perkins.

"My nickname was Cracker Jack in college."

"Just be careful, Cracker Jack."

* * *

I pulled into the parking lot of Luke MacFarlane's apartment building on my way home. No BMW sitting on his unit. No one surveilling the area at all that I could see. Good. But had the bad guys quit

for good or just taken a day off? Or, were they way ahead of me and had already found Luke's hideout? I buried the thought and what the outcome would be if that were true and went up to Luke's apartment and knocked on the door. Silence. A few more knocks. Nothing.

Luke MacFarlane was still in the wind.

Or buried somewhere beneath it.

CHAPTER TWENTY-EIGHT

I CALLED MOIRA.

"How did it go with Hartunian and Shane?" I asked by way of greeting.

"Okay, I guess." Not the machine-gun delivery, but the words still had hard edges. "They didn't seem too impressed with the bag of trash I gave them."

"Did you give them the things we set aside in the basket?"

"Of course." Irritated.

"What about the envelope? The one that had the money in it."

"Is that the only reason you called? To ask about the trash we took from Luke's apartment?"

"I'm on your team, Moira. Luke's team." Matter-of-fact. "I'm all in, but you have to tell me everything, so I'll know how to play things with the police."

"I don't want you to play anything with the police."

"Cut the bullshit. If you held back the envelope, you're playing games with them. Something I have much more experience at than you. Something I'm willing to do again. For you. I just need to know the score. Did you hold back the envelope?"

"Yes."

"Okay." Moira told the police the truth, but not the whole truth. I'd done that even more times than she knew about. Just not for a while. The police and I hadn't crossed paths in almost two years. The only wrongdoing I'd found during my background check gigs was people lying on their resumes. A capital crime to corporate human resource departments, but not to the police. "Did you tell them about the two guys in the BMW at Luke's apartment? One who is supposedly named Dan Williams?"

"Yes. They took notes, but weren't enthusiastic. I can tell they think I'm just a worried mother who's drawing at straws and I'm pretty sure they still think Luke killed Jim Harkness." Tentative. "Do you still feel the same way?"

"No. I'm convinced he didn't kill Harkness. I learned some things today that we need to talk about. But first, tell me how the rest of it went with the detectives."

"There is no rest of it. They weren't impressed with Luke's trash, but took it anyway. End of story."

"What about the receipt from Walmart's? Are they going to follow up on that?"

"I don't know."

"I sure hope they do."

"Why?" Brighter emotion.

"I'll tell you, but let's do it in person. I'm already in the car. I can be at to your house in fifteen minutes."

"No. Not here. This place feels like a dungeon to me. I need to get outside. How about the lookout above Boomer Beach in Scripps Park?"

"I can meet you there in fifteen." If I could find a place to park at the crowded tourist spot near La Jolla Cove.

"I'm going to walk. I'll be there in twenty, twenty-five minutes."

"I can pick you up."

"I'm going to walk." A command.

"See you there."

*   *   *

The lookout above Boomer beach was a six by eight-foot open air structure at the edge of a grassy expanse in Ellen Browning Scripps Park just south of La Jolla Cove. Painted green, it sat above a sloping limestone cliff that ran down to the ocean below. The view was spectacular. I had to park up the hill on Girard Street a half a mile away. Moira was already seated alone on the organically, not commercially, distressed wooden bench that looked out over the ocean.

There were fifty or so people walking along the cement walkway and milling about on the grass. The sun had burnt off the remaining marine layer and glowed golden overhead. Another day that reminded me I was blessed to live in San Diego.

I stepped inside the lookout and Moira threw a stink eye to my left. I turned to see a twenty-something couple holding hands outside the entrance. They looked at each other and continued along their way.

Moira's good cheer might explain why the lookout was all hers. I sat down next to her on the bench and watched a wave crash along the rocks below. White on tan with a blue background. A handful of artists in the park stood in front of canvases holding oil paint palettes and tried to catch a snapshot of paradise for posterity. Or a few hundred bucks.

I took a deep breath and let the scene fill me up. Something I'd done far too little of in all the years I'd lived in paradise adjacent.

"Are you going to meditate or tell me what you found out today and why you hope Hartunian and Shane follow up on the Walmart receipt?" Moira, Zen not so adjacent.

"I made a trip up to the Walmart in Encinitas and talked to the manager." I proceeded to tell her about the manager's refusal to let me see the security footage of Luke making a purchase last Saturday morning, but his willingness to tell me that Luke's receipt pointed toward him buying two Tracfones and two prepaid minutes cards. Burners with untraceable minutes. "Luke planned his disappearance. He's hiding from someone and it's not the police. It's the operators in the BMW and whoever hired them. The detectives will be able to get a look at Walmart's security footage of Luke's purchases to see if he was alone or with someone."

"Why hasn't he called me to let me know he's okay?" Moira slammed her hand down on the wooden frame of the lookout. "He has to know I can help him. Not just because he's my son. This is what I do. Help people out of difficult situations. He knows that."

"There are some things a son can't tell a mother." Moira had to sense the same thing that I did. That Luke had broken the law. "Not even one who's the best P.I. in San Diego."

"Don't try to cheer me up or puff me up." Moira looked out at the ocean. "It comes across as bad high school drama club from you."

"I could break out in a song and dance routine." I stood up and threw jazz hands in front of myself.

"Asshole." A tiny smile.

"He may not be talking to you, but he's talking to someone. And he probably gave that person the matching burner phone before he took off. Or mailed it to them later."

"Probably." Moira pursed her lips and squinted. "Or he could have bought both phones for himself."

"Maybe." I looked out at the blue horizon and spoke without thinking. "Which could mean . . ."

"That he's planning to stay missing for a long time." She stared down at the floor.

"I made one more stop today." I needed to bring Moira back to the present, not let her drift out in the stark future I'd just painted for her. "I saw Sheila Perkins again. Luke's friend from ConnectTech. Turns out they were more than just friends before Luke started dating Gabby."

"They were? Luke never mentioned her."

I took out my phone and pulled up a photo I screenshot of last year's ConnectTech beach party that I'd found on Facebook. The photo was of Luke and Sheila sitting at a picnic table. I handed my phone to Moira.

"That's her. She still has a crush on Luke and is going to try to find out what he was working on for Jim Harkness the last month of Harkness' life."

"She does look a little familiar. Luke took me to a family company event right after he started with ConnectTech. I think I met her there." Moira handed me back the phone and looked to the side. "That was back when he still included me in his life."

"He will again after we find him." I gently touched her chin and turned her face toward me. "If he doesn't, you can feel sorry for yourself then."

Moira lifted her right hand up to my still slightly swollen left cheek, gave it three soft taps.

"Point taken, asshole." She dropped her hand to her lap. "But it's a joke coming from you, the biggest drama queen I've ever worked with."

"Thus, I know from whence I speak."

"Like I said, Shakespearian." Moira raised her eyebrows and pursed her lips. "So, how is Sheila Perkins going to try to find out what Luke was working on?"

A seagull flew right in front of the lookout, then swooped down over the ocean and plunged into the water and back up to the sky with a wiggly afternoon snack.

"She's going to try to hack into Luke's work email. His computer is still sitting on his desk in his cube at ConnectTech."

"Hack?" Moira tilted her head.

"Yeah. She's got skills and she's all in."

CHAPTER TWENTY-NINE

I DROPPED MOIRA at her home on Fay Avenue, got onto Torrey Pines Road, and drove north to the Golden Triangle.

Historically speaking, the Golden Triangle was originally the residential community of University City located north of Clairemont and east of La Jolla in the triangle between Highways 5, 805, and 52. When the massive retail mall University Town Center opened before I was born in the late seventies, residential and office development soon followed. The northern sector of UTC and business offices is still a part of University City, but many people think it's part of La Jolla. Landholders in the area are happy to roll with the misconception.

Linda Holland's charity, A Hand Up, had an office in the Golden Triangle. It was located on floor nineteen of a twenty-story office building a couple streets back from La Jolla Village Drive. The building was all glass modern and had an east to west roll to it, almost like a wave breaking sideways. I drove around the parking lot searching for a white BMW X6 before I parked. Clear.

A Hand Up could probably have contributed a couple extra hundred grand to its own charity if it sold off its furniture and furnishings. I told the receptionist in the sparkling glass lobby that I was there to see Linda Holland.

"Do you have an appointment?" The woman looked like a super-model who'd just finished a walk down the runway in chic executive attire. She wore a yellow silk business suit and black stilettos under the see-through glass desk. Her brown hair was slicked back into a bun above a face of sculpted symmetrical beauty. She wore a matching symmetrical smile that exuded all the warmth of a protractor.

"I have a standing appointment." I gave her a power smile. "Please tell Linda that Rick Cahill is here."

The supermodel touched a button on the Bluetooth device draped elegantly around her ear and stared at me through noncommittal brown eyes. "There is a gentleman named Rick Cahill out here who claims to have a standing appointment with you." A pause while she listened. "Yes, Ms. Holland."

The receptionist touched the button on her Bluetooth again and warmed up her smile to room temperature. "Please have a seat, Mr. Cahill. Ms. Holland will be out to greet you soon."

I took "soon" to mean sometime less than an hour, but that was okay. I had nowhere else to be. The seating options were all made of some space-age see-through acrylic material that looked about as comfortable as a block of ice. Everything you could touch at A Hand Up was transparent. It was the things you couldn't touch, or even see, that I was worried about.

I sat in the rounded model space chair nearest the window that looked out over the tree-lined plaza between office buildings. The chair was surprisingly comfortable. I settled in for the wait and ran over the strategy for my chat with Linda Holland.

Moira and I had devised a plan while we sat above the ocean by La Jolla Cove. Maybe not so much devised as sketched. We'd tell the police everything we learned, as long as it didn't incriminate Luke. We'd already held back the envelope that we suspected had been full of cash and the special project I'd now engaged a reformed hacker to hopefully uncover. If the clock sped up or we learned something new that put Luke's life in danger, we'd tell the police everything, front to back. His safety was sacrosanct. But until then, the police had their investigation and we had our own.

And my part was to do what I did best. Annoy people. Unsettle them. Force them to do things they didn't want to.

I was a pest.

I hadn't gotten too deep into my strategy for Linda Holland when she appeared in the lobby after only five or so minutes. Which was fine, because I didn't need a set strategy. I'd use my natural strengths. Abrasiveness and gut instincts. The two had gotten me a handful of concussions and a similar number of scars. But they'd also gotten me the truth more times than not.

"Rick. So nice to see you again." Linda Holland's smile looked more convincing than her supermodel receptionist's had, but I knew the points on her perfect white teeth were sharper than they looked. She wore a gray blazer over a cream blouse and flowing navy-blue trousers. Her two-inch pumps put her at six feet, eye level with me when I stood up. Beacon blue eyes. And coral-covered lips like on the Pannikin cup. "Let's chat in my office."

I followed her down a long hall. She turned into an office just as another woman came out of it. The woman was dressed in jeans and a blouse. Brown hair, no makeup. Nothing about her stuck out except that she and Holland didn't even look at each other as they passed. The woman gave me a flat smile.

I entered the massive corner office that had a view of University Town Center and University City beyond. I'd been in offices like it before. Inhabited by executives of billion-dollar companies, not non-profit charities.

Holland sat behind a large desk, glass, of course. The rest of her of-fice furniture wasn't see-through and I sat in an armed chair across from her. There was a mug of something hot on her desk. Steam rising, but not the smell of coffee. Something more floral. Tea.

"So, what can I do for you, Rick?" She maintained her pleasantness from the lobby. "Any news about Luke MacFarlane?"

"I'm here for that exact reason. To see if there is any news about Luke." I matched her pleasantness. Or as close as I could come. "Has he called you?"

"Sadly, no." She shook her head convincingly.

"Did you and Luke ever meet at his apartment for your counseling sessions?" My voice didn't give any inflection to the embedded implication about her counseling sessions.

"No." She shook her head once, her eyes held at a low blue simmer. "Why?"

"Oh, probably just a coincidence, but I found a Pannikin to-go cup in Luke's trash that had once had tea in it. And your shade of lipstick on the rim."

"That is a coincidence, although my lipstick is Charlotte Tilbury and can be found at any Sephora or online."

"Good to know." I smiled like I might purchase some for Leah. "Why did you lie to me about the reason Luke came to your condo last Friday night?"

"I don't know what you're talking about. I told you the truth. Luke was seeking my counsel about his job and his girlfriend." Stern, square-jawed countenance. "When Francesca told me you were here, I agreed to see you because I thought you'd come by to give me some good news about Luke. But you don't have any. All you have are specious accusations. Time for you to go so you can crawl around in someone else's trash. Can you find your way back out or should I call security?"

"Security for a charity?" I slouched down in my chair and crossed my right ankle over my left knee. "I didn't know there was such animosity in this world to need protection for an organization that does such good work."

Holland pressed a button on her office phone. "Security, please send someone to my office. Now."

"Maybe you should call the police instead." I took out my phone and pulled up the screenshot of Dan Williams, the driver of the rental BMW. Time to take a flyer and go with my gut instead of any verifiable intelligence. I held up the phone for Holland to see. "Maybe they can help find this guy and ask him why he was staking out Luke MacFarlane's apartment building last night."

Holland looked at my cell phone. Her eyes widened, then blinked.

Two hard knocks on the office door, then a brusque male voice. "Ms. Holland? Security."

She bolted up from her desk and went to the office door. I stood up and braced for violence. She had a legal right to toss me out of her office. I wasn't going to fight my removal, but I needed to be ready if security led with fists instead of words.

Holland opened the door a crack. "It's okay, Robert. False alarm. You and Steve can go back to your office."

"Are you sure, ma'am? I mean Ms." The unseen security guard. "We can wait right here in case you need us."

Something about the man's voice sounded familiar. I hadn't caught it the first time through the closed door. I couldn't place it, but I sidled over to the door behind Holland to get a look at Robert from security.

"Yes, I'm sure." Holland shut the door before I could get a look. She turned and looked at me, unsurprised by my presence. She'd felt me behind the door and didn't want me to see Robert.

Why?

Was he Dan Williams? No, not his voice. Then it hit me. Williams' partner. The few words he'd spat at me last night in Luke's parking lot had been a threat still etched in my memory. That voice could match up with the one I heard attributed to Robert from security. Not one hundred percent, but close enough for a second listen. Or a first look, after I was done with Linda Holland.

"I'll give you two minutes, Rick." Holland sat back down behind her desk. "Then I'm calling security back for real. What's this about someone staking out Luke's apartment? Is he in danger? Do the police know about it?"

She rebounded nicely. Turned her fear for what I'd discovered about her involvement in Luke's disappearance into feigned fear for his safety. A pro move that would only fool an amateur. Now I knew how she rated my abilities.

Good. Always best to be underestimated.

"I do think he's in danger and, yes, the police were notified about the two men in the rented BMW surveilling Luke's apartment."

Holland didn't blink this time, but I felt, as much as saw, her mouth grip tighter.

"What do the police think?" She was studying me now. Trying to get a read on the low-rated P. I.

"Detectives Hartunian and Shane from the San Diego County Sheriff's Department aren't very free with information, but I know they're investigating Luke's disappearance and his boss's murder."

"Murder?" She faked surprise convincingly. She even made her eyes go round and eyebrows rise up.

"Yeah. You know, Jim Harkness, the founder of ConnectTech? The same company you hired Luke from to write a program for your charity." I faked my own surprise about her faked surprise. "You must have seen it on the news. Harkness was found dead in his office on Monday morning, no more than ten miles from your Encinitas home."

"I think I heard something on the radio yesterday on my drive to work." Now concern etched on her angular face. Her radiant blue eyes trying to pierce my defenses. "I guess I didn't pay attention to the name of the business. The news may not even have given it."

"The Sheriff's Department is all over it. They initially thought Luke was the killer, but they're also looking into this Dan Williams guy and his partner." I wished.

"Partner?" Her voice and face were blank. Too blank.

"Yeah, Williams has a partner. Male Latino. Late thirties. Black hair. Solidly built. Both of those guys are suspects in Jim Harkness' murder." I leaned forward in my chair and put my hands palm down on Linda Holland's see-through desk. "Have the police talked to you yet? I told them that you were Luke's mentor and one of the last people to see him before he disappeared."

Holland suddenly typed something on her laptop, then stopped abruptly and looked at me.

"Why are you really here, Rick?" She tilted her head and dropped the façade, blue flames burning at me from her eyes.

"You caught me." I sat back in my chair. "I came here to shake the tree and see if anything fell out. Luke's mother is worried about him and I have no idea how to find him. I'm getting desperate and I think you know more than you're telling me."

"I've tried to be polite. I've told you everything I know, even though I have no obligation to do so." She stood up. "But now it's time for you to leave."

"You didn't exactly tell me everything." I stayed seated.

"This is long past tedious." She put her hands on her hips. "What did I miss?"

"You didn't tell me that your husband had invested in Sequence Corp, the company where Luke's girlfriend works. Seems kind of important, considering the Luke connection and the fact that he's now missing."

I went all in on a bluff. Holland was already booting me from her office. I had nothing to lose. It was an educated bluff. I didn't know if I was in the ball park or just letting my imagination off the leash. It didn't really matter. I had no other ideas, so I held onto that tree and kept shaking.

A little of the tan faded from Holland's face, but her eyes remained blue lasers. If possible, even more intense.

"You have quite an imagination, Rick." But the pause before she spoke and her lighter shade of tan put the lie to her statement. I'd hit another nerve. Holland was using Luke as some sort of in with Sequence Corp through Gabby Dates. Or not. But something was wrong about their relationship.

"I'll take that as a yes to the rumor that Scot is an investor in Sequence Corp." A rumor I started thirty seconds earlier.

"I can't comment on my husband's business dealings and I'm not even informed on most of them, but I'm confident that this supposed rumor is completely false." She walked over to the office door and opened it. "Now, would you like me to call security or the police? Or can you behave like a gentleman and leave on your own?"

I stood up and walked over to the door, then stopped in front of Holland.

"How long do you think Luke can stay hidden with that wad of cash you paid him?"

"What wad of cash?" Her face pinched tight and she sounded sincerely confused.

"The money in the envelope you paid him to go away. How much was it? It can't last forever. He's going to have to come in out of the cold sometime."

"You're delusional."

"Say hello to your husband for me. I look forward to talking to him again soon. Or reading about him in the newspaper." I stepped out of the office.

Linda Holland's office door almost hit me in the ass on my way out. I heard the click of a lock behind me. I didn't gather much new information, but my job as a pest worked. Linda Holland may have only been more stirred than shaken, but I'd gotten under her skin. She wasn't the cipher she pretended to be. She knew more about Luke's disappearance than she let on. My bet was that it had something to do with Sequence Corp.

But Newton's law of motion was about to come into play. I'd taken action against Linda Holland. She'd respond with an opposite reaction that I feared might be more than equal of mine.

I'd take the chance. I'd done it before. You can't play in the game unless you step onto the field.

CHAPTER THIRTY

I TURNED RIGHT instead of left outside Holland's office. The lobby
and the elevators were to the left. I guessed security was to the right. I
passed a couple offices with well-dressed women sitting at desks staring at computer screens.

The third office door down the hall was open and had a placard
with "Security" on it. I peeked inside. A buff twenty-something white
dude with a crew cut sat behind a desk. The sleeves of his tan short-
sleeve shirt were rolled up a couple inches to show off his bulging bi-
ceps. He lifted his head up and eyeballed me.

"Can I help you?" He didn't sound like he really wanted to.

"Yes, you can. Thanks." I smiled like I thought he'd been sincere.
"Is Robert around?"

"Nope. Would you like to leave your name so I can tell him who's
looking for him?" He made "looking for him" sound like a bad thing.
With negative consequences if the looker found him.

I debated leaving my name. If Robert was Dan Williams' stakeout
partner and Linda Holland hired both of them to find Luke
MacFarlane, she would undoubtedly tell him all about her meeting
with me and my identity would no longer be a secret.

"Sure. Tell him Dan Williams dropped by to see him." Why not
keep shaking that tree?

Crew Cut humphed and wrote something down on a pad.

I thanked him and retraced my steps back to the lobby. The supermodel receptionist didn't even try faking a smile this time. I faked one instead then took the elevator down to the parking lot. My car was a few rows back. I scanned the lot before I approached it. Still no white BMW X6. No Robert from A Hand Up security either. That is, if he was the same guy I saw with Dan Williams in the BMW in front of Luke MacFarlane's apartment last night. I'd bet my pink slip that he was.

I sat in my car and watched the entrance of the office building for thirty-five minutes. Neither Linda Holland nor Robert from security exited. I sat for another couple minutes and mulled over the Luke MacFarlane disappearance case.

All I had was a jumble of jigsaw pieces without a box to show the big picture. Which puzzle piece went where? I didn't know. But instinct told me they fit together to form something illegal or evil and I knew someone who might be able to give me some direction. I pointed my car down La Jolla Village Drive toward the Interstate 5 exit and made a hands-free Bluetooth call to that someone.

"Rick Cahill, private detective." A slight southern accent. "To what do I owe this pleasure?"

Odell Donohue. A wealthy private investor for whom I'd done some work last year. He was about to invest in a chain of nutritional supplement stores, but wanted me to run a background check on the owner. I did and discovered that he was into supplements. Just not the ones he sold. His nutrition consisted of steroids for breakfast and fentanyl for dinner. Dessert was a skim of the profits.

Donohue claimed I'd saved him millions of dollars as the stores went out of business within six months of my investigation. My reward beyond my fee was his endorsement to some of the heads of companies he'd invested in. I now had the somewhat cushy job of freelance background check specialist for some of the largest companies and corporations in Southern California. Leah was even more thankful to Donohue than I was.

She liked having me working from behind a computer in the safety of my home office. Working Luke MacFarlane's disappearance reminded me how much I missed the streets. But raising a child with Leah would be the final, most important adventure of my life.

"The pleasure is all mine. Especially since I hope to be able to pick your brain when you have a few minutes."

"I'm finishing up some business. Can you give me an idea what it is you'd like to pick my brain about, as you say?"

"Sure. I need to know as much as I can about a VC named Scot Sandstrom and his wife, Linda Holland, and a medical research company called Sequence Corp."

"Sure enough, my friend. I'm familiar with all three." The syrupy cadence of his Birmingham roots. "I'm a bachelor for the next couple weeks. Aliyah took the kids to Mandeville, Jamaica, to see her mother. Let me finish up what I'm doing, make a few calls, then maybe you could come by the house this evening for a drink and a little chat? Seven thirty work for you?"

"Perfectly. Thanks, O. D."

"Pull down underneath and park in the garage."

"Roger." Odell Donohue had worked hard enough and made enough correct decisions in his life to have an underground garage with his house in La Jolla.

My next Bluetooth call was to Moira. I gave her the play-by-play of my encounter with Linda Holland and some color commentary, as well.

"Do you think it was wise to tell Holland so much about what we know?" Her tone told me she didn't think so. Not the response I'd expected or hoped for.

"We know a lot less than I made her believe we do." A snick in my voice. "We agreed that I needed to push Holland to get a read on her. And my read is that she and her husband are the catalyst for Luke's disappearance. Their involvement has something to do with Luke's relationship with Gabby and her connection to Sequence Corp. I'll have a better idea after I meet with O.D. tonight."

"O.D.?"

"Odell Donohue."

"Oh, your investor friend. How can he help?"

"I don't know yet." But I was sure I'd know more about Scot Sandstrom and his wife and about Sequence Corp after I talked to him.

Knowledge was power. And right now, I didn't have much of either. "How did your talk with ConnectTech go?"

"Not great, but they agreed to meet with me tomorrow to discuss Luke." Her voice eased, like she let go a pressure release. "I had to play hardball, but I got their attention."

Moira was a lifetime .500 hitter at hardball. A much better average than I had. She was a hall of famer and I was a journeyman. But a plucky journeyman. And I always went down swinging.

CHAPTER THIRTY-ONE

ODELL DONOHUE LIVED in a custom-built contemporary modern house in La Jolla on Silverado Street, about a quarter mile from the Pacific Ocean. The house took four years to build and was a swash of limestone, wood, and metal that had as much outdoor space in its footprint as indoors. It ran three stories, including the garage. Even four if you counted the rooftop deck with an ocean view.

I drove down the driveway and the wooden garage door with horizontal slatted windows opened as if by magic. I parked on the Batman-style steel turntable platform because Donohue's Bentley convertible, Mustang GT, Range Rover, and Tesla Roadster were parked behind it.

And because it was a turntable platform.

Odell "O.D." Donohue approached me as I got out of the car. Tall, athletic build, with a pencil mustache etched above his mouth. A tight fade haircut framed a handsome chiseled face. He wore gray slacks and a crème collared shirt that offset his caramel-colored skin. I knew he was fifty-three years old, but without that knowledge would have guessed early forties.

"Rick." He stuck out a hand. "Thanks for coming by."

"Thanks for seeing me on such short notice." I shook his hand.

"My pleasure." O.D. led me into a glass elevator. He pushed the button marked two and we silently rose through the living room that featured vertical glass sheet waterfalls. We stopped on the third floor, which housed the kitchen and living room and opened up to the outdoors, which had its own kitchen/grill area, a glass dining table that sat eight, and a limestone deck with a handful of seating areas that wrapped around the entire structure. O.D. chose a couple of expensive patio chairs in the front corner of the deck that sat above the street. There was a bottle of twenty-year-old Laphroaig scotch and two rocks glasses on a table between the chairs.

"Have a seat, Rick."

I did as told, and O.D. poured two fingers of $800 scotch into a glass and handed it to me. I was tempted to grasp the glass containing the expensive liquid with two hands so I didn't dribble ten bucks' worth over the side. Donohue poured himself the same and sat down.

"Cheers." He reached his glass toward mine and we clinked them without loss of even a dime's worth of amber liquid.

I took a sip. Rich and smoky, with a hint of red meat. I didn't smoke, but suddenly had a hankering for a cigar. Something Cuban. Thankfully, there weren't any on the glass table.

"Let's get down to business. Who do you want to start with, Scot Sandstrom and Linda Holland or Sequence Corp?"

"Sandstrom and Holland. I think everything starts with them."

"It would be helpful for me to know what that is so I can focus on particular areas to talk about."

Normally, I wouldn't give up that information on a case, but Donohue had knowledge and access to information that I didn't. I trusted him and knew he needed direction to tell me what I needed to know.

I spent the next ten minutes telling Donohue about Luke's disappearance, his boss's murder, Gabriela Dates and Sequence Corp, Scot Sandstrom and Linda Holland.

And how important my client, Moira, was to me.

"That's a lot to digest." O.D. sat back in his chair and took a sip of scotch.

"Yep. And the police think my friend's missing son is a suspect in Jim Harkness' murder."

"How much do you know about Harkness?"

"Just that he was the founder and CEO of ConnectTech, which is some sort of facilitator in helping non-competitive small tech companies work together. Or something like that. Over my head."

"As an investor, it's over my head, too, and not investable." Donohue set down his glass, his cadence picking up steam. "But the interesting thing about Jim Harkness is that he used to own an online publication called *Tech Watchdog* that exposed unscrupulous and corrupt tech companies. His e-zine torpedoed at least two potential IPOs that I know of. *Tech Watchdog* was a great tool for tech investors, but Harkness had a hard time attracting advertisers and it went out of business after only two or three years in publication nine or ten years ago. Most of Silicon Valley didn't want anything to do with him. Bad juju."

This information opened things up for at least a couple new suspects.

"Do you think his murderer may have been someone who was burned by an aborted IPO, ten years ago?" Seemed like a long time to wait without the anger dissipating. But I didn't know much about the rich. I adhered to the F. Scott Fitzgerald maxim. They're different than me.

"You're the detective. That's your field of expertise, not mine. Just thought you might find that bit of information interesting."

It *was* interesting, but murder investigations were law enforcement's field of expertise.

Mine was agitating people until they showed who they really were. Sometimes that spilled over onto murder investigations. And got me into trouble.

"I do. Thanks." At least it would give the sheriff's department someone other than Luke to take a look at. Maybe they already were looking at it. "Do you happen to know the names of the people who were burned by Harkness' publication?"

"Well, there was Rachel Karpinski who tried to take Syntech public, but then she went on to form another startup in Silicon Valley that's doing quite well. The other would be Marvin Breakstone of Clash, but he went into online gaming overseas eight years ago. Lives on an island in the Bahamas now."

Both would be a long shot to hold a grudge that long, especially since they each landed on their feet and then some.

"What can you tell me about the power couple, Linda Holland and Scot Sandstrom?"

"Yep, a power couple. They're one tag team that's a piece of work. Each formidable by themselves. Together, they're as dangerous as the 1985 Chicago Bears defense."

I was born in 1979, but even I remember the 85 Bears.

"How so?"

"Scot Sandstrom likes to cut in line by leveraging insider information. He was an unknown player with no notable wins until he started dating a Miss Linda Rose Holland who happened to be the chief of staff for Congresswoman Irene Rivers who sat on the Financial Services Committee in 2007. All of a sudden Sandstrom starts shorting housing stocks and makes tens of millions with the crash of 2008. A coincidence?"

"What made Linda Holland smarter than everyone else? How did she anticipate the housing crash when few others did? I didn't read anything about insider trading regarding Congress and the housing collapse."

"First of all, by all accounts, Linda Holland is damn smart. Secondly, you're right, you didn't read anything about congressmen and -women making a killing off the housing collapse. Congress members don't have to put their investments into trusts like Presidential candidates do. The shady ones hide them with family members or friends so when they get juicy insider information, their financial windfalls can remain hidden from the public. Why do you think so many congresspeople enter Congress as paupers and retire as sultans?"

"I always wondered about that." I took another sip of scotch. "Is that why Holland resigned from Congresswoman Rivers' staff? Somebody figured out that she fed insider info to Sandstrom?"

"That's my guess. Scot Sandstrom is not the most understated person. Very soon thereafter, he traded in his Mazda Miata for a Lamborghini. Word got around. He has since started his own VC firm and invests mostly in tech startups and medical research companies."

"And pharmaceuticals? I read about his investment and exit of Stemtech."

"Yes, that was a big winner for him." O.D. nodded. "But, rumor has it that he needs another winner soon. He has a hard time keeping up with his and his wife's lifestyle."

"It's quite a lifestyle. I was at his home in Encinitas last week."

"Sea Breeze."

I wasn't sure what he meant. "Yeah, they get a nice one up there hanging over the ocean."

"No." He shook his head and chuckled. "That's its name. Every custom house has to have its own title now."

"What's the name of this one?"

"The Arc House." He made it sound regal, then laughed and shook his head.

"After Noah?"

"I think a different kind of arc, but I never asked. Architects and realtors think up that kind of marketing spin." He settled back into his chair and exhaled loudly. "I just call it home."

I thought about the bat cave garage two stories below and wondered, not for the first time, about my career and life choices. But that ark had sailed. My future was set. My own home would soon have a family. I'd have new responsibilities. Luke MacFarlane was my last case that mattered.

And I owed it to Luke and Moira to get it right.

"It's cozy." I took a sip of liquid gold. "You think Holland and Sandstrom got their hooks into Luke because of his relationship with Gabriela Dates at Sequence Corp?"

"I wouldn't put it past them. I met both Holland and Sandstrom at a Google event a couple years ago. Impressive, but I wanted to check my wallet and wipe my hand on my pants after my handshake with Sandstrom. Slippery. That impression and what I've told you tonight are all I really know about him. As for Holland, all I know is that she's smart and knows how to leverage relationships."

"What about Holland's charity, A Hand Up? Do you know anything about it? She has the kind of security you'd expect for a monarch. Or the leader of a drug cartel, not the head of a charity for underprivileged families."

"As far as I know, the charity does some good work, as any serious, non-political charity does. But if you take a look at the list of its benefactors, I think you'll discover the real reason she started it."

"To rub elbows with the wealthy elite and glean an occasional insider trading tip?"

"Yup, but it's a symbiotic relationship. Fred Willis from Wellness Health and Kym Cameron of Velvet Hammer Technologies, among others, get to show everyone that they're good corporate stewards by helping the underprivileged and they get to sit on the board. It's a win-win."

"But Holland and Sandstrom aren't winning enough lately."

"That's what I've heard."

"What do you know about Sequence Corp?"

"A little. When the company incorporated seventeen years ago, it was as a research lab that studied DNA mutations for cancer research. What's new is that they claim to be able to predict if someone will get cancer in the future and what kind. They say all of this can be found years in advance from a single DNA mutation and from that they can determine what drugs pre-cancer patients can be put on to prevent the cancer from ever developing. They call the test Cancer Sweep."

"Holy crap. A cure for cancer. Sequence Corp must be worth billions." I blew out my own loud exhale.

"Not quite a cure, but a predictor and a way to fight cancer early." O.D. finished the last of his scotch. "And the company is not worth billions quite yet. From what I was able to find out earlier this evening, they're still in the clinical trials stage. And that sucks up a lot of money. Millions and millions. I don't know how close to market they are, but, apparently, there's an internal struggle within their board whether to go public or sell to one of the pharmaceutical giants."

"So Big Pharma could sell you the DNA test, then when the results come back pre-cancerous, it also sells you the drug that will keep the cancer from ever forming?"

"Correct. And, possibly, sell you the drug for the entirety of your life. And if that drug works well, your life will be longer and the company's profits higher."

"That is a win-win." I took a last sip of the smoky scotch and set my glass down onto the table. "I already checked Sequence Corp's website trying to find out if Sandstrom has invested in them, but they don't list all their investors. If he is, this could be that big win that he's looking for. Whether they go public or sell, he will make a fortune when he cashes out."

"Correct." Donohue held up the bottle of Laphroaig to me. "Another one?"

"No thanks." It wasn't every day I turned down a second round of $800 scotch. Tonight was the first time I'd been given the opportunity. "I'd better stop after one because I won't be able to stop after two."

I had to drive through La Jolla to get home and LJPD liked to pull me over every once in a while, just to remind me they could. I didn't want to blow .0799 on a breathalyzer and have them round up.

"Suit yourself." O.D. poured himself another drink.

"What do you think the Sandstroms could get out of Luke to enhance their chance at a big score?"

"It may be strictly a defensive play." Another sip.

"Defensive play? What do you mean?"

"Sandstrom and Holland, obviously, would squeeze Luke for anything he knows about Sequence Corp, good or bad, ever so delicately so that he doesn't even feel the vice tightening. But, in my experience, the kind of back-and-forth between couples, like Luke and Gabriela Dates, regarding work usually involves one or both venting about perceived or legitimate slights and spreading company rumors. Thus, a lot of negative information about Sequence Corp could have been passed from Miss Dates to Luke and then to

Holland and Sandstrom. They would then determine what was and wasn't consequential negative information, so they could hedge their bets if needed."

"How could they hedge their bets?" Eight years as a private investigator and I was still mostly ignorant about the smoky backrooms of high finance.

"Well, if things don't look as rosy internally as the public perceives, they might sell their equity in the company before the IPO or the sale to Big Pharma. They probably would at least recoup their initial investment and even make a few bucks instead of holding on and selling after the IPO or sale and hope whatever bad news they knew about wouldn't become public until after they sold."

"But, under this scenario, they'd be unlikely to make that big score that you say Sandstrom needs, right?"

"Correct."

Offense or defense, I still believed that Sandstrom and Holland used Luke to their advantage and then paid him off or scared him away. Maybe both. Right or wrong, Odell Donohue had given me valuable information that I might never have found on my own.

"This has been really helpful." I stood up and Donohue did the same. "Thanks for all the information and insight."

"My pleasure, Rick." We shook hands. "I'll escort you down to the garage."

"And spin the turntable?"

"And spin the turntable." He laughed.

We took the glass elevator down two stories. I watched one level, and then another, of a lifestyle I'd never live pass by me.

We shook hands again and I got into my car, which was pointed one hundred eighty degrees in the opposite direction of the garage door. O.D. put his hands on the car windowsill and leaned toward me. I rolled down the window.

"Next time, bring Leah and we'll have dinner on the roof with Aliyah and sip more scotch and solve some of the world's problems."

"Deal." I was about to roll up the window, but O.D.'s hands were still on the windowsill.

"I hope you find your friend's son." His face hardened. "But be careful how you look for him. People like Scot Sandstrom and Linda Holland take any interference in their accumulation of wealth very seriously."

He tapped the hood of the car, then walked to the back of the garage and pushed a button next to the elevator.

My car spun slowly around and the garage door disappeared into the ceiling. I pulled out of the five-car garage underneath the seven-million-dollar home and drove into the moonless night.

CHAPTER THIRTY-TWO

I PARKED ON the right side of my driveway. My home gym took up space on the same side in the garage. I did this out of habit so Leah could park her SUV in the garage next to the gym. Midnight barked inside the house. He knew the sound of my car, but rarely barked when I came home unless I'd been away for a few days. I could just make out his head through a break in the curtains in the front window.

I got out of the car and started for the front door.

"Hey, Rick." Friendly male voice from my right, slightly high pitched.

I turned to find the voice. A figure walked toward me in the cover of the night and waved. "Rick."

Midnight barked louder.

I spun in the opposite direction. Too late.

My head exploded in pain. I turned, staggered, and swung wildly at another dark figure. My momentum bounced me off the side of my car. I stopped spinning but the world kept spiraling around me. A shadow arm swung. A shock of pain. Darkness.

I regained consciousness to the sound of Midnight's snarled barks and his paws clawing at the window. Trying to get out. Trying to protect me.

My head throbbed in a nightmare as my brain woke up. I had no idea how long I'd been unconscious. A hand grabbed the lapels of my shirt and lifted my neck up. Hard slap to my face. I opened my eyes to real-life boogeymen. One, in a ski mask and dark clothes, held my shirt. He wore leather gloves. The other, dressed the same, stood next to his partner. A black rectangular object dangled from his right hand. They didn't need the disguises. The second blow to my head knocked my glasses off. Legally blind and illegally beaten. All I saw was dark against dark.

"Luke MacFarlane says hello." A deep, gruff voice from the man holding my shirt. The same man who'd used a high-pitched voice to get my attention a minute ago was now a baritone. Trying to conceal his identity. He punched me in the right eye before I could get my hands up. Pain. Stars. My eye shut involuntarily. "Consider him found. Tell his mother he's okay and he'll contact her soon. But only her. For your own health, Cahill, stop looking for Luke. He doesn't need your help. And he doesn't like you."

I flipped up a wavering arm to partially block the next punch I felt coming. But not his partner's kick to my side. A jolt to my ribcage. I rolled over onto my side and went fetal. The men were gone when I finally raised my head. No sound of a car peeling out. They might still be out there. I scanned the night but all I could see was smudged darkness.

My ribs and my head seesawed for pain supremacy. Cold sweat chilled my body. I wanted to stay balled up and pass out. But I couldn't. I was defenseless and couldn't stay that way. My glasses. My vision, now more precious to me after not having it for almost a year, my first line of defense.

I struggled to all fours. Pain stabbed my ribs and concussed inside my head. Bile rode up my throat. I swallowed it back down and took ragged breaths. Sweat dripped down my forehead. I took five deep breaths that hurt my ribs, but my breathing began to smooth out. The nausea dissipated.

I slowly took my phone out of my pocket and turned on the flashlight app. Pain vibrated inside me with each slight movement. I pointed the flashlight at the cement driveway and searched for my glasses, one small area at a time. Between each search I stopped, steadied my breath, and fought the pain.

No glasses on the driveway between the car and the lawn. I still had to check under the car. I gently lowered my body to the ground. My ribs grabbed. They screamed when I army crawled on my belly under the car. My mouth almost did, too.

I pushed further under the car and the flashlight beam caught a glint of something. My glasses. I slowly reached forward, grabbed them, and inspected them under the light. A slight scratch on the lower part of the left lens. The glasses survived better than I did.

I put them on and slowly backed out from under the car. Pain tore at my ribs with each movement. Finally, I backed all the way out, next to the right rear tire. Now I had to figure out how to get up to my feet. Again, I went up on all fours. More searing pain.

I put the phone back into my pocket and grabbed the top of the rear tire with one hand and mashed my other against the side of the car. I pushed off the tire and shimmied up to my feet, still in a crouch. Sweat poured off my forehead and underneath my arms.

Halfway home. I pushed up to my feet and moved my hand off the tire to the underside of the wheel well for support. My hand bumped against the edge of something that protruded from the underside of the well. Something hard. Metal.

I made it all the way to my feet without throwing up or passing out. But I had one more task that would reverse all the progress I'd just made. I took out my phone again and slid at a glacial pace down to my knees. Somehow, I twisted my body to the side without screaming and pointed the flashlight app beam at the underside of the wheel well. There it was.

A GPS tracking device.

CHAPTER THIRTY-THREE

I stared at the GPS tracker for ten solid seconds, even though I had to keep my body in a painful position. I reached for the device, but stopped before I touched it. If I took it off, whoever put it there would know I was onto them. If I left it on, I might be able to use it to my advantage.

Whoever the people behind the tracker were, they sent two thugs to send me a message. Hand delivered. I didn't believe the "they" was Luke. The "Luke MacFarlane says hello" bit was a weak attempt at diversion. My guess was the charitable Linda Holland and her husband. The effort by one of the thugs to conceal his voice pointed to him being Dan Williams and the other his partner in the BMW.

I pulled my hand back and slowly straightened all the way up. Still painful at whatever speed. I scanned the neighborhood and didn't see any more boogeymen.

I trudged to the front door and keyed my way inside my house. Midnight paced in place in front of me. I scratched his head and told him everything was okay. It wasn't. He must have heard or sensed my attackers outside before I arrived. I should have reacted to his barking and the diversionary "look this way" greeting on the sidewalk sooner. Could have saved myself some pain. And delivered some of my own.

I was out of practice. Dulled by my stationary daily computer search life. Dangerous, when events beckon you out from behind the desk.

Tonight was a dangerous reminder.

I shuffled into the kitchen with Midnight at my side, looking up at me. Sensing my injuries. My vulnerability. I grabbed two plastic freezer bags from a drawer under the counter and filled them with ice cubes, then wrapped a dishtowel around one of the bags. I used to keep readymade icepacks in my freezer for incidents such as tonight. I'd thought I didn't need them anymore.

I walked into the living room and eased down into my La-Z-Boy recliner. My ribs poked at me and my head felt like it was being reverse vised outward from the inside. I reclined the chair slightly so my lower body was horizontal, but my head was at forty-five degrees. About the resting position of a hospital bed. I wedged one ice bag between the arm of the chair and my ribs.

Pain caught my breath. I felt the two welts on the left side of my head where the second thug hit me. Judging by the size of the lumps and the object I'd seen in the attacker's hand, I guessed he'd hit me with a sap. A pouch filled with lead at the end of a stiff leather strap. I pressed the dishtowel-covered ice bag against the left side of my head with my left hand. Cold pain on top of pain.

If Leah were here, I'd already be on my way to the emergency room. Then make a complaint to the police. Driving myself to the emergency room was doable, but would be painful and probably unnecessary. I'd dealt with these kinds of injuries before. On my own.

Calling the cops was another matter. Rarely a good choice for me. But they'd be hard pressed to put me in the wrong tonight. Even so, they wouldn't be able to track down my attackers. I couldn't give them anything beyond speculation or any description except blurry black masses and one friendly, then not so friendly, voice.

So, for now I had ice bags and time. A little time, at least. The ice would ease the pain, but wouldn't give me any idea how much internal damage had been done to my ribs. And my brain. I'd had bruised ribs before. That was my best guess tonight. The level of pain was familiar. Even a little less than the last time someone kicked me in the side. I didn't wince when I breathed tonight. The pain was manageable. There was no real treatment for bruised ribs. Slow down, ice, Tylenol or ibuprofen. And take deep breaths to avoid pneumonia.

Midnight sat down next to the recliner and stared at me some more. He'd seen me in this position before. Many times. Now it seemed to be taking its toll on him as much as on me. Maybe he sensed the internal damage all the beatings had wrought. He finally lay down and sighed. My protector by my side. Neither of us able to reverse the ravages of time, but both willing to continue the fight.

And think.

A thought pushed its way to the front of my concerns. How long had the GPS tracker been hidden on my car? My guess was that it was put there by Robert, the unseen security guy at A Hand Up who I couldn't find after my talk with Linda Holland. She typed something on her computer before I exited her office. An email directive to security to place a GPS tracking device on my car? Maybe.

But what if it'd been on my car longer than that? My car was easy pickings to stick a GPS device onto. I parked it outside on the driveway every night. Anyone could have attached a device at night while I slept upstairs in my bedroom. And while Midnight did the same.

And however long the device had been attached to my car, had someone been using it to follow me or just keep track of my whereabouts remotely with a computer?

I used to have a sixth sense about being followed. Didn't work all the time, but I'd sensed, and discovered, cars, and people on foot, following me more than a handful of times. Even when I couldn't see. It came with always being aware of your surroundings and being open to your primordial sense of fear. Fear kept you alive. Monotony could get you killed.

Had someone been following me and I'd been unaware due to my dulled survivor skills? Or had my CTE caused me to be paranoid? No. The GPS device was real.

Was it on my car when I went to ConnectTech and took Sheila Perkins to lunch? If someone was following me, not just watching my car icon move around an animated map on a computer, they'd seen me pick up Sheila. If they knew as much as I did about Luke MacFarlane, they knew she was a friend of his.

Had I put a bull's-eye on Sheila's back? Was she in danger? I pushed my arm into my jeans pocket for my phone and ate the pain the movement caused. The walls of my house inched in on me. Sweat pebbled my forehead and my mouth slacked open. My breathing quickened as my mind slowed. I stared at the phone I held in my lap. The walls pushed in tighter. Everything turned gray.

* * *

"Rick? Is that you? Rick?"

I stared at my lap. Noise came from the phone in my hand. The walls slowly pushed away and the fog lifted.

"Rick, Goddammit! Answer me." Moira's voice.

I stared at the phone. Somehow I'd put it on speaker.

"Moira?"

"What the hell is the matter with you?" Concern mixed with anger.

"What do you mean?"

"What do you mean, what do I mean? You called me and wouldn't say anything. I could hear you breathing. It sounded like you were hyperventilating. Why didn't you answer me? Are you okay?"

"I thought you called me." A mistake. My mind wasn't yet hitting on all cylinders. I didn't know how long I'd been in a fugue state. I must have hit the last number dialed when I opened the phone app. "I mean I butt dialed you and didn't realize it. But I do need to talk to you."

"Where are you?"

"Home, but we can just talk on the phone."

"I'll be there in fifteen minutes."

*　　*　　*

Midnight barked. His happy bark. The one where he knew there was someone outside he wanted to see. And sniff. Then a knock on the front door. I rolled the recliner up to horizontal and set the ice bag I'd held against my head on a side table on top of the morning newspaper. I left the other ice bag on the chair and struggled to my feet. The ice had muted the pain. Slightly.

Moira gave the front door a second knock before I was able to shuffle to it. I opened the door and tried to look like two thugs hadn't beaten me to the ground an hour earlier. And kicked me while I was down.

"Holy crap." Moira stepped inside and peered up at me as Midnight nuzzled her hand.

"What happened to your eye?"

My eye? I'd forgotten about the punch to my eye. I put my hand up to my cheek and felt a growing swell. It had half closed my eye and I hadn't even noticed because of the hierarchy of pain manifested in my head and ribs. I should have made three ice bags.

"I got mugged by a couple toughs who claimed to be sending a message from Luke."

"What?" Moira's eyes went wide.

She started to waver. Then I realized it was me. My vision mushroomed in and out of focus. More sweat peppered my hairline. Despite the constant pounding, my head suddenly felt untethered. "Let's go sit down and I'll tell you all about it." I turned to let Moira pass in front so she wouldn't see me walk. Or stagger.

My legs went jelly.

"Whoa!" Moira wrapped her arms around me before I could fall down. She shifted so her right shoulder was under my left armpit and her right arm went around my waist.

I steadied under her support. She turned me toward the front door instead of the living room.

"Wait. Where are we going?" My voice sounded in slow motion.

"The hospital."

"No. I'll be fine." The last word came out in three syllables.

"Shut up, Cahill." Five feet and a hundred pounds of attitude led me out the door and into her car.

CHAPTER THIRTY-FOUR

Scripps Memorial Hospital in La Jolla was only a ten-minute drive up Interstate 5. Moira did it in considerably less time. I began to tell her about my ambush and what the goon said about Luke, but gave up when I realized it would take all my concentration not to puke on the dashboard.

All of a sudden, Moira was pulling me out of the car. I didn't remember us stopping. Or getting off the freeway.

"Put your arm around my neck." She pulled at my waist and I tried to help her by moving to my right.

Somehow, we made it out of the car. Moira acted as a two-legged crutch and walked me into the curved glass Scripps Emergency and Trauma Center building. I had a little of both: emergency and trauma. She eased me down into a chair next to a woman holding a crying baby. A nervous man next to her touched the baby's head while two small children next to him watched. A groaning, disheveled man with a ten-foot stink radius was seated two chairs down from me.

Moira went to the front desk and I tried to hold my breath and close my ears. And not slip out of the chair onto the floor. A minute later she came back to me and said something about moving her car, then disappeared.

The baby cried louder and the man stunk harder. I remained upright.

*   *   *

Twenty minutes later, the baby and the family and the malodorous man had been shuffled out of the waiting area to examination rooms. My turn came a couple minutes later when a woman in blue scrubs called my name. Moira helped me up and we walked over to the woman. This time, mostly under my own power.

"Rick Cahill?" She had a friendly voice. I hadn't had much luck with friendly voices tonight. Hopefully there wasn't another nurse hiding nearby waiting to hit me with a sap.

"That's me."

"Hi. My name is Rhonda. Do you need a wheelchair to get back to the examination room?" Rhonda was short and looked to be stocky under her scrubs. She wore her long brown hair back and had a pleasant smile on her round face.

"No. I'm fine. Thanks." I disengaged from Moira.

"Okay." She smiled nervously at Moira. "This way."

The nurse walked next to me with her left hand in front of her to show the way and her right hand behind me waiting to make a catch. Moira bracketed me on the other side, ready as well. We walked into a large room with a row of individual open three-walled bays. A hospital's version of office cubbyholes. No complaints. The last time I'd gone to an emergency room, there were just beds separated by thin vinyl curtains.

The Barbey Family Emergency and Trauma Center was new and comfy and nice. And I hoped never to visit it again.

Nurse Rhonda directed me to the first vacant bay and I gingerly eased my way onto the examination table in a sitting position. She took my blood pressure and asked me why I came to the emergency room while Moira eyed me, arms folded across her chest.

The pain from the blows to my head morphed with a CTE headache, but the fog had cleared and I was able to give her the specifics about the mugging through the pain. I showed her the lumps on my head and lifted my shirt to show her my ribs. I couldn't see if there were visible bruises because it would have hurt too much to twist and look. Rhonda typed in notes on a computer that was on a metal cabinet with wheels. She asked if I'd been drinking or taking drugs. I told her about the two fingers of scotch I drank at Odell Donohue's house. I left off the part about it being $800 a bottle. Didn't want to brag and give off the wrong impression.

"What about your right eye?" Rhonda asked.

I'd forgotten about my eye again. I closed my left eye and felt like I was looking through a mail slot with my right one. Then it hit me. My right eye. Every other black eye I'd ever received from someone's fist, outside of a boxing ring, had been my left one. My attackers' dominant hands had always been their right. The punches always hitting my left eye. The only exception had been when I got two black eyes together from a broken nose. The thug with multiple pitches to his voice was a southpaw. Lefthanded.

"One of my attackers punched it."

"You took quite a beating." Nurse Rhonda sounded sympathetic, but I knew she'd seen worse. Probably tonight. "Dr. Martinez will be in soon."

"Thanks."

"Have you talked to the police?"

"No."

"I can call them for you, so that they can talk to you here and the doctor can also consult them about your injuries."

I looked at Moira who squinted and pushed her head toward me.

"I'm good for now. Thanks."

Nurse Rhonda squeezed her lips together and exhaled from her nose, then looked at Moira, who shook her head.

"The doctor will be in shortly." Rhonda left the bay.

"You need to report this." Moira, hands on her hips.

"I didn't get a decent look at either one of the fuckers who did this to me." I kept my voice down so none of the other ER inhabitants could hear. "They were geared all in black and wore ski masks. The cops wouldn't know where to start. The guys were pros, not street toughs with long rap sheets. Muggers usually just rob you. They don't put GPS trackers on your car either."

"What GPS tracker?" Moira's eyebrows went up.

I told her what I'd found in the wheel well of my car.

"You think Linda Holland and her husband are behind this?"

"It makes the most sense. The two guys who ambushed me were probably the same two we saw in the Beemer in front of Luke's apartment."

A tall, thin, tan man in a lab coat walked into the bay and extended his hand to me.

"Rick? I'm Doctor Martinez." The name on his coat matched. He had an angular face with high cheekbones.

I shook his hand. He and Moira then went through introductions.

"I'm going to pull up the nurse's notes for just a second." Dr. Martinez typed something into the computer on the metal cabinet and studied the screen for a solid thirty seconds. He typed some more and studied the computer monitor some more. He finally turned away from the computer and looked at me.

"Your records show that you saw Dr. Andrews last month?"

I shot a side eye at Moira, but she caught me because she was already looking at me. "Yeah, that sounds right." I tried to sound nonchalant, like Dr. Andrews was a pediatrician who took a splinter out of my thumb. Not the head of the Neurology Department.

"Let's have a look." Dr. Martinez listened to my heart with his stethoscope, then checked my pupils with his penlight and had me dance my eyes around the room. The he gently felt the lumps on my head and the tenderness of my ribs.

He had me stand up and go through a couple balance drills. I was a little wobbly, but never lost my balance completely. Next, Dr. Martinez pulled a rolling stool away from the wall, sat on it, and hit my knees with the little rubber triangle hammer while I sat on the edge of the bed. My legs moved. Barely. He put the hammer in his breast pocket and stood up.

"Well, Rick." He smiled his doctorly concerned smile. "You've obviously suffered a dramatic event tonight. You have a concussion and bruised ribs, which normally wouldn't worry me too much. But considering your situation, I think you should get in to see Dr. Andrews, tomorrow, if possible, or in the next couple days."

"What condition?" Moira snapped her head toward the doctor.

"Oh, I'm sorry." Martinez looked at me. "I thought . . ."

"That's okay, Doctor." I looked at Moira. "It's a private matter."

Dr. Martinez didn't run a CT scan to check for a skull fracture or bleeding on my brain. He didn't think it was necessary. He didn't state it, but damage had already been done in there, anyway. Tonight was just another layer. How much more sand had it knocked out of the hourglass? No way of knowing even if I wanted to. I didn't want a hypothesis or a certain date. The countdown had started without my approval. I shouldn't have to be the timekeeper.

*   *   *

Two uniformed police officers walked up to the bay right after I gingerly got off the examination table. White male, forties, tall and broad shoulders. Latina, thin, and younger than her partner.

"Mr. Cahill?" The male. His brass name tag read "Saller." The woman's was "Ramos."

I looked at Moira.

"I called them when I moved the car." Resolute. "I knew you wouldn't."

"Do you have something to report?" Ramos, thumbs cinched under her Sam Browne duty belt, irritation in her voice. She sensed my recalcitrance.

"Yes." It's what a citizen who's soon to be a family man should do.

I spent the next fifteen minutes going over my entire day. Moira chimed in with backstory about Luke's disappearance and our suspicion that the guy with the ID of Dan Williams and his partner in the Beemer were the assailants and that they'd been hired by Linda Holland and Scot Sandstom. I left out the GPS tracker. Moira eyeballed me when I omitted it, but didn't say anything. We gave the cops the names of the sheriff's detectives working Jim Harkness' murder when we were done.

"Thanks." Saller. "A detective will contact you to update you soon. Here's my card if you need to contact me."

Officer Saller handed me his card and he and officer Ramos left.

*   *   *

Moira didn't say a word for the first few minutes of the drive. Not that difficult as she was seething mad. She often gave me the silent treatment when she was mad at me. But she had to battle her concern for me and her natural curiosity. She finally broke when we exited the freeway. Close. Another three or four minutes and I'd have been safe at home.

"What condition was the doctor talking about, Rick?" She turned down the burner on her anger and sounded almost normal. For her.

"Look, I'm tired and beat up. Let's talk about this some other time." Time. The most precious and finite thing in life.

"I looked up Dr. Andrews on the Scripps website while you were finishing up with Dr. Martinez." She turned left on Balboa. Only a couple more minutes until I was safe at home. Alone, except for Midnight. And he didn't ask questions. "There were three. A general practitioner, a pediatrician, and the head of Neurology."

"Good to know."

"What's wrong with your brain?" She stopped at the red light at Moraga Avenue. Thirty seconds after the green, at most.

"No one's ever been able to figure that out." I laughed like life was one long sitcom. "You've probably come the closest. Maybe you should burn your paper badge and become a shrink."

"This isn't a joke, Rick." Emotion pitched her voice higher. The light changed and she turned left up Moraga. "Dr. Martinez was concerned. I heard it in his voice and saw it in his eyes. You're seeing a neurologist and something is seriously wrong. Please tell me what's going on."

I didn't say anything. She turned left onto Cadden Way and then into my driveway and turned off the ignition.

"Thanks for taking care of me tonight. You've been . . . my friend." The words got stuck in my throat and came out heavy. The events of the night caught up with me and carried with them other events of my life. The damage. And a reminder of the ebbing tide of my time left on earth.

"Rick . . ." Moira's voice, still tight with emotion.

I sat silent a full minute. Moira didn't say anything, either. I opened the door, but stayed in the car.

"I can't tell you. Leah doesn't even know, yet." I finally eased my way out of the car and left Moira alone in the driveway.

CHAPTER THIRTY-FIVE

My phone woke me up the next morning at 7:00 a.m. Leah. Our daily morning call when we were apart. Normally, I'd have been up for an hour by now. Rest was the best treatment for a concussion. Rest and no heavy thinking. Today, I didn't want to think at all.

My head hurt so badly that I didn't think I'd consider getting out of bed until noon. Even the idea of reaching over and answering the phone seemed impossible. But I didn't have a choice. If I didn't answer, Leah would worry about me. I didn't want her to worry about anything. Worry led to stress and stress could trigger a miscarriage.

I grabbed my phone off the nightstand and my ribs grabbed at me. My head continued to split in half.

"Rick? I wish you could see me right now." Leah's voice, bright and bouncy even in the morning. And full of affection. She'd always been more upbeat than me, by a hundredfold, but since we found out she was pregnant there was a joy in her that I'd never seen before. Ebullient. Untamable. "I'm looking in the mirror right now and I officially have a baby bump!"

The joy in her voice made me forget the pain in my body. I sat up in bed and was quickly reminded. I didn't care.

"Really?" A smile spread across my face. "A bump? Send me a picture. I want to see that fat belly. I wish I could be there to rub it."

I'd only been able to say the word "baby" out loud a handful of times since we found out about the pregnancy. I wasn't exactly sure why. I thought of the fetus growing inside Leah as human from the first notice. My child. Our child.

Maybe I didn't want to jinx the miracle happening in my life. Our life. Maybe if I called the being growing inside Leah a baby, it would change from reality to a wish. A dream. A hope.

I hadn't had much luck with any of those.

"Okay. Hold on." She giggled then the phone went quiet for a few seconds. "On its way."

My phone chimed the arrival of a text. I opened the attached photo. Leah stood with her body in profile in front of the full-length mirror in her bedroom in Santa Barbara. One hand held up the bottom of one of my white T shirts, the other held the phone pointed at the mirror. She looked in the mirror, beaming. The raised shirt exposed her belly. Sure enough, there was a slight swell to her trim stomach. Unnoticeable to anyone who didn't know she had a life growing inside her.

Our miracle baby.

I looked at her face in the photo. Morning hair the color of the sun, wavy and bedhead spiked in different directions. Unglamorous beauty. Her smile radiated joy. Life.

My eyes welled with tears.

"Did you get it?"

"Yes. You look beautiful." My voice fluttered. Tears ran down my cheeks.

"Rick, what's wrong?" Her voice now heavy with concern.

I'd worried her. The opposite of what I wanted to accomplish.

"Nothing." I put the phone on mute and took a long deep breath and let it out slowly.

"Rick?" Leah's voice through the phone.

I unmuted my volume.

"Sorry. Sometimes I get a little swept away." Leah had seen me cry. Once. She'd been crying too at the time. "I never thought I'd have a chance to be a father after . . ."

"After Colleen died. I know." Tears in Leah's voice now. "I never thought I'd have the chance to be a mother, either, after the miscarriages. God's giving us another chance."

The pain of my head being cleaved in half returned. A reminder that the Lord giveth and the Lord taketh away.

CHAPTER THIRTY-SIX

I GOT OUT of bed at 11:30 a.m. I'd turned off my phone after Leah and I ended our conversation. Last night and this morning combined, I got almost ten hours sleep. About two nights' worth for me. The only times I got more sleep than that over a twenty-four-hour period as an adult was when I was in the hospital on pain medication recovering from gunshot wounds. Twice. And, later, a stabbing. For once, I was following doctor's orders to the nth degree. Sleep. Rest. No undue mental stimulation.

I got out of bed and got dressed. Both slowly. The pain in my ribs had eased a bit from last night, but my head still throbbed. Every movement magnified the throbbing. Midnight danced in place in anticipation of some activity. Any activity. I hated to disappoint him. He'd spent most of the morning lying at the foot of my bed as he did every night. I fed him after my talk with Leah then went back to sleep. He was free to roam the house and the backyard via a doggie door in the kitchen. But he'd stayed by my side.

My protector.

I grabbed my phone and went downstairs, Midnight leading the way. When we got to the kitchen, he went through his doggy door into the backyard. I made myself a couple one-eyed sandwiches with eggs and sourdough bread and then some juice by pushing carrots, apples, and strawberries through my juicer.

The early fall sun was bright so I stayed inside and ate at the butcher block kitchen island instead of my preferred table out on the deck in the backyard. Bright light was my enemy with a concussion. Even with sunglasses, it was safer inside.

After I finished eating, I pulled my phone out of my shorts pocket and turned it on. Midnight stuck his head through the doggie door and looked at me. He chomped a tennis ball in his mouth.

"Sorry, buddy. Maybe this evening."

He dropped the ball on the kitchen floor and stared at me. I shook my head and he snapped the ball back up and disappeared into the backyard.

My phone powered up. Two texts and a voicemail from Moira. A text and a voicemail from Sheila Perkins. Sheila. I'd forgotten to check up on her last night after I discovered the tracking device on my car. I jabbed her number, then scanned Moira's texts while Sheila's phone rang. I hung up.

Moira's second text demanded that I call her before noon. I tapped her number. The text had the feeling of a threat rather than something urgent. She picked up on the first ring.

"About damn time." By way of greeting. About what I expected.

"What's so urgent? News from Luke or the police?" I was ninety-nine percent certain it was neither.

"Dr. Martinez told you to make an appointment with Dr. Andrews. Have you done that yet?" Her voice challenging. I knew she called out of concern for me, but her voice had no affection or concern in it. Just anger. Moira was smarter, more measured, and less neurotic than me. But sometimes, when it came to me, I don't think she knew how to manage all the contrary feelings she had. I guess I couldn't blame her.

"No. I've been following his other orders by getting as much rest as possible. I just got out of bed."

"So, when are you calling Dr. Andrews?" Steam.

"Soon, Nurse Ratched, soon." I knew I needed to heed Dr. Martinez's advice and make an appointment to see Dr. Andrews again. It's what a responsible person who was going to get married and be a father should do. But I just got tired of hearing bad news.

"If you can't give me confirmation in the next hour that you made an appointment, I'm going to call Leah and tell her that you're seeing a neurologist for a serious condition. Something you should already have told her. I mean it, Rick."

She was right on both counts, of course. And wrong about blackmailing me.

"I'll handle things at my own pace. You don't know everything that's going on in my life." Not a good excuse, but the best I had.

"I know there's something wrong with your brain and you need to tell Leah about it. Playing the strong silent type and locking people out who care about you isn't fair or admirable. It's fucking selfish. Call the doctor."

Moira hung up.

I was about to hit Sheila Perkins' number again, then stopped. Selfish? I didn't really care about being fair or admirable. Life wasn't fair and I'd done things that would be termed despicable if seen through any other lenses than mine. But I couldn't be selfish with Leah, the woman who gave me her everything without conditions even while I stubbornly held onto my own.

I found Dr. Andrews's phone number and made an appointment with his office. At first, the best they could do was two weeks. I told them it was urgent and they might want to check with Dr. Martinez in the ER. A couple minutes later, I had an appointment for next Tuesday. Five days from now. The day Leah returned from Santa Barbara.

I had five days to decide if I'd go to the appointment alone or with my fiancée and future mother of my child by my side.

Scripps Hospital emailed me an appointment reminder from their My Scripps website immediately. I took a screenshot of it with my phone and texted it to Moira. Not because I really thought she'd call Leah, but because I wanted her to know so she'd worry a little less. And stop bothering me until at least after the appointment.

Sheila Perkins picked up on the third ring.

"Are you okay?" I blurted out before she could tell me why she'd called me.

"Yes. I'm fine." I heard the bustle of people in the background. Maybe a restaurant. I forgot it was lunchtime. Breakfast was my lunch today. "Why?"

Why? How much should I tell her. How much was "fair"? In all likelihood, the GPS tracker was put on my car at A Hand Up after I met with Sheila. No one probably knew that she and I had lunch together and I didn't want to needlessly worry her. I didn't want to worry anybody but just found out that that was unfair.

"It's possible that somebody may know we met for lunch yesterday." I kept my voice as light as seemed reasonable. "I think the odds are against it, but I thought you should know."

"You mean the people who killed Jim?" Anxious, in a hushed tone. Another failed mission.

"I don't know who the people are, but it's possible that they're responsible for Jim's death. I told you yesterday that you can quit this deal anytime. Maybe now's anytime."

"Not yet. Did you read the text or listen to the voicemail I sent you?"

"No." I'd jumped right from talking to Moira to calling Sheila and skipped the voicemail and text. "What's going on?"

"Read the text and come by my house tonight at six. I have copies of emails to give you."

"I will, but be careful."

"I am careful."

"Good. What are on the emails?"

"Read the text." Hurried. "I have to go."

"Will do. If it's okay with you, I'm bringing Luke's mom with me tonight."

"Sure. See you then." Sheila hung up.

I opened the text and read it.

Heres a summary of what Ive learned so far. The special project Luke was working on had something to do with Sequence Corp, a medical research company where Gabriela Dates works. Luke thought they had faulty data on a test they were running on one of their projects.

Sequence Corp. Test data. Could it be the Cancer Sweep test Odell Donohue told me about?

I tapped Moira's number on my phone. My head hurt more and more with each new phone call and text. Apparently talking and reading a three-sentence text used a lot of concentration. At least, for me.

"I got the text about your appointment with the neurologist." Rapid fire. Old Moira. "Congratulations on being an adult."

"Thanks for blackmailing me, but that's not why I called."

"Asshole." Back to our accustomed affection. "But how are you feeling? I should have asked you that earlier. Sorry."

"I'm fine." Grading on a warped curve. "No need to apologize."

"I know you're lying to me."

"Just a little. How did your meeting at ConnectTech go?" I'd forgotten that today was the day that Moira was to meet with upper management at ConnectTech to talk about Luke. I'd forgotten a lot of things over the past couple months. My beating last night didn't help.

"Not great. We met at a lawyer's office instead of ConnectTech. I talked to the vice president of sales and the chief financial officer and neither of them seemed to know much about what Luke did in general or what he did for Jim Harkness with the special project."

"Do you think they were playing dumb to cover the company's ass and their own or did you believe them?"

"I mostly believed them. Harkness was a one-man hierarchy. It looks like he ran the show alone and only told those who worked for him the minimal they needed to know to perform their jobs. They seemed to be scrambling about how to lead the company."

"Well, I got a little luckier than you did. I found out about the secret project Luke was working on. Read this."

I sent her the text I got from Sheila Perkins.

"Luke was checking up on Sequence Corp for Jim Harkness?" Her voice pitched high with anxiety. "And now Harkness is dead?"

The reality that Luke was in the worst-case scenario that we'd feared sank in.

"Right, but the good news is that the police are already looking for Luke." I tried to sound upbeat.

"Yes, but for the wrong reasons."

"Everything will get worked out." I hoped. "Anyway, we're meeting Sheila Perkins at her house tonight. She's going to give us the emails she's uncovered so far."

"I don't think you should leave your house tonight." Luke's mother's voice. "You still need to take it easy."

"I will. That's why you're driving. Plus, I want my friends from last night, and their employers, to think that I'm home for the night."

"Oh, yeah. The tracking device." She let out a breath and, in my aching imagination, I could see her shaking her head. "Why didn't you tell the police about that. The device will have a serial number that they can track and find out where it was sold. Maybe even to whom it was sold."

"Maybe, but I doubt they bought it from a spy shop on the corner of University and Fifth. Anyway, I want whoever put it on my car to think they know where I am when I'm someplace else."

"You're such a stubborn idiot."

"I didn't get a chance to tell you about what I learned from Odell Donohue last night." I wasn't going to call Officer Saller. She'd have to deal with it. "Some interesting stuff."

"Tell me." A hint of enthusiasm in her voice. Back on the case. Hopeful for her son.

I recited the information Odell gave me about the Sandstroms and Sequence Corp. last night. Before the tough guys ambushed me.

"So, he's on the same page as us? That the Sandstroms were pumping Luke for information on Sequence Corp because of his relationship with Gabby?" Moira's words sped out of her mouth.

"Yup." I moved in my chair and breath shot out of me. My ribs reminded me that they still deserved their spot on the hierarchy of pain.

"Are you okay?"

"Fine," I said through a grimace. "O.D. thinks the Sandstroms might have been pumping Luke for info to take a defensive position to protect their investment in Sequence Corp."

"What does he mean by a defensive position?"

I explained that Donohue thought the Sandstroms might be gathering negative information so they could sell their Sequence Corp shares before the news became public and tanked an IPO or sale to a pharma giant.

"It seems like Luke was almost a double agent, working for Harkness and the Sandstroms all at the same time. Did he ever talk to you about Sequence Corp or conversations he had with Gabby?" I asked.

"No. He didn't talk to me about much of anything the last couple months."

"The other interesting thing that O.D. told me was that Jim Harkness founded an online magazine a few years back called *Tech Watchdog* that sussed out stories on corrupt tech entrepreneurs and helped put the kibosh on a couple IPOs. The magazine went out of business nine or ten years ago, but it may show where Harkness' heart was."

"And maybe he sensed that something was off about Sequence Corp's claims about pinpointing early cancer warnings." Energy of the chase in her voice. "If the information was true, it could have gotten him killed."

"Yup. Hopefully Sheila Perkins will have more on that subject when we meet her tonight."

CHAPTER THIRTY-SEVEN

MOIRA PULLED UP in front of Sheila Perkins's duplex on Bannock Avenue in Clairemont at 6:00 p.m. The car ride was tolerable. My ribs still hurt when I moved, but not as much as last night. Or this morning. The headaches were about the same. Progress.

We knocked on the front door and Moira got to see the painted tulips on it.

"She's got a thing for tulips," I said.

"Apparently."

"Wait and see."

Moira twisted her head askance and looked at me. The door opened and no further explanation was needed. Sheila Perkins wore jeans and an orange shirt with purple and blue tulips. She micro-recoiled when she looked at me. The black eye.

"Hi, Sheila. I bumped into something and am fine. Nothing to worry about." I pointed at my eye, then at Moira. "This is Moira MacFarlane."

"Nice to see you again. We met at a company party last year." Sheila stepped back and held the door open for us to enter.

"Oh yes." Moira sounded sincere. "Thanks for all you're doing to help us find Luke."

The living room was again neat and tidy. The smell of peppermint tea wafted from a large mug on the coffee table sitting next to a vase of white tulips. She led us over to the love seat across from the table.

"Please, have a seat." Sheila swept her hand toward the only option, minus her rocking chair. The love seat.

Moira and I looked at each other, both of us probably thinking the same thing: was there a love/hate seat we could share? She sat down first and I followed. We didn't touch. Moira was so small that we each had plenty of our own love space.

"Can I get you anything? Tea? Water? Almond milk?" Sheila, again, the perfect hostess.

"I'll have some tea if it's not too much trouble." Moira, the perfect guest.

"No. It's fine. I've already got hot water on the stove. Oolong? Green? Peppermint?"

"Peppermint, please."

I'd never known Moira to consume anything peppermint or mint of any kind. But, aside from the perfect guest, Moira knew that mirroring Sheila was the best way to make her feel comfortable.

"Rick, anything for you?" Sheila smiled.

"No thanks."

A couple minutes later, we were having a proper tea party minus the crumpets and biscuits.

"So, what did you find out?" I asked before anyone could start speaking in British accents.

"I'll show you." Sheila got up and disappeared down the short hall into a room. Five seconds later, she returned with two manilla folders and handed one to each of us. "This is what I've gotten so far. I didn't have a chance to go through all of them and categorize everything. This is just raw data. Emails between Luke and Jim. It looks like the special project Jim assigned Luke to was to learn as much as he could about the testing Sequence Corp was doing on their pre-cancer DNA test they call Cancer Sweep," Sheila said.

Moira and I exchanged looks. Connecting dots we'd laid out as a possible path Linda Holland and Scot Sandstrom were using to gain knowledge about Sequence Corp. Jim Harkness and the Sandstroms were after the same information. Probably for different reasons.

"What did Luke know about DNA and cancer? He was a programmer, right?" I said.

"That's like calling da Vinci a house painter." Sheila scowled at me. "He wrote the most beautiful programs I've ever seen. Writes, I should say. And, he already had some insight into Sequence Corp's Cancer Sweep because he wrote a program for their internal testing."

"What?" I fought not to jump out of my seat. "Luke worked for Sequence Corp?"

"No. That's not how it works. Companies contract ConnectTech for specific computing purposes or to get third confirmation on their own work. Sequence Corp wanted an independent programmer to write a program to test their results." Sheila was comfortable, calmly giving a tutorial on the contractor-based economy. "Sequence Corp is a medical research company that, of course, has an IT division, but it's not their strength. They are really there to solve systematic problems and to try to streamline the existing system. Their internal programmers didn't have the bandwidth to create a program to test Cancer Sweep."

"When did Luke work with Sequence Corp and for how long?" Moira asked.

"I think the first day was August 16th and he was only there for about three weeks."

"Is three weeks normal for a project of that complexity?" Moira, ahead of me.

"No." Sheila shook her head. "Luke originally thought it would take about a month. We'd made the contract for six weeks so Luke would have time to run checks on the program and make sure there were no discrepancies in the results. Standard operating procedure for us, but they said they didn't need Luke anymore and paid the full contract. So, we had no complaints."

"What about Luke? Do you think he was happy to be done with the project or would he have preferred to have the extra time to check his work?" Most people that I knew who were truly great at something wanted their greatness to be tested.

"He would have wanted to test his program. Multiple times. But, as I said, Sequence Corp was fine with it and that was all that mattered."

"If Luke was only there for three weeks, then he was back at ConnectTech the first week of September, right?" I asked.

"Yes."

"So, a week or so later, Jim Harkness put Luke on this secret project to monitor Sequence Corp?"

"Yeah, I thought the same thing." Sheila nodded.

"How could Luke provide any new information on the Cancer Sweep test if he stopped working at Sequence Corp?" I asked.

"Gabby?" Moira.

"I didn't see her name mentioned in any of the emails I read." Sheila took a sip of tea. "Luke just talked about trying to deconstruct the data he had on the testing and figure out how they arrived at their numbers."

"This is very good work, Sheila." Moira smiled. "Is there anything else we should know about as we look through the emails?"

"Two other things." She set down her mug. "Jim mentioned a podcast in one of the emails. He said, 'this will launch the podcast with a bang' and he told Luke he could be his first guest."

Jim Harkness had learned his lesson with e-zines. Now he was moving onto podcasts, the ubiquitous form of citizen journalism, entertainment, or self-promotion that exploded in the second decade of the 2000s. Not easily monetized, but a much smaller footprint and overhead than an online magazine.

"There was also an email from Bryson Basquez, the CEO of Sequence Corp, to Jim that sounded like a conversation continuing from another email, but the original wasn't attached." Sheila kept giving.

"You go into Harkness' email account?" I asked.

"No. It was an email he forwarded to Luke."

"Was it confrontational?"

"Not really. He said something like, 'I share your concerns about medical ethics and that's why our testing continues.' You'll see it. It's in the file."

"Do you remember the approximate date of this email?" I asked.

"It was a week after Luke completed the job for Sequence Corp."

Moira and I glanced at each other.

"Right about the time Luke started on the secret project." Moira. Not a question.

"Yes." Sheila answering for all of us.

"Do you think anyone at work is onto you?" I asked.

"No." Definitive. I hoped she was right. "I'm going to keep trying to get into Jim's files."

"I appreciate all that you're doing, Sheila." Moira leaned across the coffee table. "Just be careful. Whoever killed Mr. Harkness may be after Luke, too. They're dangerous people. If what you're doing gets back to them, they might come after you. You can quit now and Rick and I will use what you've given us to find Luke. I don't want you to endanger yourself."

"I want to find Luke, Mrs. MacFarlane. Almost as much as you do."

CHAPTER THIRTY-EIGHT

THE NEXT MORNING, I Ubered to the Sequence Corp office. I didn't tell Moira I was going there. I didn't want to get a lecture about lying low. I felt better and I was antsy. Moira was home going over and over the emails between Jim Harkness and Luke that Sheila Perkins gave us last night. There were about a hundred of them going back five weeks. Right after Luke completed his project for Sequence Corp. More precisely, right after they thanked him and sent him on his way.

The first correspondence between Luke and Harkness was a forwarded email from Bryson Basquez of Sequence Corp to Harkness on September 3rd, Luke's last day at Sequence Corp. It was very complimentary about the work Luke had done. Harkness forwarded it to Luke on Tuesday, September 7th, the day after Labor Day.

Luke's reply was stilted and probably the first email he'd ever sent to ConnectTech's founder. But the subject matter was clear. He was upset about not being able to work longer with Sequence Corp to test the viability of his program. He said his own reputation was at stake if a fault in the program was discovered without him being able to beta test it and make adjustments.

Harkness responded immediately and asked Luke to come into his office. That meeting must have birthed the secret project to check up on Sequence Corp.

There wasn't a smoking gun in the emails that could prove that Sequence Corp was faking test results. Most of the emails were cryptic like Luke and Harkness were communicating in coded words. I had the feeling most of their discussions were done face-to-face and that Luke was doing most of his calculations on his home computer. Which was missing from his apartment when Moira and I went there.

I entered the Sequence Corp building and walked to the receptionist's desk in the small lobby. The man behind the counter was dressed in a sport coat and tie and wore a headset attached to a phone on his desk. No supermodels with Bluetooths in their ears at Sequence Corp. The place had a professional and sterile vibe, which is what you'd want from a company researching DNA.

"Can I help you?" The man stared at my black eye, then gave me a professional smile. He had a shaved head and red-framed glasses. His silver name tag read, "Crispin."

"Yes." I gave him a semi-professional smile. "I'm here to see Bryson Basquez."

The man who'd written Jim Harkness the email about the great job Luke did and the other one about medical ethics.

"Could you give me your name, please?"

"Rick Cahill."

He punched some keys on his computer keyboard, studied the monitor for a couple seconds, then looked back at me.

"I don't see an appointment for you, Mr. Cahill." Sterile smile. "Did someone at your office forget to make one?"

I had an place. In my house. And a booth in a restaurant when I had to meet a client. But I didn't have a someone in either office. Strictly a one-man band. And one that made noise instead of music.

"I don't have an appointment, but I'd still like to see Bryson Basquez." No smile at all, this time.

"Mr. Basquez is very busy." Still professional with a side of a patronization. "If you'd like, I can make an appointment for you to see him. The first thing I have open is a week from next Tuesday."

"I apologize for dropping in without an appointment, but I'm a private detective working on behalf of Luke MacFarlane's family and I need to speak with Mr. Bazquez."

I fished out my wallet and flipped it open to the picture window that held my P.I. license.

"He's currently in a meeting and I can't disturb him. I will check and see if he has time for you once his meeting adjourns. That's the best I can do."

"That will be fine. Thanks." I sat in a cushioned chair nearest to Crispin's desk.

After about five minutes, a man and woman emerged from a hall behind the lobby. Both were dressed in business attire. Expensive business attire. The man was in his fifties and filled out his tailored suit like a well-dressed walrus. The woman was in her early forties with flowing blond hair. Silky, like in a shampoo commercial. Her blue pinstriped suit accentuated her body much more attractively than the man's did his.

One word came into my mind. Money. My guess was that they were potential investors and were the participants in Bryson Basquez's meeting. They exited the building.

I glanced at Crispin. He had his hand over the headset microphone in front of his mouth and was speaking quietly. I heard my name. He had to say it twice. A couple seconds later, he dropped his hand and looked at me.

"Joanne will be out shortly to show you into Mr. Basquez's office."

A full ten minutes later, an attractive woman walked into the lobby from the hallway. Her brown hair was cut short and she wore a blue pencil skirt suit. She looked to be in her mid-thirties, but could have been older.

"Mr. Cahill? I'm Joanne Murphy, Mr. Basquez's executive assistant." A micro wince when she saw my black eye. "Please follow me."

She led me out of the lobby and down a long corridor. We ended up in an office at the end of the hall. The room was modestly appointed and had a door in the back. Joanne sat behind a desk and offered me a chair against the wall. Bryson Basquez's office must be behind the door.

"Can I get you something to drink?" Pleasant smile.

"I'm fine. Thanks." I gave my most earnest smile. "How long have you worked here?"

"Eight years."

"Exciting times, huh?" I asked.

"It's a fun job if that's what you mean." This smile was pasted on.

"I'm sure it is, but I'm talking about all the rumors about an IPO or a possible acquisition by a big pharmaceutical company." Rumors that, if they weren't already out there, I just started. I leaned toward her. "I'm guessing you probably have company stock after being here for eight years. You should make a killing when the IPO goes down."

I felt a little guilty for starting a rumor that could make Joanne worry about her job stability. But I was a disrupter.

"I'm not really sure what you're talking about. And I would never discuss Sequence Corp business with anyone outside the company." No smile this time. "Mr. Basquez will see you shortly."

"Sure. Okay. Thanks." I leaned back in my seat, blunted at my attempt to validate my suspicions.

Joanne Murphy frowned and started typing on her computer keyboard. Loudly.

A second later the door to Basquez's office whipped open. A man stood in the doorway smiling at me. Almost as if he'd been listening to my talk with Joanne and leapt up from his desk to cut it off before she gave anything away.

However, the man in the doorway wasn't the Bryson Basquez I'd seen online when I checked him out. About forty years too young and forty pounds too light.

And I'd seen this man before. At Gabby Dates' condo the night Luke visited Linda Holland. The thirty-something preppy-looking guy who drove up in a Tesla. He wore jeans and a tweed jacket, just as he had that night. Different tweed jacket, though. He probably had a walk-in closet full of them.

"Mr. Cahill?" A friendly greeting. He ignored my eye. "I'm Bryson Basquez. Come on in and have a seat."

I walked into his office and Basquez closed the door behind me. The office was large, about four times the size of Joanne's. There was a door in the middle of the front wall that must have opened directly into the corridor I took to Joanne's office. Plaques and photos of the man who claimed to be Bryson Basquez covered the walls. One of the plaques stated that Bryson Basquez Jr. had a PhD in pharmacology while another said he had one in finance. A very accomplished man. School smart.

The desk he sat down behind was sleek wood and curved into the floor like a waterfall. I studied him for a couple seconds before I spoke. Up close, I could see narrow crow's feet around his eyes and flecks of salt in his pepper hair. I put him in his early forties, not the ten years younger I thought on first glimpse from binoculars that night on La Jolla Boulevard.

"You're not the Bryson Basquez I expected to see." I smiled and raised my eyebrows.

"I completely understand." An affable smile. "I'm Bryson the 2nd and I run the day to day operations for Sequence Corp. My father still maintains the title of CEO and Chairman of the Board, but I'm the top report."

Bryson, the 2nd. I thought the numbers kicked in on the third iteration.

"So, what is your title?" I didn't see junior, or the 2nd, listed as one of the officers on the website.

"You can call me the Chief Operating Officer, if titles are important to you."

"Do I look like a title guy to you?" I smiled like a back-slapping beer-drinking bro and took out my phone. But I'd remembered seeing someone else's name for COO when I researched Sequence Corp online. I pulled out my phone and did a quick internet search for Sequence Corp and held the phone so the 2nd could see the screen. "Your website says a guy named Phillip Dewey is the COO. See?"

"He used to be. I'm afraid we haven't updated the website. Sadly, Phil died of a massive heart attack." His eyes cast down to the desk. They came back up looking mournful. "We miss him dearly."

Dewey looked to be in his late sixties and obese in the company photo online. A massive heart attack couldn't have been a big surprise.

"Sorry to hear about Mr. Dewey. How long ago did he die?"

"Oh, it's been about two or three months." Now a respectful smile. "As good a guy as Phil was, I'm very busy and can only give you ten—" He looked at a Hublot watch on his wrist. "No, eight minutes. So, what can I do for you? Crispin said you mentioned you were here on behalf of Luke MacFarlane's family."

I ran over the dates in my head that we'd gotten from Sheila Perkins about when Luke wrote the Cancer Sweep testing program for Sequence Corp. Two months ago would have overlapped his time there with Phillip Dewey. I wondered how much contact a COO would have with an outside contractor writing a program to test

Cancer Sweep results. If Dewey had died three months ago, there'd be no overlap.

"And thanks for squeezing me in when you're so busy. I don't know if you're aware, but Luke has been missing for about a week and his mother hired me to find him."

"I do know. We contracted ConnetTech to write a program we planned to use to test the accuracy of our DNA cancer predetermination test called Cancer Sweep. They said Luke was their best programmer so they put him on the project. I was sorry to hear that he was missing."

Luke's disappearance hadn't been mentioned in the press. Moira recorded all the local news to watch later and keep track of in case the police started publicly calling Luke a person of interest. They hadn't so far.

"Really? How did you hear about it? It hasn't been on the news." I studied Basquez for a tell.

"One of our employees used to date Luke. She told me about it." Nothing. Like he was discussing what to order for lunch.

"Gabby Dates?"

"Yes."

Something clicked in my brain regarding what Basquez said about Luke's program.

"You said that you had planned to use Luke's program to verify your test results. Is that what you're using now?"

"Unfortunately, no. It was faulty and we ended up hiring an expert programmer to come on full-time and write a new program. He's excellent and we haven't had any problems." Basquez looked at the Hublot on his wrist again. Ready to give me another countdown.

I jumped back in before he could.

"The contract was for six weeks and you released Luke after just three, but paid the full sum." I tilted my head and peered at Basquez.

"Luke complained to Jim Harkness that he didn't get the chance to refine the program. Isn't it standard procedure to give a programmer time to work out the kinks? Wouldn't another couple of weeks have been helpful for both you and Luke to get everything perfect?"

"We're developing a test that will save millions of lives, Mr. Cahill." Basquez hunched forward and clasped his hands together on his desk. His face, a mask of earnest certainty. "Every day lost getting Cancer Sweep in health professionals' hands could mean thousands of people will die that we might have saved."

When the test went to market, Basquez was going to be the perfect pitchman. Hell, I almost believed him myself. But I believed Sheila Perkins more. Unlike Bryson Basquez, Sheila had nothing to gain by disseminating information. And she'd called Luke a rock star programmer. The best she'd ever seen.

"What was the problem with Luke's program?" I asked.

"Mr. Cahill." A disarming smile. One he probably used on investors. "I gave you time out of my busy day in hopes that I could somehow aid you in your search for Luke MacFarlane. I didn't think I'd be able to, but an innocent life is always worth the effort. Unfortunately, you've spent all your time questioning me about Luke's failed program. I don't see how this will help you find Luke and I'm afraid I'm out of time."

"It's all connected, Bryson." I didn't want to call him Mister Basquez or the 2nd.

"I don't see how any of it is connected." He stood up. "Good luck with your search. I sincerely hope you're successful."

I stayed seated.

"Please. Just a couple more questions. All of this has been very helpful." I wasn't sure how much of a lie that was yet. "Let me ask you again, what was the problem with Luke's program? Too many false positives? Or a complete failure?"

Basquez remained standing.

"Complete failure." Basquez crossed his arms.

"That's what's baffling."

"Why is that?"

"Because Luke was a genius programmer. A real whiz kid."

"He had talent. That is undeniable, but my IT people and one of our geneticists told me that he was difficult to work with and unable to see his own faults."

"Yeah. I've met him. He's not too likeable. But here's the thing." I leaned forward and rested my elbows on the waterfall desk. "I saw an email you sent directly to Jim Harkness that said you were extremely happy with Luke's work and that it was so good that it would be the de facto bar that all your pre-cancer testing would have to reach before the product went to market."

"It seems strange to me that you have access to ConnectTech's company emails, but I'll leave that to them to figure out." A paternalistic smile now, even though we were roughly the same age. He sat back down and rested his hands on the desk. "My driving force in life is to help people, not crush their dreams. Luke MacFarlane is a talented young man with great potential. I didn't want to poison the well for him over at ConnectTech, so I gave him, perhaps, an overly effusive endorsement. Very unprofessional on my part. I have to admit that the fact that Luke was dating an important member of our team influenced my decision to shade the truth, as well."

"Gabby Dates, again."

"Yes." He stood up again. "I hope this has somehow been helpful, but I'm late for a meeting."

I debated whether to ask him if his relationship with Gabby was strictly professional just to see how he'd react. But I had a better question.

"Of course." I stood up and walked over to the door, which Basquez now held open for me. I stopped just short. "Did you know that Jim

Harkness, Luke's boss, used to publish an online magazine called
Tech Watchdog?"

"That doesn't sound familiar." He stepped through the door and
faced me. "I'll walk you out. I have someone waiting to meet me in the
lobby."

"Okay." I let him lead me down the hall. "So back to *Tech Watchdog*,
apparently reporting in the magazine helped quash a couple IPOs."

"That's interesting." He seemed to quicken his pace.

"I know. And Harkness was about to start up a podcast before he
was murdered." We hit the lobby and I stopped parallel to Crispin's
desk. "Were you aware of that?"

Basquez stopped and looked at me. The mask slipped for a micro-
second and I caught a glimpse of anger. He righted himself and smiled
at me, then at a man in an expensive suit who stood up from a chair.
His next meeting. Money. Investor.

"I was very sorry to her about Mr. Harkness. Tragic. But I don't
know anything about a podcast." He stuck out a hand and I shook
it. "Should I have Crispin arrange a ride for you or did you drive
yourself?"

An odd request. Unless he knew I hadn't driven my car there because a GPS device he could track on his computer showed my car
parked at home.

"I'm good on my own." I smiled long enough to make him uncomfortable. "For now."

I left Sequence Corp knowing more than when I came in, but not
nearly enough.

CHAPTER THIRTY-NINE

MIDNIGHT GREETED ME at the door when I arrived home via Uber. I bent down and scratched him behind the ears. My ribs told me I shouldn't do that. I did it anyway.

Priorities.

He followed me upstairs into my office and found his favorite spot under my desk. I liked having him there. He calmed me. Restored order. Outside, the world whirled and evil spun out of it, talons grasping at me. My home was my sanctuary, guarded by Midnight. Twice, the evil penetrated my safe harbor. Each time, Midnight saved my life. I had no more loyal friend. I reached under my desk and scratched him behind the ear and the tension of the day oozed out of me.

I added what I'd learned at Sequence Corp to my case notes on my computer, then called Moira.

"What?" Her greeting.

"Find anything new in the emails?"

"No, but Sheila sent me another one that Harkness forwarded to Luke. An email that Harkness sent to a medical research company called American Health Innovations in Washington, D.C."

"Who are they? Are they connected to the federal government?"

"No. They're similar to Sequence Corp, but much bigger." Moira's words ricocheted into my ear. She was on to something and excited.

"Apparently, they are doing something similar to Cancer Sweep. Harkness emailed their Research Compliance Officer and asked him about their protocols for testing. The guy responded a week later and, of course, told him he couldn't discuss proprietary information. But it's clear that Harkness thought there was something irregular about Sequence Corp's testing."

After my talk with Bryson Basquez Jr., so was I.

"That's interesting. So is what I learned from Bryson Basquez at Sequence Corp."

"Why didn't you tell me you were going there?" Now her excitement was directed at me. Not in a good way. "You should have stayed home. I would have gone or taken you with me. You can't go rogue. We're supposed to be a team. Especially when you're injured."

"I'm feeling better." She was right, but going rogue had gotten results. "Do you want to hear about my chat with Bryson Basquez?"

"The CEO?" Calmer now. Moira had done the same research I had.

"Not quite." I spent ten minutes telling her about my talk with Bryson Basquez, Jr. Complete with everything I observed from the plaques and pictures hanging from the office walls, down to his story about Luke's program supposedly being defective. And his offer to have his receptionist arrange a ride for me.

"Do you believe him about the program?" Moira asked.

"No. And I found it interesting that he offered to have someone drive me home like he knew that I didn't drive there myself."

"He could have just been using a polite way to get you out the door by offering to get you a ride." Devil's advocate.

"I doubt it. I'm ninety percent that he had the tracker put on my car."

"But why would he? How would he even know that I hired you to find Luke before you talked to him today?"

"Gabby Dates. The day I ambushed her at lunch. She must have told Basquez about it. Which means she's complicit in whatever Basquez is up to. Or trying to cover it up."

"We don't know that. But I think everything revolves around Cancer Sweep." Moira's voice was a dart hitting the bull's-eye. "Luke must have figured out that the test was either inconclusive or just didn't work. His program must have found a flaw in their testing. When he showed it to Gabby or Basquez or whoever over there, Sequence Corp thanked him and cut his contract short, but still paid the full amount so that there'd be no argument about the efficacy of the work done."

"Luke takes what he knows to Jim Harkness, who's about to launch a tech watchdog podcast and thinks he's found the perfect corrupt company to expose on his first show. Harkness starts snooping around and gets killed. Luke figures out who killed him and goes into hiding."

"But how did Luke know Harkness was dead?" Moira, skeptical. "He bought the burner phone at Walmart early Saturday morning and Harkness' body wasn't discovered until Monday."

"He must have gone by the office early Saturday morning." The scenario took form in my head. "He only lives a mile away from ConnectTech and the office is between his apartment and the beach and a lot of restaurants. We found a lot of to-go boxes in his trash. Maybe he was on his way to the beach or to get something to eat and he saw Harkness' car still in the parking lot and stopped to check it out. He found the body and got the hell out of Dodge."

"Luke does sometimes go for runs on the beach on weekend mornings." Moira starting to buy into my scenario. "But what about the envelope full of cash? Where did that come from? Do you think Harkness gave it to him?"

"Two things. One is that we aren't a hundred percent certain that there was money in the envelope." My turn to play devil's advocate. It came naturally. "And it was either a payment or a payoff. I don't think Harkness would pay Luke for the information. Harkness was secretive, but I don't think he was a cash in an envelope kind of guy. He was the guy trying to expose people who gave underlings envelopes full of cash to do their dirty work."

"There was cash in that envelope, Rick. You know it as well as I do." I heard a rustling away from the phone. "I can still smell the scent of money in it. But I agree with you about Jim Harkness not giving it to Luke."

"Okay. Can we agree that the cash could only have been for one of four things? Blackmail payoff, hush money, an under-the-table work payment, or payment for a hit."

"What!" Her voice rocketed out of the speakerphone and bounced around my office. Midnight jerked to attention under the desk and banged his head. "My son is not a blackmailer or a murderer. Goddamn you!"

I could hear her breath through the phone.

"I'm taking Luke out of the equation and just looking at the facts. If it wasn't Luke, you'd come up with the same conclusions."

"But it is Luke, you asshole, so we can eliminate those conclusions."

She had a point. But I wasn't Luke's mother. With a blind spot, or at least lack of acknowledgment of his potential for violence. A parent's prerogative that I hoped to never have to use.

"Okay. Blackmail and murder are out." Just for the purpose of our conversation. "That leaves hush money and payment for work done under the table."

"What's the difference between hush money and blackmail?"

"I guess one is offered and one is demanded."

"It has to be payment for something Luke did." Moira, adamant.

"If we both agree that it didn't come from Jim Harkness then I think the arrow goes back on the Sandstroms. They must have paid Luke to solicit information from Gabby, or however he could get it, about Cancer Sweep. That's the only thing that makes sense. Either that or hush money from Bryson Basquez."

"It's not hush money." Moira, firm.

"If the Sandstroms paid Luke for inside information, and if we're right about there being some flaw in Cancer Sweep that his program revealed, then they have to know it isn't ready to go to market, yet." I was working out the angles as I spoke. "If so, they've probably sold off their private shares of Sequence Corp or are in the process now. If they haven't, then they have to be betting that Basquez will either get the flaw worked out soon or will be able to hide it long enough for an IPO or the sale of the company. That would make them very nervous about what Luke knows."

"You're right." Tight voice. "Maybe Luke told them about the podcast Jim Harkness was creating and that he knew about the Cancer Sweep flaw. They'd want Harkness dead, and Luke, too, as much as Bryson Basquez would. We need to find out if the Sandstroms really are investors in Sequence Corp and whether or not they dumped their equity."

"I might know how to do that."

CHAPTER FORTY

I CALLED ODELL "O.D." Donohue after I hung up with Moira. His voicemail answered and I left a message. I had the rest of the afternoon to myself and decided to hit my garage gym. Until I stood up and my ribs reminded me that I wasn't ready yet.

The ache in my head made itself known. With a vengeance. My ribs would heal, but my head wouldn't. Was this the state of my remaining years on earth? More fugue states? Less memories until they all drifted away?

I sat back down in my chair and Midnight put his head on my lap and looked up at me with his soft Lab eyes and brought me back to the here and now. If I worried too much about the number and quality of the days I had left, I'd just be wasting the ones right in front of me.

Then I remembered something. Not a memory from my childhood I hoped to hold onto. One from my talk with Bryson Basquez Jr. at Sequence Corp. The name Phillip Dewey. The COO who died right around the time Luke was writing the Cancer Sweep testing program. Did they or didn't they overlap their time at Sequence Corp? And if they did, did it matter?

I googled Phillip Dewey on my computer and found a few links about him. He'd worked at Sequence Corp since its inception seventeen years ago. He started as Chief Compliance Officer, then graduated to COO seven years ago. He had three adult children and was still married to his wife of thirty-eight years at the time of his death. He died of a heart attack on August 31 at the age of sixty-three.

August 31st. Six weeks ago. Bryson Jr. said that Dewey died two or three months ago. Did he lie on purpose or just not remember? Based on my talk with Junior, my guess was he lied. Either way. Luke's time at Sequence Corp *did* overlap with Phillip Dewey. But did that mean they even met?

My phone buzzed, interrupting my thoughts. Odell Donohue.

"Did you find that young man?" Odell asked after our greeting.

"Not yet. But I could use more help."

"I don't have time right now, but what do you need?"

"Anything more you can find out about a potential Sequence Corp IPO or sale." I let out a breath. "The next one is tougher. I need to know if Scot Sandstrom has shares of Sequence Corp company stock and if he recently sold some or all of them."

"And this all has to do with your friend's missing son?" His voice rose at the end, like he was dubious.

I didn't blame him. Seemed like a long way around, but I knew in my gut it was a direct path.

"It does. I can explain if you want me to."

"That's okay." Slightly grudging, like I was asking a lot. I was. "I have some business to take care of, so I may not be able to get to this until tomorrow or the next day. Even then, it's going to take some digging from people who know where to dig. If Sequence Corp was public, you could easily get the information yourself. Private corporations are a whole different ballgame."

"I understand. I really appreciate this. And, I owe you."

"Not yet. But you might. I'll let you know what I get as soon as I can." O.D. hung up.

I went back to reading about Phillip Dewey on my computer. The article I'd read earlier was a press release from Sequence Corp. I found an obituary, which didn't add much, other than Dewey was born and raised in Gaithersburg, Maryland, and served five years in the Navy after attending the U.S. Naval Academy in Annapolis. His military service was an interesting omission for the Sequence Corp press release. Corporations usually try to tout the military service of their employees or management. Red, white, and blue sells in most parts of the country. But the press release was only six sentences long. Apparently, Sequence Corp had more pressing matters than lengthy press releases for a fallen comrade.

The only other article I found was by an online medical research industry magazine. The writer noted Dewey's death, his service to our country, and his employment record over his lifetime. Which had only been two employers as an adult. Sequence Corp for seventeen years and its competitor, American Health Innovations, the previous twenty. The same company that Jim Harkness emailed about testing protocols a few weeks before he was murdered. Dewey joined that company right after he was honorably discharged from the Navy in 1984. He worked his way up to Chief Compliance Officer for American Health Innovations after six years on the job.

I didn't know much about compliance of any kind. Most of my life I'd been non-compliant. But I imagined to become the chief compliance officer for a large medical research company at the age of thirty-two was rare and a big deal. He led the compliance department for fourteen years until he moved all the way across the country to take the same position for a brand-new medical research company.

Maybe Sequence Corp paid better and Dewey was sick of the East Coast and wanted to see the West one. Or maybe Sequence Corp dangled the COO job as the next stepping-stone. I did a quick google search on my computer and learned that Washington, D.C., was only twenty-six miles from Gaithersburg, and Annapolis was only fifty.

I didn't know where Dewey served his five-year hitch in the Navy. I'd have to send a request to the National Personnel Records Center to find out. But it didn't really matter. The majority of his forty-six years of life before he ventured west had been spent in a fifty-square-mile area in Maryland. That wasn't unusual to me. I'd spent all but about seven years of my life in San Diego. Granted, it's San Diego. But home is home and Dewey had spent a lot of time near his before he made the break.

Why leave? Maybe a more important question was why did it matter in relation to Luke's disappearance? Because my instincts told me there was something hinky about Bryson Basquez Jr and that meant there might be something hinky about Phillip Dewey's death. The longtime compliance officer who died soon after Sequence Corp hired Luke to write a program to check the accuracy of their DNA pre-cancer test.

Dewey's wife was mentioned at the end of the article. Her name was Charlene Alice Dewey and the article said she lived in La Jolla.

I got onto a paid people finder website and quickly located Charlene Dewey's address and phone number.

CHAPTER FORTY-ONE

I PULLED UP in my Honda Accord in front of a sprawling ranch house on Hartley Drive in La Jolla. Charlene Dewey's home. I took the GPS tracker off the car before the trip. Maybe whoever attached it was alerted when it was disengaged or maybe they thought I was still home. Whoever my attackers were, they reminded me that I was back in the game. If they came for me again, I'd be ready. I had my Ruger .357 Magnum snug in the pocket of my bomber jacket.

Hartley Drive was tucked back from La Jolla Scenic Drive in an area that had a rural vibe. The lots were large and many of the homes were the original ranch house builds. A couple miles from the beaches with no ocean view, the homes would still go for $2,000,000 and above on the open market.

The Dewey home fit into that category. A small white furry dog greeted me with yaps when Charlene Dewey opened the door. My black eye could jangle any dog's nerves. And any human's. The frames of my glasses hid a little of the swelling, but none of the discoloration.

Charlene Dewey looked me square in my good eye and didn't flinch.

"Skipper, hush." She picked up the ten-pound dog, which continued to yap, and held it against her chest. "You must be Mr. Cahill."

Her white blond hair was up in an old-school bouffant do that had so much hairspray in it I feared for her life if she smoked or cooked over an open flame. She wore gray capri pants like Mary Tyler Moore's on *The Dick Van Dyke Show* that I'd watched reruns of with my dad as a kid. She wasn't as svelte as Laura Petrie, but thin enough for the pants to work with an untucked navy-blue blouse. I'd told her on the phone I was investigating a case that had bled over to Sequence Corp and had some questions about the company and her husband's work there.

She looked to be around Dewey's age when he passed. Early sixties. Attractive, even with her retro vibe. But there were purple circles of grief under her pink-rimmed eyes. Her husband had only been gone for six weeks. That's just a blink after thirty-eight years of marriage. She'd grieve him for the rest of her life.

"Yes." I refrained from sticking out a hand. It's the small dogs that bite. "Please call me Rick. Thanks for seeing me on such short notice."

"Not a problem, hon, come on in. I'm happy to talk about Phil anytime." Her voice was sweet and motherly and she dropped a few syllables like a guy from Baltimore I played college football with. "I'm gonna put this little man outside, then we can sit and talk."

She led me down a hall past a kitchen opening, a family room, and into a living room and let the yapper out a sliding glass door that opened into a large grassy backyard and a cement patio with a kidney-shaped swimming pool.

Charlene sat on an avocado-colored sofa. I sat across from her in a matching chair.

"Oh, where are my manners?" She pushed forward on the sofa. "Can I get you anything to drink? Coffee, tea, water? I even have some of Phil's leftover Natty Bohs."

"Natty Bohs?"

"Oh, sorry, hon. National Bohemian Beer. It's a Baltimore thing."

"I'm fine, thanks."

"Okay." She settled back into the sofa. "Now what did you want to know about Phil? You said something about his employment at Sequence Corp."

There was a photo of Phillip Dewey on a side table next to Charlene. A burly man with a barrel chest. He sat at a table in front of a home-made cake afire with birthday candles. A cardboard crown sat askew on his head. His smile was as bright as the candles.

Likeable.

"Phil's sixty-third birthday in March." Charlene caught me looking at the photo. She smiled, but there was a slight quaver in her voice. "I put all sixty-three candles on the cake. The smoke alarm went off. Scared Skipper so bad, he tinkled on the carpet. We had to open the sliding glass door and my son, Ben, waved a towel at the smoke detector for five minutes before the darn thing would stop screeching. I laughed so hard I almost tinkled on the carpet, too."

"Sounds like a lot of fun." I wasn't just being polite.

"One of the best nights of my life. But they were all great nights with Phil." Tears filled the bottom of her eyes.

"You two were lucky." I thought of the first year of my marriage and my parents' early years together when I was a kid. Both marriages had started the way Charlene Dewey's was every day. Neither ended that way.

"Oh, now look what I've done." She wiped tears away from her eyes. "You didn't come over here to watch me cry. Please, what would you like to know about Phil?"

I took a breath. I felt like an interloper on her grief. And fond memories. But I had a job to do. My best friend, who was also a widow, needed to find her only son.

"Was Phil happy working at American Health Innovations?"

"Oh. I thought you wanted to talk about Sequence Corp."

"I do. But I also want to know about Phil's work history before he started at Sequence Corp."

"He loved it at AHI. They respected his work and treated him great and we could visit our families on weekends. He was happy as a clam and so was I."

"Why did he leave?"

"Well, it was a tough decision. He went to the Naval Academy with Bryson Basquez. The 1st." She raised her eyebrows and tilted her head. Like she didn't have such a high opinion of Bryson Basquez, The 2nd. "They remained good friends and when Bryson retired from the Navy to start his own company Phil couldn't turn down the offer to help him set it up."

"Did Phil enjoy his time at Sequence Corp as much as he did at American Health Innovations?"

"For the most part."

"What didn't he like?"

"Is this confidential like a lawyer/client type of relationship?" Charlene squeezed her hands together.

I'd lied often while working cases. I rationalized that it was for the greater good. My interpretation of it. Greater or lesser, grieving Charlene Dewey deserved the truth.

"It doesn't always work that way." I looked Charlene in the eyes and let her see whatever she could in me. "I'm here because my best friend's son is missing. His name is Luke MacFarlane and he wrote a program to test the results of the Cancer Sweep test. Did Phil ever mention him?"

"Oh." She put a hand to her cheek. "I am so sorry to hear that. No, I don't think I ever heard that name before."

"Thanks. So tell me what Mr. Dewey didn't like about Sequence Corp."

"Well." She twisted her rear end, burrowing deeper into the couch. "Phil thought Bryson Jr. influenced his father to move Phil up to COO so he wouldn't be as close to the Cancer Sweep compliance. Bryson Jr. thought Phil was overly strict."

Bingo.

"Why did Junior think that?"

"Phil wouldn't allow anyone to cut corners in methodology or practice. Bryson Jr. thought Phil always took an extra step that wasn't needed and that it would delay getting Cancer Sweep to market. They clashed and Bryson Jr. was able to get his father to be on his side more and more. Phil thought that he had his own agenda."

"What agenda?" I asked.

Charlene Dewey sat quietly for an instant, then unfolded her arms and grabbed the front end of the couch cushion to scooch herself forward. Locked and loaded.

"He had the idea that Sequence Corp should be run like some Sillycon Valley startup instead of a legitimate medical research company."

I thought I heard her say Sillycon Valley.

"Are you saying that Cancer Sweep isn't legitimate?"

"No. They're getting closer and closer to viability, but not as close as Junior, as you call him, would like. He jumped from test tubes to animals in the testing before the initial tests results were even verified. He's been hyping the test to investors and selling private shares of the company. He's raising huge amounts of private capital, but diluting the equity of everyone who's worked there for years and years."

"Like Phil."

"Yes, but he wasn't just looking out for himself." Her face turned sour. "We would have been fine if the company went bankrupt. Phil had a large 401(k) and we own real estate in Maryland. Phil was worried about the everyday employees who had set aside money from their paychecks to buy company stock towards their retirement."

"Yeah, but if Sequence Corp goes public or is sold, they also stand to make a lot of money, even with their diluted equity. Right?"

"Yes, if they can beat American Health Innovations to the market."

"Can they?"

"I don't know, but Phil thought they were at least two or three years away." She slowly shook her head. "But he thought Junior was telling potential investors that testing would conclude by the end of the year and they'd be able to launch the product by the end of June."

"That seems pretty quick. Doesn't the FDA or HHS have to give approval?" I didn't know how much Charlene knew about governmental oversight of her late husband's business, but I knew it was more than me.

"Not exactly. The regulatory agencies are still playing catchup with genetic testing. Most of it is still unregulated."

"Did Phil think that Junior was going to rush the product to market in order to beat American Heath Innovations and then set up an IPO?"

"Yes. That or privately sell the company."

"How much did Phil think the company would sell for or get in an IPO?" An article I read online had Sequence Corp's worth at $460 million.

"Probably around three billion dollars."

A lot of things were starting to make sense. Luke MacFarlane disappearing and hiding out somewhere was at the top of the list. Billions. This was real money. White-collared crooks had killed for a lot less. Or paid someone else to do the killing.

"What if American Health Innovations goes to market first?"

"If they are able to patent the technology, that could be the end of Sequence Corp. When Junior came onboard he put almost all of

Sequence Corp's eggs in the Cancer Sweep basket." She scooted up to the very edge of the sofa. "But this is the important part; he doesn't even have to get the test to market. He just has to make investors, the public, or some pharmaceutical giant think that he will soon."

"But if he chooses an IPO, he has to get past the SEC."

"Phil thought his real target is to sell to a pharmaceutical giant. They could get people on specific cancer-curing drugs before they even came down with the disease, if they ever did. That's why Phil was so adamant about properly doing the clinical trials. The IPO talk might just be a ruse to get a pharmaceutical company to make an offer before an IPO can happen."

"What does Bryson Senior think about all of this? He's Phil's friend. Doesn't he have a say in the company anymore?"

Charlene squeezed her lips together and shook her head.

"Alzheimer's. He's degenerating rapidly. The company hasn't made an official announcement yet. He got the board's approval to give Junior free rein to run the company. Phil hadn't seen or talked to Bryson for at least two months before he died."

"How long has Junior been with the company?"

"Four years. He worked in Sillycon Valley before that." She sneered when she said Sillycon Valley. I'd heard her correctly the first time. "He had a couple failed startups while he was up there. He came down here as soon as his father started showing early signs of dementia."

Bryson Basquez Junior was either a scheming opportunist or an overeducated son who'd never found his own path in life and was now trying to do right by his father. My bet was on the former. Junior had a chance to set himself up for life via the DNA cancer test. Was that enough for him to kill someone who could have squelched his dream right when it was on the cusp of coming true?

If Moira was ever going to get her son to come in out of the cold, I had to find out. Or help the police do it.

Charlene Dewey was a font of information. Old-fashioned in the best of ways. And a lovely hostess. Even with a broken heart. A heart that was healing one stitch at a time. What I had to ask might rip it open anew.

"I know your husband died of a heart attack." My eyes softened when I looked directly into hers. On their own. "If you don't mind me asking, where was he when he died?"

"Why do you need to know that?" She sunk back into the couch and hugged her chest. "Why does where my husband died have anything to do with your investigation?"

"I think Luke MacFarlane went into hiding because he thought whatever was going on at Sequence Corp put his life in danger."

"What do you mean?" She hugged herself tighter.

All I had was a game of connect the dots with too many of them missing. The momentum of the case told me the missing dots connected, too. But I wasn't alone anymore. Moira and Sheila Perkins were passengers along for the ride. Would I put Charlene Dewey in danger if I told her what I believed? Maybe, but if I was fighting for the truth, Charlene had a right to know what it was.

"The founder of ConnectTech, the company Luke works for, was murdered a week ago." I leaned forward in my chair and rested my forearms on my knees. "Luke went missing the next day. We think he's still alive, but in danger."

"What does that have to do with Phil?" But I could see it in her face. She was already putting the pieces together. She just wanted someone else to say it out loud.

"Was there an autopsy performed on your husband?"

"No. Do you think someone killed him?" Her voice was steady, but the knuckles on her hands holding her arms against her chest were white.

"I think it's a possibility." I had to tread lightly. "Had your husband ever had a heart attack before?"

"No, but they say that the ones that kill often happen to someone who's never had one before."

A widow maker. Phillip Dewey had been a large man. Big boned, not all fat. But he was significantly overweight. Certainly, a classic candidate for a heart attack.

"Did heart disease run in his family?"

"No." The word left her mouth right as I finished speaking. "His father died of lung cancer. His mother is still alive. But three of his four grandparents died of hereditary cancer."

"So Cancer Sweep was important to him."

"Yes. Very much so. That's why he was so adamant about doing things the right way. If it works, it could save millions of lives."

A righteous quest that takes time versus a quick buck. Humanity's loss if the wrong person held all the power. And maybe Jim Harkness and Phillip Dewey's loss, too.

"Were you with your husband when he passed?" A violation of her grief, but a question I had to ask.

"No. I was with family on vacation in Maryland." She rubbed her chin and stared at her lap. "My sons and daughters-in-law were with me. I had to call my neighbor, Kevin Alpert, to check up on Phil because he hadn't answered his phone since the day before and he didn't go to work that day. We each have keys to each other's houses. Kevin . . . Kevin found him that afternoon."

"I'm very sorry."

"I know." She pursed her lips and nodded her head. "Everyone is."

I didn't have an answer to that. Just a job to do.

"If you don't mind me asking, why didn't Phil go with you on vacation?"

"He was supposed to." Her lips quivered. "We vacationed at Deep Creek Lake every year. We plan our whole summer around it, but

Junior asked Phil to stay to talk to the Sequence Corp board of directors about Cancer Sweep. Phil was going to come out the next week."

"Had he ever talked to the board before?"

"Yes. A couple times."

"Did Junior know about your vacation ahead of time?"

"Yes. Bryson Senior was Phil's boss, but he had to report to Junior the last six months or so. Junior knew about the vacation well in advance and Phil reminded him a month before we were supposed to leave."

Charlene's eyes flipped wide open and she thrust her hand to her mouth.

"What is it?"

"I wasn't going to go until Phil could go with me." Her face turned ashen. "Junior heard about it and offered to pay for both our flights if Phil stayed the one week and I flew out early with my kids. He called me to apologize and promised he'd have Phil on a plane the next week."

Another bloody dot connected. And Charlene connected it, too.

"Had Junior ever called you before?"

"No, but . . ." She frowned. "He's always been very friendly to me. And he actually treated Phil well. They just had disagreements on the direction of the company. Phil actually liked Bryson until he started fast-tracking Cancer Sweep. I don't think he's capable of . . ."

People surprise you. Especially when multiple billions are at stake.

"Phil was all alone when he died." Tears welled in Charlene Dewey's eyes and ran down her checks. I went over and sat down next to her on the couch. I put my arm around her shoulders. She wept quietly. I held her and didn't say anything. There wasn't anything I could say that would help. She tilted her head against my shoulder for a moment, then lifted it up and patted my hand.

"I'm okay now, hon." She leaned against the sofa back and I returned to my chair.

"Did you . . ." Delicate. "Were Phil's remains buried or were they cremated?"

"He was buried." Her back tightened and her head rose. "With his family and friends around him. We had to have two memorial services. One here and one in Gaithersburg. That's how much he was loved."

"I'm sure he was a wonderful man."

"He was."

I'd thought a lot about death lately. With my headaches, my fugue states, my ticking clock. But about what I'd miss, not about who'd remember me. The list of mourners would be short. They'd only need a couple rows of pews at my memorial service.

I'd mourned the dead for over half my life. My father, Charles Cahill. My wife, Colleen. My partner on the Santa Barbara PD, Krista Landingham, Leah's sister. And the people who'd died on my watch. The ones I couldn't save and the ones who died because their lives intersected with mine at the exact wrong time. Timothy Buckley. Trey Fellows. Naomi Hendrix. Alicia Alton. Audrey Hastings.

All gone. All mourned. All remembered.

A tainted legacy. But in the past. My life started over the day I learned Leah was pregnant. Less life in front of me now than behind. A new life. A family to build a new legacy around. A child to make a better world than I'd left behind.

"And he deserves justice," I said.

"What do you mean?" But her eyes knew the truth. And it frightened her.

"There should be an autopsy."

"He needs to rest in peace." Charlene stood up. "I'm not going to let some pathologist desecrate his body."

"That's up to you." I stood up and Charlene started pacing in front of the sofa. "But you know that something's not right with your husband's death. I can see it in your face. Isn't it worth the chance to find the truth?"

"It's been six weeks." She wrung her hands in front of her as she paced. "What could they possibly find now?"

"A lot of things. Drugs that can simulate a heart attack."

"But who could have drugged him? Phil was home alone. He died in his sleep. He was in bed when my neighbor found him." Charlene thrust both hands to her face. "Oh, god."

"What?" I took a step towards her and gently put my hands on her shoulders. "Did he meet someone that night?"

"Yes." She looked at me, wide-eyed, and nodded her head. "I forgot."

"Who? Bryson Jr?"

"No. A woman who runs a charity."

The blood in my veins turned to ice, but sweat boiled out of my forehead.

"Linda Holland?"

"Yes."

CHAPTER FORTY-TWO

LINDA HOLLAND. THE woman who took Luke MacFarlane under her wing. Wife to Scot Sandstrom. One half of the power couple who always found a way to end up on top. And the last person Luke saw before he met with Jim Harkness the night Harkness was murdered. The night before Luke disappeared.

"How did your husband know Linda Holland?"

"Through her charity, A Hand Up. Bryson Senior was on the board of directors and got Phil involved and eventually onto the board."

"Where did they meet that night?"

"I don't know." Charlene's brow furrowed. "They usually had dinner at Duke's in La Jolla."

"Just the two of them or the whole board?"

"I'm not sure. Sometimes the whole board or just a few would get together. Sometimes her husband tags along. He's an investor in Sequence Corp and was always picking Phil's brain about Cancer Sweep. Bryson Junior also started going in his father's place."

That answered the question about whether Scot Sandstrom was an investor.

"Could Junior have been there that night?"

"I don't know. Phil just told me when we talked that day that he was having dinner with Linda. That was the last time I spoke to him." She sat back down on the couch.

"Do you have access to his credit card records? Would he usually pay for dinner or would Linda? Or would they go Dutch?" If I knew where he had dinner, I might be able to track down the staff and show them photos of Dewey, the Sandstroms, and Bryson Basquez to see if they remembered any of them dining together that night. The last night of Phillip Dewey's life.

"Linda would usually pay and write it off to the charity. But that bothered Phil. He thought that was depleting money that should go to helping needy families. He always liked to say that the board had to eat whether they talked about the charity or not. Anyway, I'll go look up his credit card records online."

She got off the couch and started to leave the living room, then stopped and looked at me.

"Well, come on, hon. The office is down the hall."

I followed her into a masculine office with dark wood paneling on the walls and a massive polished mahogany desk with one of those old-fashioned desk lamps with the green shade. Plaques with naval commendations hung on the walls. A minibar with bourbon and scotch, from sipping to guzzling and a humidor was part of the cabinetry behind the desk. Six weeks later and the smell of tobacco smoke still oozed from the pores of the wood panel and leather furniture.

Charlene sat down in the executive leather chair behind the desk and started typing on the keyboard of an iMac computer. I sat in a leather chair across from her. She looked comfortable there. I had the feeling she'd spent a lot of time in the office since her husband died, drinking in his remaining essence after thirty-eight years of marriage.

"There's nothing on any of his credit cards for that date." Charlene peeked around the side of the computer at me. "But wait a second. There's a charge on his American Express card for $33.00 on September 1st, the day after he died. That's impossible. I tried to get a hold of him all day and he didn't go into the office. The coroner said he died the night before, on August 31st."

"Did you get his possessions from the morgue?"

"Yes."

"His wallet? Did it have his credit cards?"

"Yes, they gave me his wallet. It's right here." She opened the middle desk drawer and pulled out a man's leather wallet. Square and worn. She opened it and her hand came out with a black credit card. "Here it is. His American Express card. No one took it."

Then it hit me.

"Not all credit card charges show up on the statement on the day they were used. Especially when they're run at night, like at a bar or restaurant." I'd noticed that before with my own credit card charges. "Where was the charge from?"

"Muldoon's Steak House."

Muldoon's. The restaurant I used to manage and own a tiny piece of and that now served as a makeshift office when I had to meet a client. The owner, Turk Muldoon, and I were still friends. And it was only a couple hundred yards down Prospect Street from Duke's. A nice place to go for a nightcap. But did Phil Dewey go there alone or with someone else? And if so, who was it?

"I know the owner there. And the bartender who works five nights a week." I stood up and checked the calendar on my phone. "August 31st was a Tuesday night. The bartender I know was probably working then. Can you email me a recent photo of Phil? Not the birthday one. I need one where he's not wearing a hat and has a good shot of his face. I'll talk to the owner and the bartender tonight and see if they remember Phil and if he was with someone that night."

"We used to eat dinner at Muldoon's about once a month and listen to the blues in the bar." She came out from behind the desk. I'll get on my phone and find a good photo of Phil."

"Great. Thanks." I put my hands on her shoulders again. A personal space invasion, but I felt close to this woman I'd only known for a half hour. We shared a bond. The loss of a spouse. Something you never get over. Even when you fall in love again. "But I need you to do me one more favor."

"Okay." She looked into my eyes and nodded her head. All in.

"Think about going to court to get your husband's body exhumed and an autopsy performed. Tell your sons about what we discussed tonight. See what they think." I let go of her shoulders and gave her my card with my phone number and email address on it. "You can all call me anytime."

"I think I'm going to do it."

"Was your husband buried out here or in Maryland?" I didn't know about the legality of investigating a potential crime in one state and having a body exhumed in another.

"Here in San Diego."

"Charlene, this is important." I held her eyes. "Don't tell anybody else about what we discussed today except your sons. And tell them not to tell anybody else. Talk to a lawyer, but nobody else. No friends, not even family other than your sons. Do you understand?"

"Yes." She patted one of my hands. "I do, hon. Don't talk to anybody. If someone really did kill my Phil, they're still out there somewhere."

"Yes, they are."

CHAPTER FORTY-THREE

Turk Muldoon greeted me at the hostess station of Muldoon's Steak House when I arrived at six o'clock that night. He shifted his weight to the wooden cane in his left hand when he saw me. A lot of weight to shift. Turk was six three and now carried a few more pounds than the two-hundred-fifty he threw around the Rose Bowl as an All-Pac 12 linebacker at UCLA twenty-five years ago. The cane was compliments of a bullet meant for me, not an old football injury.

"Amazing Grace," he said and winked at me. He'd tabbed me with the song's title ever since my eyesight returned after going blind for nine months. *Was blind, but now I see.* "What happened to your eye?"

My eye. Again. Funny how everybody could see the injury that was the least painful to me and not the ones that hurt the most.

"Just a hazard of the profession, Peg Leg."

"Peg Leg? That doesn't even work." He squished up his freckled face and shook his head. "Fred Astaire would be much more clever."

He lifted the cane and twirled it deftly.

"Impressive, Tinkerbell." I took out my phone and pulled up the picture of Phillip Dewey that Charlene emailed me and showed it to Turk.

"Do you recognize him?"

Turk looked at the photo. "He eats dinner in here every so often, but I couldn't tell you the last time I saw him. Sorry."

"That's okay." The bartender was my best hope. "Is Pat here?"

"Yup. Just like I told you he would be when you called." He three-legged down the short hall into the bar and I followed in his wake.

Muldoon's Steak House still had the old-school vibe Turk's late father had started almost fifty years ago. Dark wood-slatted walls, polished brass. The bar was a microcosm of the entire restaurant, except for the stained-glass underwater ocean scene behind the top shelf liquor. A tiny stage sat to the left of the bar for musicians to use four nights a week.

I still felt like a member of the family every time I went into Muldoon's. But as the estranged son. Not the favored one.

There were only a handful of customers in the bar. Six o'clock on a Friday night in October was still early for Muldoon's. The live music didn't start until nine.

I'd struck out at Duke's before I went to Muldoon's. A waiter recognized the photos of Linda Holland and Phillip Dewey, but not Scot Sandstrom or Bryson Basquez Jr. And he couldn't remember the last time they'd been in for dinner. Muldoon's was my last chance.

"Rick!" Pat Sawyer gave me a moon-faced smile from behind the bar. "How's it going?"

"Good." I lied. I was good at it.

"Really? Your face doesn't look so good." Pat had to be creeping pretty close to forty years of age by now. His short curly brown hair caught a little gray around the temples. I hired him over a decade ago when I was Muldoon's manager.

"I bumped into something. No lasting damage." I sat down on a barstool right next to the cocktail waitress station.

"I have to play host for a little while until Jeannie gets here. Don't take up all of Pat's time." Turk slapped me on the shoulder harder than was necessary and walked back to the hostess station.

"Turk tell you why I needed to talk to you?" I asked Pat.

"Yeah. Something about remembering a customer. Get you a Macallan's neat or a Ballast Point IPA while we talk?" He smiled and swung an arm over the bar. "On the house, of course."

An important trait of any good bartender was remembering people's faces and their drinks. Pat was the best bartender on Prospect Street, La Jolla's Restaurant Row, and his memory was flawless. That was the one reason I thought there might be a chance that I could find out if Phillip Dewey had been drinking alone or had company the night he was in Muldoon's.

The charge on Dewey's credit card had been for $33.00. A bar tab that could have been for two or three people having a nightcap, Dewey drinking a couple shots of single malt scotch alone and a tip, or he could have had dinner for one and no tip if he didn't meet Linda Holland at Duke's.

"I'm good. Thanks."

"So, what do you want to know?"

I showed him the photo of Phillip Dewey on my phone.

"Do you recognize this man?"

"Yeah. Big guy. Glenfiddich neat or Bud on tap if he's drinking beer." He handed me back the phone. "He comes in with an older blond lady every once in a while to listen to the blues on Saturday nights. And a few times alone for a quick one after work. Nice guy."

The best bartender on the block.

"His name was Phillip Dewey. Can you remember the last time you saw him in here?" A much tougher ask. Pinning drinks to faces was part of the job. It became routine, rote. The bar was Pat's universe and people rotated through it five nights a week, year after year. Pulling specific nights out of that sequence was a completely different story.

"What do you mean *was*?" Pat's already round eyes bugged wider.

"He's dead."

"Dead? What happened?" Even wider.

"He died of a heart attack." Officially. For now.

"That's a shame. Nice guy." A frown on Pat's expressive face.

"Do you remember when he came in last?"

"Not the specific date, but it was a month or so ago."

Pat didn't have to remember the specific date. I already had that. He just needed to be close, and he was.

"Have you missed any shifts in the last three months? Vacation? Sick?"

"No. I went to Europe last year for a couple weeks, but haven't missed a shift since."

"Great. Do you remember if Mr. Dewey was drunk that night?"

"No." Pat pursed his lips and shook his head. "Seemed fine. Under control."

"Was he alone or with other people?"

"I think he was with some dude." He nodded his head. "Yeah, there was somebody with him."

Some dude? That ruled out Linda Holland. I pulled up Sandstrom Capital's website on my phone and found a photo of Scot Sandstrom on the homepage.

"Was it this guy?" I showed him the photo.

"No. The dude was younger and had dark hair."

Younger and dark hair. Bryson Basquez Jr. had brown hair. He was only a handful of years younger than Sandstrom, but read much younger from a distance. I pulled up the Sequence Corp website and found a photo of Bryson Jr.

"How about his guy?" I enlarged the photo and showed it to Pat. Just seconds away from confirmation of my theory.

Pat took the phone and looked at the picture.

"No. The guy who was with him that night was younger. I'd say in his early twenties."

A hole sucked open in my stomach. The person Pat saw with Phillip Dewey could have been anyone. Somebody who worked under Dewey at Sequence Corp. A success story from A Hand Up charity who'd had dinner with the board at Duke's earlier that night. The son of a friend. Anyone.

I took back the phone and pulled up one more picture, then showed it to Pat. He looked closely at the photo for three or four seconds.

"Yeah. That's him. That's the guy who was with Glenfiddich neat that night." A big smile on his face because he'd helped me pull a needle out of a haystack.

The one needle I'd been looking for, but didn't want to find in this haystack.

I took the phone back and closed the screen on Luke MacFarlane's photo.

CHAPTER FORTY-FOUR

I SAT IN my car for a solid ten minutes after I pulled up in front of Moira's house and recycled what I'd just learned at Muldoon's for the fifth time since I left there.

Luke MacFarlane. With Phillip Dewey on the last night of Dewey's life. Coincidence? Maybe. Another coincidence when he just happened to be the last person to see Jim Harkness the night he died? I didn't like coincidences in my personal life. I liked them even less as a private investigator.

But if Phillip Dewey was in fact drugged to simulate a heart attack and Luke administered the drug, how did he do it? Slipped it in his drink at Muldoon's? Some sort of time-delayed release poison? Pat said that Dewey wasn't drunk when he was in the bar. Under control. If so, when and how did Luke administer the drug? If Dewey wasn't drunk, what excuse would Luke have had to go to his house? Did he follow him home and sneak up on Dewey when he went inside his house?

Dewey was a large man. Luke was thin and maybe five feet eight inches tall. How could he subdue Dewey to administer the drug? Unless he had it in a hypodermic needle and stuck it in the back of Dewey's neck at the front door. Even then he'd have to somehow haul Dewey into his bedroom, undress him, then put him in pajamas and into bed.

Impossible for one person Luke's size.

Even if all that were possible, where did he get the drug and how did he time it perfectly so that Dewey died in his sleep? Luke was intelligent. A computer whiz, but that didn't necessarily translate to other fields. Like medicine. Whoever hired Luke to kill Dewey may have given him the drug and told him how to use it. But Luke wasn't a professional hit man. He was just a nerdy guy with an anger problem.

I thought about the empty envelope Moira and I found in Luke's trash. A payoff for something. Couldn't have been for a hit. Luke wasn't a pro. But somebody killed Jim Harkness. And probably Phillip Dewey. And Luke was the last person to be seen with both of them. Unless . . .

What if Luke was paid to help out with the murders of Phillip Dewey and Jim Harkness? Maybe he slipped something into Dewey's last drink at Muldoon's. The one for the road. And by the time they got to their cars, Dewey was too out of it to drive so Luke drove him or maybe he handed off Dewey to the killer or killers right there.

The two men in the Beemer. The same two who ambushed me. Who worked for Linda Holland. Or Bryson Basquez Jr., who had a PhD in Pharmacology.

I got out of the car and knocked on Moira's door.

"You look awful," she said by way of greeting.

"You don't look great, either." I wedged into the house between her and the doorjamb.

Moira closed the door and followed me into her living room. I sat on the sofa and she stood in front of it, arms folded.

"Did you tell Leah yet?"

"About what?" I knew, but my response was a reflex.

"Don't be an ass."

"Not yet. I will when she gets home next week."

"You promise?"

"Yes."

"How long have you known there was something wrong?" Moira sat down in the armchair opposite the couch.

I found out a week to the day after Leah and I learned she was pregnant. A sweet, bitter celebration. I'd kept the bitter part to myself. The time for the whole truth was almost at hand.

"A little over a month."

"And you haven't talked to anyone about it?" Concern in her voice. She knew I had very few *anyones* to choose from. Leah, her, and, maybe, Turk.

"We're talking now." I moved forward on the sofa. "But I didn't come by to talk about me. I spoke with Charlene Dewey today."

"Who's Charlene Dewey?"

"The wife of the COO at Sequence Corp who died of a massive heart attack while Luke was working with them."

"Why did you talk to her and why didn't you consult me ahead of time?" Her voice had a barb in it.

"I talked to her because she was as close as we were going to get to someone who knows anything about behind-the-scenes stuff at Sequence Corp."

"You just said 'we.' There is no *we* if you're talking to people without me or without me even knowing."

"You were working the emails. This could have been a complete zero. I didn't see the need to have both of us involved."

"You. Always you." She shook her head and her voice softened. "You should be home and resting, anyway."

"Charlene Dewey was kind enough not to throw any punches. Would you like to know what she told me?"

"Okay. Let's hear it." She folded her arms and crossed her legs. A tight, impenetrable wall.

I told her that Luke's time at Sequence Corp overlapped with Phillip Dewey's before he died and what I'd learned from Charlene about her husband. His concern about the direction that Bryson Basquez Jr. was taking Sequence Corp. That Scot Sandstrom *was* an investor. The rush to get Cancer Sweep to market before American Health Innovations did. Junior holding Dewey back in La Jolla while Charlene flew to Maryland for a family vacation. Dewey's sudden life-ending heart attack. The fact that there was no autopsy to positively confirm the death diagnosis and rule out other possibilities. And, finally, the dinner with Linda Holland the night he died.

I stopped there to hash over things to see if Moira believed, as I did, that Phillip Dewey had been murdered.

"We won't know for sure unless his wife is able to get his body exhumed and then have an autopsy performed." Moira had unwrapped her legs while I spoke and now her hands were loosely in her lap. "All that could take weeks, if not months, if she gets pushback from the city. Getting a body exhumed isn't easy."

"The quicker all of this comes together, the quicker we find Luke." I pressed my lips together and hoped Moira would take to heart what I had to say next. "We need to show Detectives Hartunian and Shane what we've discovered over the last couple days. There's enough here for them to listen and they could help expedite the exhumation and autopsy of Phillip Dewey's body."

"Hartunian and Shane?" Her voice pitched high and her body tightened back up. "All you have is a bunch of speculation. They're not going to do anything with this. They're going to think we're just trying to direct them away from Luke."

"Don't forget about the emails."

"The emails don't mean anything unless we can show them some real facts, not just supposition."

"My read on both detectives is that they want to find the truth. We can give them information that, hopefully, can lead them there. Lead us there, but we don't have badges."

I didn't say anything about guns. We both had those.

"You've got nothing concrete. Can you even verify that Linda Holland and Dewey actually had dinner together that night?"

She was wrong. I had at least one thing that was concrete. The one thing she didn't want to hear.

"No, but there was a charge on Dewey's credit card that night." I let out a long breath. "Thirty-three bucks on his American Express card at Muldoon's that same night. And the bartender remembers him being in the bar with someone else."

"Linda Holland?"

"No." The pain in my ribs and head suddenly exploded and my throat tightened up. "Luke. He was with Dewey a few hours before he died."

CHAPTER FORTY-FIVE

"What?" Moira shot up from her chair.

"I showed the bartender a photo of Luke. He confirmed that Luke was the person he saw with Dewey that night in Muldoon's."

"Why the hell did you do that?"

I told her the sequence of events of what happened in Muldoon's. How Luke's was the last photo I showed Pat because he fit Pat's description of who he saw with Phillip Dewey.

"How the hell could he remember who was in his bar on a random night six weeks ago?" A shout, her face red. "That's impossible."

"Bartenders remember their customers and Pat Sawyer is remarkable at it." I remained calm. This was hard enough on Moira. I didn't want to escalate. "Dewey went into Muldoon's often enough for Pat to remember him."

"Okay." Her voice now down to a simmer. "But how could he possibly remember a specific night?"

"He didn't have to. I had the night with the credit card receipt. I asked Pat the last time he'd seen him and he thought it had been a month or so, which fits in with the actual date. It was on a Tuesday night in August and Pat works Tuesday nights."

"How do you know he wasn't sick and missed a night?"

"Because I asked him."

"How can anyone be a hundred percent certain of someone they don't know, but supposedly saw six weeks ago in a crowded bar?" Back to full boil.

"I believe him." I stood up. "And instead of denying that Luke was with Phillip Dewey the night he died, you need to help me figure out why."

"Shut up, Rick! I don't have to figure anything out." She started pacing across the living room.

"Look, I can't unknow what I found out tonight. All I can do is work it." I took a deep breath and opened my hands in front of me. "Let's do this: I'll work the Phillip Dewey and Sequence Corp angle and you work the emails and ConnectTech with Sheila Perkins. You'll be a good team. I know she likes you."

"Don't patronize me." She squinted and shook her head. "And you don't have to work anything because you're off the case."

"No. I'm not." I shook my own head. "I'm working this case with or without you. Luke's not going to come out of hiding until this thing gets resolved or he gets arrested. Or killed. If you don't want to work with the sheriff's detectives, then you'd better work with me so we can keep your son alive."

"You can leave now." More weary than angry. She swung her arm toward the front door.

Moira didn't want to acknowledge what she had to know, down deep, was true. I needed to jar her out of her denial.

"Do you want to worship a dead son who you convinced yourself could do no wrong or do you want to support him when he goes on trial for murder and get him the best lawyer you can?"

"Fuck you, Rick."

I walked to the door, but Moira's voice stopped me before I opened it.

"Are you going to go talk to Hartunian and Shane?" Her voice, shredded of life.

"Not yet." I opened the door and left.

CHAPTER FORTY-SIX

LEAH CALLED ME a couple minutes into my drive home from Moira's.

"I just landed another client in Montecito!" Her voice, wind chimes of unbridled joy. The flip side to the last couple of days I'd had. "Ten thousand square feet of Spanish Colonial Revival on a ten-acre lot up in the hills."

Montecito was an uber-wealthy enclave in Santa Barbara County that claimed estates owned by Oprah Winfrey, among other celebrities. A happy client up there could add a crooked number with many zeros behind it to Leah Landingham Design's ledger. Much needed with her upcoming two-year baby hiatus only months away.

I was going to be the sole breadwinner soon. I should have been setting more corporate background check jobs that kept me safely behind a computer instead of working a case on the street without a helmet.

And I was on week two of a one-week payday, now working for free on my own. As happy as I was to become a father and get married again, I was still in Rick Cahill lone wolf mode. That wasn't fair to Leah and our child-to-be.

But Moira needed my help to find her son and keep him alive. Even if she didn't want it.

My last lone wolf case.

"That's great. Congratulations! We'll celebrate when you get home." One of many celebrations to come in our new family life. Birthdays, anniversaries, first steps and words. The pounding in my head reminded me that I had to drink them all in because they had a finite number. "How's the belly? Huge? Can you even see your feet anymore?"

"So, I have six months of fat jokes to look forward to?"

"Yes. And get ready for some food craving jokes, too."

"Can't wait." A pause, then her voice dropped. "Is everything all right? You sound a little tired."

"I'm fine." Is a white lie just a lie when you use it to keep a loved one from worrying, but also to avoid a difficult conversation? But I was just avoiding a conversation I'd have to have eventually. In a few days if I kept my word to Moira. "Any movement on the bump?"

"No, but we get to see the little urchin next Wednesday."

Our first sonagram. Too early to determine the sex, but used to get an accurate due date. I couldn't wait to see our child growing inside the woman I loved. My blood mixed with Leah's to give birth to greater promise.

I didn't take Leah with me to my CT brain scan last month. Nothing to celebrate. I had to take her to the next one. And explain to her the need for it.

"Can't wait." Something clicked inside my head. The flip side of the flip side. "With this new client, does that mean you'll have to work on the house late into the pregnancy?"

"Only if the project isn't completed by then." No wind chimes. "But don't worry, my water isn't going to break all over the client's White Staturio marble floor."

The joke was also a jab. A stiff left to keep me at arm's length so I'd end the stop working discussion. I knew that women often worked until the last few days before their due date. But I also knew how precious life was and how easy it could be snuffed out. Leah had already lost two children to miscarriages. I wanted our child to have a fighting chance. He or she would have to be a fighter. They'd have my genes, but they probably wouldn't have me around into adulthood.

"I just want to—"

"I know, Rick." Forceful, but not angry. "I want the same things that you do. The baby will be fine. I'll be fine. You know I'd never do anything to jeopardize the pregnancy. You have to trust me. I love you. Talk to you tomorrow."

She hung up. No chance for further discussion.

She ended the conversation on trust. My weak spot. My trust had been breached enough times that I rarely gave it anymore. Certainly, to my wife-to-be. But even then, my instinct was still to verify. Maybe due to the darkness in my own soul, my faith was weak. With Leah. And with my maker.

Both had given me a second chance. But I had to have faith.

CHAPTER FORTY-SEVEN

THE RING OF a phone cut through the fog. I sat in a chair in a familiar room I couldn't place. I grabbed the phone off an end table.

Letters that I couldn't make sense of populated the phone's screen. I pushed the green button and put the phone to my ear.

"Hello?" A groggy voice. I think it was mine.

"Rick. It's Odell." I recognized the name and the voice. I just couldn't put them together. "Did I wake you up?"

My awareness opened up. I was sitting in my living room. The wrought-iron clock above the fireplace read 8:39. I think it was nighttime. The lights were on. A man with spiked dyed blond hair was still talking to a chef in a restaurant kitchen on the TV.

I hadn't fallen asleep. I'd been in a fugue state. Another one. They were coming quicker and lasting longer now.

Odell? Odell Donohue, my former client. I'd asked him to investigate something for me.

"No. Sorry." My voice took form. "I'm here. Did you find something out?"

"You sure you're okay? I can call you back in the morning."

"No." I shook my head. Wisps of fog evaporated. My earlier conversation with Odell came back to me. "I'm good, really. What did you find out?"

"Your instincts were good on Sequence Corp. The word on the street, Wall Street, that is, is that they'd been positioning for an IPO, but have also been approached by the pharmaceutical companies Novartis and Johnson & Johnson. A top analyst told me that they are cash strapped and need a major influx of capital soon. They don't want to go through the due diligence and regulatory filings required by the SEC to go public. He thinks they're going to try to go the route of a sale to one of the pharmaceuticals."

"Wouldn't the pharmaceuticals' due diligence be as tough as the SEC's? They didn't get to be huge by not doing their homework."

"Yes, but Cancer Sweep is thought to be very close and the technology could be a game changer." His voice picked up speed. "For Big Pharma, it's worth the risk. Sequence Corp has already applied for a patent for the technology. If granted, and the test works, they'll put the Cancer Sweep test in every CVS and/or Walgreens throughout the country. Plus, they'll be able to have customers for life for their pre-cancer treatment drugs. This is potentially a ten-to-fifteen-billion-dollar-a-year technology. It could boost Johnson & Johnson from number five in cancer related drug sales to number one."

"What would the sale price for Sequence Corp be?"

"My guy thinks that right now it would be about three billion."

The same number Charlene Dewey gave me.

"What would the founder, Bryson Basquez's, family's portion be of that?"

"I don't know how much equity they still own, but I'm sure it's at least fifty percent. Their net after taxes, debt reconciliation, and other expenses would probably be in the area of seven hundred to eight hundred million."

"Wow." My mind was locked in now. No remnants of fog remaining. "Would the pharmaceuticals still want to buy Sequence Corp if their test was two or three years away as opposed to less than a year?"

"Possibly, but at an exponentially lower price. There's a much larger competitor of Sequence Corp's working on the same technology. They are thought to be slightly behind, but they would probably be a better risk if Sequence Corp isn't as far along as they claim to be."

"American Medical Innovations." Phillip Dewey's former employer before he went to work for Bryson Basquez Sr. And ended up with his son.

"I see you did your homework."

I didn't know what portion of eight hundred million Bryson Junior had a right to, but I could guess that he'd find a way to grab the lion's share. Enough to murder someone who could make the number go to zero.

"How much of Sequence Corp do the Sandstroms own?"

"Your instincts were good there, too. My guy thinks they own up-wards of twenty-five percent of the company stock."

"So, it's worth possibly a gross of seven hundred fifty million dollars to them for a sale to happen?"

"That's right. Of course, less after the debt is repaid. If American Health Innovations were to go to market first with an unbreakable patent, the Sandstroms' investment would be worth pennies on the dollar."

"Do you know if Scot Sandstrom has sold any shares or tried to lately?"

"That, I don't know." He grunted. "But I think the analyst would have heard about it if anyone had tried to unload a large number of shares."

"If they did or were trying to sell a huge portion of their ownership, that could tank the sale, couldn't it?"

"Absolutely."

The Sandstroms either didn't know that Cancer Sweep wasn't as advertised or they did and decided to ride it out. A gross of seven hundred fifty million dollars versus pennies on those dollars was incentive to keep the truth hidden. No matter the cost.

"Thanks, O.D. I do owe you now."

"Don't worry about it, my man. It will all come out in the wash."

I went upstairs with Midnight at my side and into my office. I sat down at the computer and added what I'd just learned from Odell Donohue into my case notes. The case of my best friend's missing son, which was now about DNA cancer testing and manipulation of a private company's value. Oh yeah, and murder. Probably times two.

I leaned back in my reclining desk chair and rested my hands behind my head. Everything I'd learned from Odell pointed the finger at Bryson Basquez Jr or the Sandstroms as being responsible for the murder of Jim Harkness and likely murder of Phillip Dewey.

Where did that leave the last person seen with both Harkness and Dewey, Luke MacFarlane? Was he a paid assassin, a blackmailer, or just really unlucky? I could drop unlucky. Whether Moira was ever willing to face the facts or not, Luke was involved. Somehow. There was an empty envelope that had once been full of cash to prove it. I couldn't put assassin on him either. When and how did he acquire the skills? But complicit in the murders? Unfortunately, that looked like a better possibility than unlucky.

But if killer, accessory after the fact, and unlucky weren't true, that left blackmailer. The cash came from somewhere and for some reason.

If I was an impartial bystander and could look down from thirty thousand feet, I'd give my case notes to Detectives Hartunian and Shane and walk away. They could take them or leave them, but I didn't know how much farther I could carry the case without getting law enforcement involved.

I rocked my chair forward, took my phone out of my pocket, and set in on the desk. And stared at it. For five, ten minutes. I didn't know how long. What I did know was that I had to pick it up and make a call.

I had information that was important to a murder investigation. All I had to do was give it to the police and betray my best friend. The friend who'd saved my life. And withheld evidence that could have sent me to prison. For twenty-five to life.

I stood up, picked up the phone. and put it in my pocket. It rang almost immediately. I pulled it out and checked the screen. The incoming phone number was blocked. I answered anyway.

"Mr. Cahill?" An agitated male voice. Vaguely familiar. But it couldn't be.

"Yes."

"It's Luke MacFarlane."

"Luke." I stayed calm, not wanting to add to his agitation. "Where are you?"

"It doesn't matter where I am." His voice, a high rattle. "I can't get a hold of Gabby. I'm worried that something's happened to her."

He was worried about the woman who had a restraining order issued against him. And he called me. He must have known that his mother hired me to find him. How?

"Gabriela Dates has a restraining order against you, Luke." Still calm, but stating the hard facts. "Maybe she's just not picking up when you call. You're supposed to leave her alone."

"You don't get it, man." Frantic now. "That was all fake so they wouldn't think Gabby was working with me."

"What do you mean? Who wouldn't think?"

"None of that matters right now! Please go check on Gabby."

"Why can't you check on her?"

"I'm already on my way, but it will take me at least an hour and a half to get there." The bleat of a car horn. He was driving. "I can't wait that long to see if she's all right."

"Why do you think something's wrong?"

"I got a call from her burner, but she hung up when I answered. Then I got a text from her phone. The deal was we wouldn't text. I called back like five times and she wouldn't answer."

The burner phones he bought at Walmart. One for him and one for Gabby. Maybe they were working together and the TRO was a ruse.

"I'll head over there right now. Give me her gate code. And give me your number so I can call you back after I check on Gabby."

"I can't give you my number. Sorry."

"Give me your damn number!"

He didn't say anything for a few seconds, then gave me the code to get into Gabby's condo complex and his phone number.

"Please make sure she's all right." His voice cracked.

"I'm on my way. Did you call the La Jolla Police Department and ask them to check on Gabby?"

"I don't trust the police." Desperate. "They probably have connections there."

"Who? Linda Holland and her husband?"

"Just make sure she's okay!"

The phone went dead.

I grabbed my keys. And my gun. Went downstairs and called Moira from my car.

"Luke called me. He's worried about Gabby. I'm heading over to her condo."

"Oh my God!" Joy and relief. She deserved both, but Luke wasn't home yet.

"He needs his mom." I gave her Luke's number.

"Did you call LJPD and ask for a welfare check?"

"Not yet. I don't think they'd check on Gabby on my word. I hope I don't find something stronger than my word when I get there."

CHAPTER FORTY-EIGHT

Ten minutes later, I parked on La Jolla Boulevard, across the street from Gabby Dates' and Linda Holland's condos. A chilled fog thickened the air and clamped down on the night. I'd circumnavigated the block before I parked. No white BMW X6 anywhere or any other car with two operatives sitting in the front seat watching Gabby's condo. Or Linda Holland's. Or me.

Luke's call to me could have been some kind of setup. There might be killers inside Gabby's condo waiting for me to walk in. But I didn't think so. The fear in Luke's voice was real. He was afraid. For Gabby. And for himself. He was a scared kid, not an accomplice to murder.

I buzzed unit one at the gate guarding Gabby's complex. Nothing. I didn't bother with a second time and punched in the key code Luke gave me to unlock the gate. No one else was in the courtyard. I walked quickly over to Gabby's condo and rang the doorbell. No answer. Then I noticed that the door was slightly ajar. Maybe half an inch. Shit. My insides throttled up. I rang the doorbell again. And waited, trying to slow my heartbeat. Nothing. No sense of movement inside. Silence. Dead silence.

I had a phone in my pocket with the digits 911 on it. But what if Gabby was inside and needed immediate medical attention? I pushed the door open with my forearm.

A metallic smell immediately hit me in the face. I'd smelled it too many times before. Blood. I grabbed the Ruger .357 Magnum from my jacket pocket, pushed the door all the way open, and rushed into the condominium.

"Gabby!"

No response.

Blood splatter streaked the wall next to the cutout kitchen. Tacky, like there was still some viscosity to the blood. More on the white carpeted floor in the living room. A trail that led to the lone bedroom.

"Gabby!" I knew it was futile even as I called her name.

I tiptoed around the blood toward the open door of the bedroom. I kept the Ruger in front of me in a triangular shooting platform as I inched my way along next to the bloodstain on the carpet. Instinct, even though I sensed no one else was in the condo. No one else alive.

I got to the opened bedroom door. Horror.

A body—a woman's—was splayed out on the bed. Naked. Covered only in blood. The sheets and comforter, stained red with blood and brain matter. Castoff droplets ran up the wall and along the ceiling above the bed.

I couldn't tell if the body was Gabriella Dates. The face of the woman was grotesque. Bludgeoned beyond recognition. Her hair was dark like Gabby's, but was so matted with blood and brains that determining the actual color was impossible.

Bile swept up my throat and sweat pockmarked my forehead. Breaths pistoned in and out of me. I fought the nausea. I'd seen death before. My wife. Other people I cared about. But it never gets easier.

And not like this.

I turned away, then turned back. Something on her left shin. A tiny red line, like the aftermath of a scab. Something that would heal completely and not scar. Gabby had been hit in the leg by shrapnel from the chair Luke MacFarlane broke in front of her. Identity confirmed.

The hole inside me bore deeper. I scanned the bedroom looking for a murder weapon. Then I saw it. An aluminum bat. Only the handle was visible. On the floor to the left of the bed, caught up in the folds of the comforter. Something about the handle was familiar. A neon green wrap.

Like the wrap around the handle of the bat I saw next to Luke MacFarlane's bed when I was in his apartment.

I edged back the way I came, careful not to step in any blood. There was a lot to avoid. I stopped in the living room and looked around for anything out of place. Not that I knew Gabby Dates' home, but I'd been in enough crime scenes to recognize something that didn't belong. Nothing.

I turned to leave and found the one thing out of place. A phone on the kitchen counter. A Rebel 4 Tracfone. One of the phones Luke bought at Walmart. It sat faceup. I put my gun back in my jacket pocket, grabbed the bottom of my t-shirt with my left hand, and pressed my right index finger firmly against the cotton. My fingertip formed a nub at the bottom of the shirt. I didn't want my fingerprints or DNA on the phone. I pressed my cotton-tipped finger against the screen of the phone, leaving it on the counter. The screen remained dark.

I'd done this before with another phone I wanted to access without leaving any of me behind. It had worked. I tried again, pressing harder this time. Bingo. Enough body heat penetrated the cotton to engage the screen. I pressed the phone tab and saw the phone call history over the past ten days. Nine or ten incoming and outgoing calls, each. The outgoing calls all went to the same phone number. The same number Luke gave me over the phone.

There were no voicemails or incoming texts. Just a single outgoing text. It read:

Luke, this has gone on too long. PLEASE STOP HARRASING ME!

The only text Luke claimed they ever sent to each other.

The text was sent at 8:37 tonight. Meaning that Gabby was alive at that time or her killer was still in her condo then and sent the text. But unless Luke lied to me, the text was sent from Gabby's killer.

I checked the call log again to see when the most recent calls were made. There was an outgoing one at 8:35 tonight. The outgoing call was only a minute. The dead air call Luke told me about. The killer calling to hear Luke's voice and confirm that the phone number belonged to him.

And then five more incoming calls every couple minutes after the text was sent. Luke's returned calls that weren't answered.

The perfect setup. The killer broke into Luke's apartment and stole the bat by his bed to use as a murder weapon. The bat would have Luke's fingerprints and DNA all over it and so would Gabby's condo. As would the TracFone he bought at Walmart. The killer makes the call, hears Luke's voice on the other end, then hangs up and sends the "stop harassing me" text. Another nail in Luke's coffin. Angry text goes to the stalking ex-boyfriend, he calls her right away, she doesn't answer, so he blows up and goes to her condo and kills her. Rage. Overkill from the man with the anger management issues.

The killer figured Luke would come to Gabby's condo after she'd called and texted him but didn't return his calls. He'd either kill Luke when he arrived or leave the perfect setup for Gabby's murder. He just didn't know Luke was an hour and a half away.

I put the burner in my pocket and exited the condo. I left the door open instead of trying to re-create things as I'd found them. That game was a loser.

I went across the street to my car and put my gun and the burner phone in the black ops duffle bag hidden in the spare tire wheel well in the trunk. I had a conceal carry permit, but didn't want to go down that road with the police when it could be avoided.

The burner was another matter. I'd just removed evidence from the scene of a crime. Evidence tampering, punishable by up to six months in jail in California. For somebody I didn't particularly like. But he was Moira's son. I'd take the risk for her. Plus, Luke was innocent.

I went back across the street and stood sentry in front of Gabriela Dates' condo. An hour too late. I pulled out my phone and made three calls. The first one was to the La Jolla Police Department. The second to Moira.

The last to Luke. Next to telling my late wife's parents that Colleen was dead, the hardest call I'd ever made.

I put my phone back in my pocket and waited for the police outside a dead woman's condo.

CHAPTER FORTY-NINE

A BLACK-AND-WHITE PATROL car, light bar afire and siren wailing, arrived at the condo within five or six minutes.

The patrol officer who questioned me was in his late forties, but buff with a gray-blond buzz cut. His bronze name tag read "Brown." Polite, but to the point. I respected that, but gave him as little information as needed to be considered cooperative. I knew there'd be a detective questioning me soon after and I wanted a consistent narrative. I only told Officer Brown a couple off-white lies to protect myself. And left a couple things out, like the burner phone. My usual when dealing with the police.

The other officer put up crime scene tape around the condo all the way to the security gate. We stood inside the fence, but outside the tape.

As predicted, a slick-top detective car pulled up and double-parked next to the squad car a couple minutes into my Q & A with the patrolman. Two detectives got out of the car and walked toward us. A man and a woman. One detective was the only cop who ever gave me a fair shake at the Brick House, LJPD's headquarters. The other one hated me and had done me wrong, or tried to, more than once.

One splintered off to the patrolman guarding the police tape and maintaining the crime scene log of all who entered. Hailey Denton talked to the patrolman, put on black nitrile gloves, ducked under the tape, and entered Gabby Dates' condo.

The male detective pulled up next to me and the patrolman who was questioning me.

"A moment, Officer." Detective Jim Sheets. "Please remain here, Mr. Cahill. I'll need to talk to you."

I nodded my head.

Sheets led the patrolman about ten feet away and they spoke to each other in low tones. A few people came out of their condos and rubbernecked. No one came out of number 4, Linda Holland's unit. I wondered if she was inside peeking through a crack in a curtain or was up in Encinitas in her palace by the sea. And I wondered if she knew about Gabby's murder before I did because she and her husband ordered it.

The police would have to sort it all out.

Another patrol car arrived and two more cops manned the police tape.

Detective Sheets walked back to me. Officer Brown went over to the condo owners milling together.

"Mr. Cahill." Sheets stuck out a hand. The good cop. Or at least a fair one. I shook his hand.

"Detective. As always, you can call me Rick."

When I'd first met Jim Sheets four years ago, he was a young detective who looked more college grad student than homicide cop. He still had short black hair and wore black horn-rimmed glasses, but he now looked like a seasoned homicide cop. It was in the eyes. Eyes that had seen too much of the evil that leaks out of some people's souls and the wreckage it leaves behind.

"Well, Rick." He put his hands on his hips opening up his gray sports coat to reveal a badge on his belt and a gun on his hip. "This repetition is troubling. Death always seems to swirl around you."

"It didn't swirl around me, Detective. I came and found it." I matched his stance. "Believe me. I wish I hadn't."

"Okay." He pulled a small notepad and pen from his inside coat pocket. "How about you tell me why you're here and how you came to find the deceased."

"I got a call from Gabriela Dates' ex-boyfriend who was out of town. He couldn't reach her and was worried, so he asked me to check on her."

"What's the ex-boyfriend's name?"

I didn't have to tell him. Legally, at this point, I didn't have to tell him anything. But, while many cops I'd encountered wouldn't believe it, I thought most were generally fair and wanted to find the truth. Just like I did. Unfortunately, I ran into a few too many cops on the wrong side of fair who were convinced they knew the truth even before it could be known.

In some ways, I wasn't much different from them. Too often, I went with my gut and tunneled in on a scent, a feeling, a premature conclusion. But, fortunately, I didn't have a badge anymore. Didn't have the power to take away people's freedom, backed up by the monolithic power of the state.

"Luke MacFarlane." I didn't give up Luke to Sheets just because he was the right kind of cop. I told him because he'd find out about the restraining order soon enough. And because a good cop on the trail for Luke might help keep him alive. "He's been missing for a week and is a person of interest in the murder of James Harkness in Encinitas last weekend. I'm sure San Diego Sheriff's Deputies Hartunian and Shane will be happy to let you see their case file."

"How did you get inside the deceased's condominium?" Sheets studied me behind his glasses. Looking for a tell? That hint of deception? Probably.

Didn't have to lie for this one. Much.

"The door was ajar when I got there. I smelled blood and called—"

"You can recognize the smell of blood?" Sheets' eyebrows went up.

"Unfortunately. I've been around it enough. I'm sure you can, too."

"Go on. Did you enter the condo?" Sheets kept writing on his notepad.

He knew I did because I told Officer Brown that I had and Sheets talked to Brown before he talked to me.

"Yes. I called out Gabby's name twice and didn't get an answer, so I went through the open door."

"You said the door was ajar, not open."

"I pushed it open and entered."

"Why didn't you call 911 first and wait for the police instead of entering a crime scene?" Sheets' cop eyes studied me. "You said you smelled blood. You had to know a crime had been committed."

"I thought that whoever was bleeding inside might still be alive. I wanted to see if I could administer CPR or stop any bleeding. But I was too late."

"Did you touch anything?"

"No." Just the phone that I hid in the trunk of my car.

"Did you see anyone leaving the condo or near it when you arrived?"

"No, but everything is set up to make it look like Luke MacFarlane killed Gabby. He didn't and the people who did also killed Jim Harkness."

"Why do you say that?" Detective Sheets stopped writing notes and stared at me.

"You have a tape recorder or are you going to make notes on all of this? It's going to take a while."

"Meet me over at the Brick House in fifteen minutes. You can tell me all about it there and how you got the black eye."

CHAPTER FIFTY

DETECTIVE SHEETS SAT kitty corner from me at the small table in the square white room. A tape recorder was on the table between us. The video camera above the door stared down at me. Angry red light. We'd been in the same positions three or four times before. I'd lost track. My big mouth had gotten me back here, but I knew it was the best way to get all the information I had recorded accurately and acted on.

Then I could go back to sitting behind a computer all day doing background checks on prospective employees who may have shoplifted when they were twelve years old. Boring, but I'd yet to stumble across a dead body sitting in my home office.

The buzzing of the fluorescent lights reawakened my sleeping headache. With a vengeance. Sweat leaked under my arms. A Pavlovian response to the square white room.

"Start from the beginning." Sheets leaned back in his chair and crossed his legs.

I told him about Moira hiring me. Gabby Dates' restraining order against Luke. Luke's visit to Linda Holland's condo. The arrival of Bryson Basquez to Gabby's condo. Luke's trip to the ConnectTech office right after. His disappearance. Jim Harkness' murder. My talk with Gabby Dates. Meeting Linda Holland and Scot Sandstrom in their Encinitas home. The men in the BMW spying on Luke's apartment and the identity of one of them. The Walmart receipt in Luke's trash that was for the TracFones and memory cards. My trip to Linda Holland's charity. The assault at my house. The GPS tracker under my car. My talk with Bryson Basquez Junior at Sequence Corp. The information about a possible Sequence Corp sale. My visit to Charlene Dewey's home and what I'd learned about Phillip Dewey's death. My trip to Muldoon's and talk with Pat Sawyer. And finally, my call from Luke MacFarlane.

I didn't tell him about the envelope that smelled of money. My promise to Moira when I called her after I called the police.

I put all the pieces together for Sheets the way I thought that they should fit.

"Wow, that's quite a scenario." He unfolded his legs, leaned forward, and rested his forearms on the table. "So, Luke MacFarlane just happens to call you out of the blue to check up on his ex-girlfriend?"

"He knew his mother hired me to try to find him and that I'd talked to Gabby. He doesn't trust the police."

"A convenient way for someone else to find the body."

"I thought Luke might be capable of murder when I started this investigation, Detective." I straightened my posture and felt a twinge of pain in my ribs. "Then I added all the puzzle pieces together. He didn't kill Gabby Dates or Jim Harkness. You'll get there, too. People with potential fortunes to protect killed them both. Take a close look at Scot Sandstrom and Linda Holland or Bryson Basquez Jr., not Luke."

"You mentioned the deceased, Gabriela Dates, as Gabby a number of times. Did you have a relationship with her?"

A quick change of direction. Right at me.

"A relationship?" I cocked my head at Sheets. "I talked to her the one time during her lunch break just outside her office. There was no relationship."

"Will we find your DNA in the victim's home?"

"Possibly, but I was careful not to touch anything."

"So, you took a lot of precautions not to leave any DNA, didn't you, Rick?"

"Yes. And then I called the police, gave my name, and waited around for them to arrive and be questioned. Anything else, Detective. It's late and I'd like to go home."

But Sheets wasn't done with me yet. He made me go over everything a couple more times. It wasn't hard. Almost all of it was the truth.

"Stay in touch." He stood up. "We may have to talk with you again."

"Always." I got up and left the square white room and the police station while the sweat under my arms began to dry.

*   *   *

The clock on the dashboard of my car read 12:11 a.m. as I exited the Brick House's parking lot on Wall Street. The streets of La Jolla were mostly empty. Only one pair of headlights behind me when I stopped at the stop sign as Wall T-boned into Ivanhoe Avenue. I made a left then turned right on Cave Street, only a few hundred yards away from Torrey Pines Road, the main artery out of La Jolla.

A car whipped out in front of me from the curb. I slammed on the brakes. Impact to my rear bumper. My head snapped back and my car lurched forward. The car that cut me off stopped and a woman got out of the driver's door.

"I'm sooooo sorry." She walked toward my car through the beam of my headlights, her hands up to her face to block the glare from her eyes. Dark hair, disheveled. She wore a leather jacket and a skirt. Her gait was a little loose and her speech was slightly slurred. Drunk. "I didn't see you."

I got out of the car and heard a door slam behind me. "What the hell, lady? You just cut out in front of that guy and now I'm going to have to deal with the insurance."

The man's voice familiar. I turned toward him. A ball cap and a hoodie obscured his face, but he carried something in his hand against his leg. His left hand.

I whipped back to my car just as a pin pricked the nape of my neck. I swung around and the woman pulled her arm away. The night sky spun above me. The last thing I saw were two shadowed faces staring down at me.

CHAPTER FIFTY-ONE

I smelled kerosene. No, diesel fuel. I opened my eyes and saw darkness. I moved my head and felt material brush across my face. Thick and abrasive. Someone had put a canvas sack over my head. I was sitting on a chair. My hands were cuffed behind my back. The binding cut into my wrists. Zip-tie handcuffs. I tried to move my right leg. It wouldn't. It was zip-tied to the leg of the chair. Same with the left. Silence except for the sound of my own breath bouncing off the sack over my face. My ribs and head strobed pain.

"He's awake." Female voice, sounded like the woman who cut me off in her car to start the ruse. The ruse that caught me in a trap that might lead to my death. If someone pulled the sack off my head, there would be no might about it.

"I guess we're not going to exchange insurance information," I said. My voice steady. No hint of the terror I felt. Human, likeable. It probably wouldn't matter. They were pros. The ruse worked perfectly. Seeing a woman lowered my defenses. Not very woke for 2021. My punishment, death.

I was already riding a death sentence. We all are the minute we're born, but my life's timeline had been shortened. My cognitive capabilities were on an even shorter leash. Right now, my remaining time on earth was shorter still. Hours. Maybe minutes.

Two years ago, I could've lived with the consequences of my mistake. Or died with them. I had a life, but didn't have very much to live for. Except redemption and revenge. My life was backward looking then. Redemption for actions I'd taken. Revenge for those taken by others.

Now with my final clock speeding out ahead of me, I was looking forward for the first time in sixteen years. I had Leah and a child on the way. Family. A chance to be a father. To love unconditionally and raise a child to be better than me. A last redemption.

I couldn't die in a warehouse, my last breaths choking on diesel fuel fumes. Not now.

"Not unless it's life insurance." Male voice. Familiar.

The bag suddenly whooshed off my face. Shit.

Death.

I saw two men. Neither wore a mask. They weren't concerned about me identifying them later. There wouldn't be a later.

The man with the San Jose ID that said he was Dan Williams stared at me. Six feet, solid. Devil's ears pointed upward. He still wore a ballcap and a hoodie, but with the hood hung down the back of his neck now. The grip of a gun on his right hip facing to the front showed beneath the furrowed bottom of the sweatshirt. The southpaw had a reverse draw holster like some sort of 1860s gunslinger.

Williams held the canvas sack that had been on my head in his left hand down by his side like he'd held something else on Cave Street, probably a gun, when his accomplice stuck me in the neck with a hypodermic needle. Behind Williams was the other man who'd been in the BMW sitting in front of Luke MacFarlane's apartment that night. A couple inches shorter than Williams, but stouter. Dark, empty eyes. He held a small sport duffle bag. No sign of the woman or her needle. She must have been behind me.

The mask was off. The two male operatives weren't wearing any. Death stood in front of me. I needed an escape. Luck. An act of God.

The chair I sat on was an old wooden desk version. Rickety. I scanned the warehouse. Cement columns supported the roof every ten yards or so. Abandoned, except for a circa 1950s dump truck about twenty yards away and a shipping container in the middle of the concrete floor. The kind that comes off cargo ships. There were also a half a dozen or so old metal gas cans on the far side of the warehouse. Must have been where the diesel smell was coming from. An office with broken windows sat in the front of the warehouse, about fifty feet away. A loading dock area with two chain hand-cranked roll-up doors that were closed was located in the back.

"No flashlight tonight, Dave?" This from the Latino guy who occupied the passenger seat in the BMW the night I rousted them in the parking lot, wearing my faux security shirt with an embossed "Dave" name tag. His voice told me he was the security guard who spoke to Linda Holland through her office door the day I visited her at A Hand Up. She'd called him Robert.

"That's my side job." Nobody laughed.

"What did you tell the police?" Dan Williams.

"That I found Gabriela Dates' body."

"That's it?" Williams slapped me in the face with the canvas bag. "You spend fifteen minutes talking to a cop and a detective at the crime scene and then an hour at the police station and all you told them is that you found the body?"

"Yeah. About a hundred times." The tips of my fingers tingled with a thousand pinpricks. My hands would be completely numb in another fifteen minutes. "I called in the body. I went inside the condo. I questioned Gabriela at her job. I'm a suspect. I don't know if you've ever been a murder suspect, but homicide detectives like to ask the same questions over and over again and then change it up a little bit. I told them that I found the body and that's it. Over and over again."

"Uh-huh." Williams towered over me. "Where's Luke MacFarlane?"

"I don't know." I shook my head. The truth was easy. I didn't know where Luke was. The rest took effort. And deceit. "Listen, I don't know who any of you are or who you work for. I don't want to know. The case is over and I'm onto the next one. That's the game. I don't take any of this stuff personally. I didn't tell the cops anything, because I don't know anything. You guys let me go and we'll call it even. No hard feelings."

"You don't give yourself much credit, Rick." The woman's voice from behind me. On the move. Her voice cut through the night. A slight Midwestern accent. "You've been a very busy beaver."

The woman appeared. Still in the dress and the leather jacket. Heavy eye makeup and lipstick. Too much. An effort to alter her appearance from the blank slate I saw coming out of Linda Holland's office Wednesday at A Hand Up.

No weapon that I could see, but her jacket pockets were big enough for a snub nose revolver or a .22 or a .25. or a folding knife. Certainly, a hypodermic needle. She wore tennis shoes. I hadn't noticed that on Cave Street. No sloppiness in her walk now. Athleticism in its place. Her brown, indistinct hair, still messy.

"Enough with the small talk." Williams looked over at his partner and nodded. The man tossed him the sports bag he'd been holding. Shit. "Let's get some honest answers."

Williams reached into the duffle bag with his black nitrile-gloved hand and pulled out a pair of gardening shears. The kind you hold in one hand and prune roses with. Short scissor blades. But powerful.

Sweat started at my forehead and my heart percussioned my chest. My breath, short, rapid.

"I told you the truth." I turned my head to the woman. "The police don't know anything. I found the body. That's it."

"Rick, I want to help you, but you keep lying to us." Her voice sounded sincere. It wasn't. She had a friendly look on her face. She wasn't a friend. "We know you talked to Charlene Dewey and then went into Muldoon's Steak House where Phillip Dewey met Luke MacFarlane the night he died."

"I don't know what you're talking about." I realized too late that I wasn't as smart, or lucky, as I thought I was.

"Yes, you do. There were two tracking devices on your car." She read me much better than I'd read her. "I figured if you were lucky enough to find one, you wouldn't bother looking for another. And you didn't bother checking your friend Moira MacFarlane's car, either. We've been tracking her, too. After all, she is Luke's mother. Still, I'm impressed. You've been busy. You're figuring things out. But now it's time to tell us what we want to know."

Shit. Moira. If they tracked her car, they knew that we'd gone to see Sheila Perkins last night. Depending upon how long they'd been tracking me, they might know that was the second time I'd been to Sheila's house and that I'd gone by her work. They would have figured out that Sheila was important in finding Luke. I had to somehow warn Sheila that she was in danger.

First, I had to survive. And tell them just enough of the truth to keep me alive.

"I didn't find out anything that helped me locate Luke." I looked at each of my captors one at a time as a defendant is taught to look at the jury while on the witness stand. "Charlene Dewey found a charge on her husband's credit card from Muldoon's Steak House the night he died. I talked to the bartender and the owner and neither of them recognized the picture I showed them of Phillip Dewey. Dead end. The whole case was a dead end and now it looks like Luke killed his ex-girlfriend. That's the cops' beat. I'm off the case."

"Why did you go to Gabriela Dates' house tonight?" The woman.

"I . . ." I had to be careful. Just enough truth to stay alive for as long as possible. "I got a call from Luke. He wouldn't tell me where he was, but asked me to check on Gabby."

They'd obviously searched me after the woman drugged me. They'd found my phone and would have seen that one of the calls I made after I found Gabby's body was to the same number they called on Gabby's phone when Luke answered.

"But you said Luke killed Gabby. Why would he ask you to check on her if he'd killed her?"

"Probably because he wanted her body to be discovered at a time when he had an alibi." I was running as fast as I could to keep my life's clock ticking. "I called him after I found Gabby to confront him, but he lied to me."

"Not really believable, Ricky." The woman walked up to me, took my chin in her hand, and smiled down at me. A smirk. "Do you need more of an incentive to tell me the truth?"

The woman looked at Williams and nodded toward the shipping container. Williams and Robert both walked behind the container. Whatever they came back with was going to make things even worse for me. The sweat under my arms and on my forehead hit full stream. I could smell the stink of my own fear.

"Ricky, you're a mess." The woman waved a hand in front of her face. "And you need a shower."

I heard a shuffle of boots on concrete, then saw Williams sidle sideways from behind the shipping container. He was carrying something. A chair. Robert appeared holding the other end.

The body of a woman sat in the chair. Her hands behind her back, her legs zip-tied to the chair like mine. A canvas bag on her head. The head jerked when the men set the chair down across from me. She wore a yellow blouse.

With blue tulips on it.

CHAPTER FIFTY-TWO

Sheila Perkins. Cuffed to a chair. Sentenced to die. Violently.

Because I'd asked her for help. I'd weighed risks I didn't have the right to weigh. I'd encountered this kind of evil before. Sheila hadn't. I understood the danger. She couldn't.

I'd put her in that chair. I had to get her out of it.

"She doesn't know anything." In command. "Let her go."

"That's where you're wrong, Ricky." The woman. "She knows a lot. She knows that Luke MacFarlane and his girlfriend were spying on Sequence Corp for Jim Harkness. She knows that Sequence Corp's Cancer Sweep test is not all that it's cracked up to be. She knows too much."

A muffled sob from underneath the canvas sack on Sheila's head.

Once the sack came off, nothing I could say would save Sheila. She'd be able to identify her kidnappers. They'd have to kill her. Just like they were going to kill me.

"Ricky, you're smart enough to know that things are not going to end well for you. Bad luck, I know." The woman squeezed my chin and batted her eyelashes. "The same goes for your friend Moira. She must know everything you do. And we know you called Luke after you called the police. We'll find him . . . with the help of his mother."

Moira. Unless there were more killers than just these three, she was safe. For now. They'd come for me first. They killed Gabby and staked out her apartment. Hoping that her angry text and unreturned phone calls would bait Luke into physically checking up on her. When he showed up, they'd kill him. Or, if they didn't get the chance, they still had the setup. Once Luke was in jail, even for only a night, there'd be someone with a shiv made out of a spoon or a bedsheet with a noose.

But they'd gotten me instead. And after they saw me talking to the police, I became target number one.

"But there's still Sheila here to think about." The woman nodded at Sheila, shivering under the canvas sack. "You can save her and end your life as a hero. Go out on a high note. Otherwise, my friends here will scatter her body parts in the ocean."

Muffled sobs from Sheila.

"And there's your pretty blond girlfriend to think about."

All the oxygen left my body.

"Yes. I do my homework. Leah Landingham, I believe. I might have the boys here throw her a little welcome-home party when she gets back in town." She bent down and stared me in the eyes. Hers dark and cold. "Tell me what you told the police and I'll cancel the party."

I fought the urge to lunge at her. She was close enough that, even tied to the chair, I could headbutt her in the nose. If I did, I'd endure a lot of pain and then death. And so would Sheila. And Leah, for spite.

I would die no matter what I told them. I had one shot. I couldn't waste it out of anger.

First, I had to even the odds a little bit.

"I'm telling you the truth. I didn't give the cops anything, but I do have information I didn't tell them about. Everything I've learned so

far is on my computer at home. I have a copy on a flash drive in my
safe, too. Take me there and I'll give you both. Just let Sheila go."

"Nice try." Williams. "You're not leaving here until someone finds
your decomposing body and some poor schlub from the Coroner's
Office has to slide it into a body bag."

Another sob from Sheila.

"The deal is my notes and you let Sheila go and you leave Leah alone,
right?" I wondered how long it would take one of them to realize that
they had an easy solution. If I gave it to them, they'd know it was a ploy.

"There's no deal." Williams. "There's an easier way."

He walked behind me with the garden shears in his hand. His partner walked toward me. I clenched my fists with all my strength. Not
my choice for an easy solution.

"Grab his right hand." Williams. "We'll start with the middle finger. One this tough guy probably uses often."

"Wait." The woman. "You have his keys, right?"

"Yeah."

"Give them to me. I'll go to his house and get his computer and the
flash drive." She looked at Williams, then turned back to me and gave
me the smile again. "Where's the safe and what's the combination,
Ricky?"

Bingo. One less captor improved my odds. But I needed the captor
who left to be one of the men. A greater physical threat. But I couldn't
just roll over. They might smell out the ruse.

"I need to go with you. That's the deal. I get you the computer and
the flash drive and you let Sheila go." I knew the only way I'd leave the
warehouse with them was as a corpse. But I needed them to think I
believed I could save Sheila and Leah if I helped them.

"Where's the safe and what's the combination, Ricky?" The woman,
a sneered smile now.

"Promise me you'll let Sheila go and leave Leah alone." My voice
cracked. Tears filled my eyes. Not part of the act. The tears were for

Leah and our baby. For what could have been. I'd been ready to die for years, but now I had something to live for. Something greater than myself.

The final quarter of my life would mean more to me than all the rest of it. The chance to be a father. To raise a child in a loving family. Something I'd missed as a little boy. I wanted my child to have a better chance than I'd had.

"Ah, Ricky, don't get upset." The woman patted my head. "I'll keep my promise. But if you lie, Sheila and blondie die."

"I think he needs a little more incentive." Williams.

I clenched my fists harder. A hand grabbed my wrist and another tried to pry open my fist. It couldn't.

"Fuck!" From behind me.

Williams walked back in front of me and coldcocked me in the right eye. Stars. Pain. Darkness.

Water splashed me in the face. I opened my eyes to see the woman holding a water bottle. She put my glasses back on my face that Williams' punch had knocked off. They were crooked and both lenses were scratched, but I could see out of them.

"You back with us, Ricky?"

I nodded.

"I want to make sure you can see me when I talk to you." A warped smile.

My head vibrated in pain. Water dripped off my face. My eye had already started to swell. Again. I closed my left eye to check my right's vision. A slit and closing fast. I needed my vision to live through the night. All of it.

Jaws cut into the tip of my right middle finger. Pinching, slicing pain. The shears.

"Now." The woman grabbed my chin again. "Tell me where the safe is and it's combination or our friend is going to give you a manicure."

More pressure on my finger.

"It's in the closet of the master bedroom. It's a gun safe. The flash drive is in there. There's a home alarm, too." I gave the woman combinations to the safe and home alarm.

"What about the dog?" Williams.

"Oh." The woman. "I forgot about the dog. One of you two has to go. I don't like dogs. Especially big ones."

"You just shoot the fucking thing." Williams. "There's an extra Glock in Robert's car."

"Don't hurt my dog. Please." I was gambling with Midnight's life, but it was the only play I had. "Call him by name and tell him to go outside. He'll do it."

He wouldn't. He'd die defending the house. Or kill to defend it. At six feet distance, he had an even chance against someone holding a gun. I prayed it wouldn't get to that.

"I don't like guns and I don't like dogs. A German Shephard bit me in the face when I was five." The woman folded her arms across her chest.

"Shit." Robert. The voice from the security guard I heard, but didn't see at A Hand Up charity. Linda Holland was behind all this. The woman who signed my death order. "Give me the keys."

This was my luck. My act of God.

I heard the jingle of keys and then caught a glimpse of Robert heading for the door.

"Listen." The woman. "Call when you get to the house, before you go inside."

"Roger." The man left the warehouse through a squeaky steel door.

I didn't know where we were or how long it would take Robert to get to my house. I had to act quickly to save the women in my life I cared about. And myself. Everything depended upon something I'd once seen on YouTube. And that I got the chance to find out if it worked.

CHAPTER FIFTY-THREE

"I THINK MR. Tough Guy needs to know we're serious." William's hand around my wrist. Steel blades bit deeper into the tip of my finger.

"Ahhh!" The slicing pain increased. I squirmed in my chair.

"That sucker doesn't want to come off." Williams.

"Gross." The woman.

The blades cut deeper into the meat of my finger. A sickening clip.

"Ahhh!" I screamed.

A muffled cry from Sheila.

"Got it." Williams chuckled.

I fell forward onto the cement floor, rolling to the side in time for my right shoulder to take the brunt of impact and not my head. The zip ties around my ankles pulled the rickety chair down on my back. Sweat boiled out of my body and nausea clawed up my throat. My finger throbbed gruesome pain.

"That's disgusting." The woman's voice above me, moving away. "You just going to leave that thing there?"

"I've seen and done worse." A frightening calm in Williams voice. Like maiming someone didn't even raise his blood pressure. Then the sound of a boot skimming across cement. He'd kicked the tip of my finger aside, like a pebble on a sidewalk. "And the prisoner has been noncompliant. He got what he deserved for that and for playing tough guy as a fake security guard in a parking lot."

I hyperventilated. Fighting the pain and the nausea. I'd lost the tip of my finger, but falling onto the floor had given me my last chance to survive.

I rolled over onto my forehead and tried to work my legs under me. Futile. Impossible with the legs of the chairs still attached to my ankles. The chair made creaking sounds. I needed it to break. Soon. I groaned with each new movement. The pain was real. The groan was for affect.

"Jesus." The woman's voice. Slightly distant, like she was thirty or forty feet away.

"Fuck him." Williams.

"Help him up. How many more indignities are you going to heap on this guy?" True irritation in her voice. The woman who threatened to kill Leah, Moira, and Sheila and who intimated I was already a dead man. "I'm going to the ladies room. He'd better be sitting up when I return."

"What about her?" Williams. A whoosh from Sheila's direction. I pivoted on my forehead and looked at her. Williams had ripped the sack off her head. Tears streamed down Sheila's face. Her nose, red and runny from crying. Duct tape was stretched over her mouth.

"Leave her for now." The woman, her voice distanced away.

But the removal of the sack from her head was Sheila's death warrant.

Footsteps to my left. I twisted on my forehead and saw Williams shoes, military duty boots, coming toward me upside down. He grabbed the back of my jacket and yanked. I went up and backwards, then fell back to the concrete. I needed more effort from him. That was my only chance to stay alive.

"Asshole." Williams. "You either have to try to get to your feet when I pull you up or you're going to die lying down like a dog."

Like a dog. Mother. Fucker.

"Okay." I rolled up to my knees, my torso still folded over. He grabbed the back of my jacket and yanked it. As soon as I felt a tug, I snapped my body upright and my head back. It smacked against something hard. A groan and thump of a body hitting the floor behind me.

"Hey!" The woman, farther away. Footsteps rushing toward me.

Sheila's eyes wide.

Now standing, but bent over and angled away from the back of the chair. I thrust my butt out and raised my arms up behind me and pulled my wrists apart. The YouTube video. The flex cuffs cut into my wrists. I slammed my wrists down on my lower back. Once. Twice. Snap.

My hands. Free.

A strangled scream through Sheila's taped mouth.

I turned and saw the woman charging me, hypodermic needle held above her head, thumb on the plunger. Sixty feet away.

Movement behind me.

I rocked forward onto my toes, then leapt backward like a diver doing a backward entry.

The chair, along with my weight, landed on top of Williams. The chair shattered. One ankle came free, still attached to the chair leg that had broken away from the frame. The other one was still connected. Adrenaline pushed past the pain pulsing through my finger.

The woman closed on me.

Williams struggled under me. I rolled off him to the right and grabbed for the gun in his hip holster. So did he. I got there first, yanked the weapon free, and fired into his side. Twice.

"Ahhh!" A guttural scream.

I stood up and pointed the gun at the woman as she jabbed the needle at me. It hit the gun barrel and broke. I grabbed the woman's arm with my left hand, pulled her toward me, and hit her in the nose with the barrel of the gun.

She dropped like an anchor.

CHAPTER FIFTY-FOUR

WILLIAMS CRAWLED ON his stomach toward the door. He'd never make it. A body-width smear of blood followed him. I cut my ankles free from the remnants of the chair with the shears Williams had used to sever the tip of my finger and walked over to him. Blood still dripping from the jagged end of where my fingertip used to be. My adrenaline ebbed. Pain and nausea blurred my vision. I took deep raspy breaths as I rifled Williams' pockets and found my phone.

I called my neighbor, then flipped Williams over onto his back with my foot.

"Like a dog," I said.

His face, pale and blank. Eyes staring at nothing. Blood pooling at his side.

I called Moira next. She answered on the first ring.

"Get out of your house and take a gun with you."

"What? Wait, I talked to Luke."

"Make sure he's safe, but leave your house. Now."

"Where are you?"

"I don't have time to explain. Get out now but don't use your car." I hung up.

Sheila struggled against her flex cuffs, eyes imploring me to free her. I walked by her. The threat first.

"You're safe now. This will just take a second," I said as I passed.

I grabbed the sport bag Williams had taken the shears from off the floor and opened it. A torture treasure chest and murder kit. The pruning shears may have only been the first round. There were pliers, a wire garrote, a hunting knife, a meat cleaver, duct tape, and more zip ties. I decided on the duct tape.

I walked over to the unconscious woman on the floor. Blood oozed out of her bent nose. I duct-taped her wrists together in front of her and checked her jacket pockets. I found four hypodermic needles in one pocket. Fully loaded. I threw them across the warehouse. Her phone was in the other pocket. Bingo. I put it in my jeans pocket.

My phone vibrated in my pocket. I pulled it out and answered it.

"Midnight's here safe with me." My neighbor's voice, brittle with anxiety.

"Thank you, Dorothy."

"Thank Micalah. She got him." Dorothy's daughter who took care of Midnight when I couldn't and loved him almost as much as I did.

"I will. I'll pick him up tomorrow morning." I hung up.

Midnight, Sheila, Moira, and I were all safe. Leah was still in Santa Barbara. But there was still a killer loose in the night.

I cut Sheila free from the chair and snipped off the zip cuffs from her wrists. She lunged up and hugged me before I could pull the tape off her mouth. Tears wet against my check. Bursts of air from her nose against my neck. Sheila leaned back and removed the duct tape from her mouth.

"Your finger! We have to call the police and get you to the hospital!" Sheila, frantic. She pulled away from me and looked at the floor of the warehouse. "There!"

She ran twenty-five feet over to a nub on the floor and picked it up.

"We can still save it." She ran back toward me, opened her hand. "We have to stop somewhere for ice then go to the hospital."

The fingertip was white with bone exposed inside the jagged cut where Williams had repositioned the shears after each failed attempt to lop it off.

A surgeon might be able to reattach it. If I got to the hospital in time.

"Help me take off my coat and shirt," I said to Sheila.

"Why?"

"Please. Just do it."

She took off my coat and pulled my t-shirt over my head.

"Oh, my god." Sheila put her hand over her mouth. Her eyes scanned my body. My scars. The bullet wounds under my left shoulder and on my left bicep. The raw L-shaped scar on my abdomen left by a knife. Matching set to the two-inch gouge in my neck from the same knife and the remnant of a surgically repaired bullet hole under my right eye.

Visual and tactile reminders from my quests for redemption and the truth. Tonight, I had one more quest.

I handed Sheila the shears.

"Cut a strip out of my shirt and wrap it around my finger, then tape it." The pain in my finger continued to throb. Bandaging it wouldn't relieve the pain, but it would allow me to do what I needed to do. "Please."

"I don't think we should do that." Sheila's brow furrowed. "We need to go to a hospital right now. Bandaging it will just waste time. And your shirt's dirty. It could infect the wound."

"I don't have time for the hospital yet." I'd moved past nausea and the bleeding had lessened to a weeping ooze, but my finger still pulsed searing pain with each heartbeat. If I could stay upright and think, I'd deal with the pain. "Please, I need your help. Now."

Sheila blinked twice, then cut a strip from my t-shirt and wrapped it delicately around my finger. Next, duct tape. More pain. After she'd secured the t-shirt bandage with the tape, she started to wrap more tape around all my fingers to keep them together. I pulled my hand away.

"I'm going to need those. Thanks."

A moan from the woman behind me. Her head lolled, but she still looked unconscious. I walked over to her with Dan Williams' Glock 23 in my hand. I held the grip of the gun with the thumb and bottom two fingers of my right hand. My bandaged finger, straight against the bottom of the trigger guard. Not a perfect grip, but good enough for close range.

I picked up the water bottle the woman had used to splash my face. About a quarter full. I poured the remaining water into her right ear. Her eyes snapped open and she shook her head. She saw the gun six inches from her forehead. And me behind it.

Fear.

I yanked her up to a sitting position with my good hand, then pulled her phone out of my jeans pocket and held it down to her.

"What's your name?"

"Gina." Quick.

I didn't believe it, but that didn't matter. It was a handle.

"You get one chance, Gina. Call Robert on speaker right now and tell him to abort my house. Tell him it was a ruse to buy time and to meet you back here to help with the cleanup. Do this and you live. Don't and I shoot you in the face and dump you where the coyotes will find your body before anyone else. Understand?"

A quick intake of air from Sheila behind me. Another peak under my mask.

The woman saw under my mask, too. She didn't need to look twice.

"Yes. Yes." She nodded, raised her bound wrists and touched the phone's screen with her index finger to bring up recent calls. She tapped one, then hit the speaker function.

"Yeah." The voice sounded like Robert's.

"Are you at his house yet?"

"No. I'm about ten minutes out. What's wrong with your voice?"

Shit. Her broken nose thickened her voice.

I pressed the barrel of the gun against her forehead. She squeezed her eyes shut.

"Cahill tried to go out a hero and headbutted me. I think he broke my nose. But listen, don't go to his house. He was just trying to buy time. Circle back here and help with the cleanup."

"What do you mean?"

"You heard what I said. Get back here."

"She's not going to like this. If Cahill has information that can hurt her, she needs me to get it. Let me talk to Alpha."

"Listen, you asshole." Gina into the phone. "I told you Cahill got heroic. He slammed Alpha's head onto the concrete before I could get a needle in him. Alpha is still unconscious. Get back here now."

A dial tone sounded out of the phone.

Another phone rang. It came from Williams, the Alpha dog.

Sheila looked at Williams' body, then at me.

I stared down at Gina, still sitting on the concrete, fear in her eyes, blood coagulating around her nose. I might have felt sorry for her and bad for having to be violent. But she was a killer. Like the other two.

"Move and I'll shoot you."

I hustled over to Williams. His eyes were open. His life over. I grabbed a phone from his pocket. A burner. The incoming call number showed as unknown on the screen. But I knew who it was. I took the phone over to Gina, received the call on speaker, and nodded to her.

"Hello?" she said.

Another dial tone.

"Is Robert on his way here or does he have his own plan?" I asked.

"He's coming here." Too sincere. Wanting me too badly to believe her.

"Is Robert on his way or does he have his own plan. Would he go after Moira?" Hopefully Moira had already fled her house. I pressed the barrel of the gun against Gina's left cheek.

"I don't know." Wide-eyed headshake.

"Guess. If you're right, you live. If not . . ."

"I don't know him. I was hired to oversee him and the guy you killed."

"Hired by Linda Holland?" I already knew the answer. I was just testing Gina's willingness to lie to me while I held a gun to her head.

"Yes."

"Take a guess. Is he coming back here or not?"

"I don't think so. He might run or call Linda."

I could take Sheila's advice and go to the emergency room and hope the tip of my finger was salvageable. But there was still a killer roaming free who, along with the dead man and the woman in front of me, had threatened the people I loved. Leah and Moira wouldn't be safe until he was brought to justice.

Or dead. My justice.

"Where are we?" I asked Gina.

"In Oceanside."

Oceanside was fifteen miles north of Encinitas. I could probably beat Robert to Linda Holland and the Sandstrom house, if that's where he was headed. It was after one o'clock, but Holland would still be awake. She was probably waiting for a report about what I told the police and confirmation that I was dead.

"Is my car outside?"

"Yes."

"What about Alpha's car?"

"It's here, too."

"What is Robert driving?"

"A Ford Explorer."

I walked over to Williams and removed the sweatshirt and ballcap from his dead body.

"What are you doing?" Sheila.

"What's necessary."

I went back over to Gina and grabbed her jacket with my left hand and yanked her to her feet. I led her out of the warehouse front door. Sheila followed.

My Honda Accord was parked next to a Volvo S60. Williams must have traded the Beemer in. There was a dent in the front bumper that matched the one in the Accord's back bumper. Robert had my keys to my car, but I had a spare fob attached to a magnet underneath the trunk. I grabbed it and pushed the button to open the trunk and got what I needed, then handed my keys to Sheila.

"Take my car and drive somewhere safe, then call the police. Tell them whatever you want to."

"Where are you going?" Sheila.

"To talk to the boss."

CHAPTER FIFTY-FIVE

I SPED DOWN I-5 South in a dead man's car, slicing through floating sheets of fog. I got into Encinitas and stopped a half mile from Sandstrom's house on a residential street away from any lights.

My teeth ground against the pain in my finger.

I wore Williams' hoodie and ballcap. The sweatshirt, drenched in semi-viscous blood, clung to my skin. I got out of the car and walked to the trunk. The cool night air slipped through the two bullet holes in the sweatshirt and brushed against my bare skin.

Gina's wide brown eyes stared up at me when I opened the trunk. I ripped tape from her mouth. She recoiled in pain. Not as much pain as my finger.

Her ankles and calves were taped together.

"How do you contact Holland?" I shoved her phone down at her.

"Text."

"Show me the last text from her."

She took the phone in both hands, her wrists still wedded in duct tape. Five seconds later she held the phone up to me.

There were a string of texts to and from an unidentified person. The last one was sent from Gina's phone at 12:21 a.m. and read:

We have the package.

No response coming back.

"Did she call the dead guy in the warehouse Williams or Alpha?" I pointed the Glock I used to kill Dan Williams at her face.

"Just A." Message received.

"Text her that A has something she needs to see and that he's on his way."

Gina did as told. I grabbed the phone from her, reapplied the duct tape to her mouth, and shut the trunk.

I got back in the car and waited. Ten seconds later, the phone pinged the arrival of a text.

Was the package delivered? Holland was asking if I was dead.

I responded: *Yes.*

I waited a minute for a reply. None.

I pulled a dead man's car onto the Sandstroms' driveway a minute later. A black Ford Explorer was already parked there. Robert beat me to the house.

I got out of the car, careful to keep the bill of the dead man's cap between my face and the security camera above the front door. I put my throbbing bandaged hand in the pocket of the dead man's sweatshirt, where the gun was, and walked up to the front door. The sweatshirt was navy blue and hid the color of the blood.

I rang the bell. A full minute and no one answered. Finally, the click of the door.

I grabbed the Glock from the sweatshirt pocket and kicked the door with the sole of my boot the instant it started to open. It banged off something. I jumped inside. Robert lay on the marble tile fumbling for his gun. I shot him twice in the chest. The deafening booms echoed down the hallway. Robert's gun clanked down onto the marble floor. I kicked it aside. The rotten egg stink of burnt gunpowder clung to the wisps of smoke floating in the air. Robert lay still on the marble tile. Eyes open, unblinking. Blood oozed from the two bullet holes in his chest. One of the bullets must have penetrated his heart.

Dead.

"Robert?" Holland's voice, frantic but muted through my ringing ears.

Quickly, but quietly, I hustled down the hall in my Vibram-soled Gall duty boots.

Holland peeked around the corner of the hall just as I got there. She screamed. I shoved her back into the living room. She fell. I rushed forward.

"Linda?" A voice I didn't expect to hear. Bryson Basquez Jr. stood up from the sofa when he saw me. "What the fuck!"

"Sit." I pointed the gun at him.

He slid back down onto the couch. Terror in his eyes. I spun the gun down at Holland on the floor, who was scrambling, trying to crabwalk away from me on her hands and bare feet.

"Stop."

She did.

"Who else is in the house?"

"No one." Her voice quivered.

I walked over to her and stuck the gun in her face.

"If you lie, I'll paint your Terrazzo tile with your brains. Who else is in the house?"

"No one!" A spat tremor. "Scot is out of town. I swear."

"Get on the couch next to Junior." I spun the gun toward him, then back at her.

She slowly stood up from the floor, wide eyes on me the whole way, and walked over to the couch and sat down five feet from Junior.

"Closer. Right next to him."

Holland followed orders. I kept the gun on the couple and walked to the edge of the living room. I angled my head toward the hall that must have led to the bedrooms. Empty. Silence. I turned my attention back to the co-conspirators on the couch who had other people killed so they could live in ten-million-dollar homes above the Pacific Ocean.

"Rick. This could be the luckiest day of your life." The sultry voice from four days ago in this very house. Somehow, Holland had gone from sheer terror to under control in five seconds. Even her posture was relaxed. Reclined back into the sofa, one leg bobbing a foot over the other.

Her partner looked like a clenched fist. Terrified.

"Really?" I lowered the gun to my side. An invitation for a charge. I welcomed one.

"Being the smart private detective that you are, you probably already know that Johnson and Johnson is going to purchase Sequence Corp. It's all but a done deal. They're just finalizing the last few details. The deal should close at two point six billion. I own thirty-eight percent of the company. I'm about to be rich beyond my wildest dreams. You can be, too."

"You own thirty-eight percent? What about your husband? Doesn't he own it, too?"

"Dear Scot is merely a tool. He functions well when used correctly."

"So, you're offering to pay me off?" My face flat. My insides at stiletto point.

"I'm offering to change your life forever."

"How much do you think it will take to do that?"

"Fifty million is a nice round figure. Think of the life you could lead. No more snooping around in other people's garbage. You can live anywhere in the world you want."

My life was already changing forever in another six months. That's the life I wanted. If I could live that long.

"Tell me how it all started first. If you lie, I'll shoot you in the knee and wait for another lie. Do you understand?"

I raised the gun and fired. The bullet punctured the couch, a foot from Holland's shoulder. She and Junior jumped. Smoke curled out of the barrel of the Glock. The gunshot echoed thunder throughout the massive living room.

"Do you understand?"

"Yes!" The sea breeze cool, evaporated.

"What's Luke MacFarlane's role in all of this?"

"I introduced him to Gabby and they started dating. I didn't expect anything to come from it, but when he was hired by Sequence Corp to write the program to check the results of the Cancer Sweep DNA test, I kept him close."

"And you paid him to keep quiet about Cancer Sweep not working?"

"I didn't pay him anything." Her head shifted backwards. "He thought we'd quietly try to sell our shares when he told me. He thought he was doing me a favor. He didn't know about my relationship with Bryson or that things were too far along with the potential sale at that point."

Gabby must have given Luke the envelope full of cash when they realized things were too dangerous for him to stay in town.

"But the test is very close." Junior jumped in. Pride of ownership. "We'll get there."

After how many more dead bodies? But it was too early for that accusation. Holland was talking and telling me the truth, best I could tell. Which my phone in my pocket was recording.

"How'd you find out that Harkness planned to talk about Cancer Sweep on his podcast?"

"Luke." Holland. "He thought I was divesting so he wanted to make sure I'd sold my shares before Harkness went to air."

"So, Harkness had to die."

Holland shrugged her shoulders like it was the price of doing business. The microphone in my phone couldn't hear shoulder shrugs.

"Who killed him? Williams or Robert or both of them?"

"Both." Holland.

"And Luke was set up?"

"Not initially. We had somebody watching Harkness when Luke went to ConnectTech that night and everything fell into place. We got lucky."

And Luke got unlucky.

"But now Luke has to die, too," I said.

Neither of them said anything or looked at me.

"How did you two get hooked up?" I waved the Glock at Bryson Jr.

"The charity." Holland.

"And each could tell the other had a little larceny in their soul."

"Yes." Holland smiled. Completely in control. "And the sex."

"Why did Phillip Dewey have to die?"

"He didn't have to." Basquez. Adamant.

"He looked at Luke's early test results and told Bryson there was a discrepancy between those and the internal reports he was getting." Holland shook her head. "He started asking too many questions. The wrong questions."

"He didn't have to die." Basquez looked down and shook his head.

"But you supplied the drugs, right?" I pointed the Glock at Basquez. "You have a PhD in pharmacology. You knew what drugs could make a death look like a heart attack and where to get them."

Basquez didn't say anything.

"What about Gabby Dates? Why did she have to die?"

Basquez looked at the floor and shook his head, again.

"She was one smart cookie." Holland, admiration in her psycho-pathic voice. "She was working with Luke and turned him against me. I think the restraining order was just to make it look like they'd split up after Bryson questioned her about her relationship with Luke. Luke even got violent to really sell it."

"She risked her job to do the right thing." I thought of Gabby's crumbled body lying on sheets crimson with her blood. "And her life."

"Some kids these days are such self-righteous do-gooders that they forget to look out for their own best interests." Holland. No hint of responsibility for Gabby's death in her voice.

"But why did she have to die now?"

"The sale is only weeks away. We couldn't take any chances. We had someone break into her condo and get a look at her computer. She emailed Luke before he disappeared that she wanted to go to the press about Cancer Sweep. We couldn't allow that to happen." Holland pursed her lips and looked at Basquez. He stared at the floor.

"Why did you go to Gabby's condo the night Jim Harkness was murdered?" This to Junior.

"She invited me over." Junior continued to stare at the area rug beneath the sofa.

"She was flirting with him to try to get information about the po-tential sale." Holland, another perturbed look. "Rumors were swirl-ing about it at their office. But, let's talk about you, Rick. And fifty million dollars."

"You put out the order to kill me. Now we're friends?"

"That was business. Nothing personal. Now we have a new busi-ness arrangement. The past is the past." Her glittering blue eyes pierc-ing mine.

"Not for me."

The walls suddenly closed in. Two people on a couch in a luxurious house. I didn't know them. I didn't know how I got there. Excruciating pain in my right middle finger. I looked at it and saw that it was wrapped in duct tape. And my hand was holding a gun.

The woman said something to me, then gave a side glance to the man next to her. Sweat ran down into my eyes. I could feel air pulsating in and out of my slack mouth. The woman got off the couch and slowly walked toward me.

I stood still.

The woman eased over to my right side. A hand on mine. Then a void in my hand. The gun. The woman stepped back from me and raised her hands.

My eyelids fluttered. The fog started to lift.

Linda Holland stood in front of me and pointed Dan Williams' Glock 23 at my face.

CHAPTER FIFTY-SIX

I LET MY mouth remain slack and my eyes blank gazing at nothing beyond Holland. I couldn't let her know I was coherent. But if she pulled the trigger, it wouldn't matter.

Bryson Basquez Jr. stood by the couch.

"What are you going to do?"

"Kill him." Holland's voice, tight. Her body, rigid.

"Maybe that's not a good idea." Basquez. "There are already too many dead people connected to us."

I kept my eyes looking beyond Holland but concentrated my peripheral vision on her hands holding the gun. The finger of her right hand was on the trigger. Her left hand was wrapped around her right on the grip of the gun. The knuckles white with tension. Her left thumb was right behind the Glock's slide. My bet was that she'd never fired a gun before. Her death grip on the gun would probably cause the barrel to rise when she pulled the trigger. When the gun fired, the slide would snap backwards and pinch the skin on the inside of her left thumb. And the recoil would force the gun upward after she fired. If she missed the first shot, I might be able to get to her before she regained control of the gun.

Low odds on a gamble for my life. The only odds I had. Doing nothing was certain death.

Then I remembered my car. Getting something out of the trunk before I gave Sheila Perkins the spare key at the warehouse in Oceanside. Advice from a partner when I was a cop in Santa Barbara. Never go into battle outgunned.

"No one's going to find—" Holland.

I snapped down into a squat and spun my arm behind my back. Holland's gun exploded above me. I grabbed the Ruger .357 from my waistband, whipped it forward, and shot Holland twice in the chest just as she yelped in pain from the Glock's slide pinching her skin.

She dropped straight down; her left leg bent grotesquely underneath her body. The Glock clanked along the marble floor.

Basquez screamed. I leveled the gun on him. He stood, hands pressed against his face. He looked at me then slumped down onto the couch. No threat.

Linda Holland coughed and stared up at me. The brilliance in her eyes dimmed. I knelt next to her, set my gun on the floor, took off the sweatshirt that already had Dan Williams' dying blood on it, and pressed it down hard on the two bloody holes an inch apart in her once white blouse.

I took out my phone with my free hand and called 911.

"Nine-one-one. What's your emergency?" A woman's voice.

"Need an ambulance now." I gave her Holland's address. "Two gunshot victims. One dead, one in bad condition. I'm putting pressure on the wound right now."

"What is your name, sir?"

"Rick Cahill. The scene is secure. I'm the shooter. Self-defense. I'll be unarmed when the police get here."

"Please stay on the line with me until the police arrive."

"No. I need to help the victim." I hung up and used both hands to press the sweatshirt against the bullet holes in Linda Holland's chest. The sweatshirt already soaked with her fresh blood. Holland coughed and expectorated blood that landed on my arm. Fear in her eyes. Then vacant. The gleam that commanded attention in life, gone. I started chest compressions. Bloody bubbles percolated out her mouth.

"Is she dead?" A screech from Basquez on the couch.

I stopped the compressions, rolled her onto her side to let the blood drain out of her mouth, then rolled her back and blew two breaths into her mouth as I pinched her nose closed. I repeated the procedure even though I knew it was hopeless.

Basquez sobbed alone.

I'd killed before. Dan Williams wasn't my first, but, hopefully, Linda Holland was my last. I'd killed enough people that I had to think before I could come up with the number. And remember all their faces. Most had been in self-defense. Three had been murder. Cold-blooded, warm-blooded, it wouldn't matter if I was ever arrested for them. Life in prison, either way. The three I murdered had killed innocents and would have again if I hadn't killed them.

I'd lived my life by my late father's code. Sometimes you have to do what's right even when the law says it's wrong. The law, those who enforced it, and those who judged it, had different ideas.

I had regrets. Not about the people I'd killed. About the innocents I couldn't save. Those who were sucked into my vortex and died on my watch. I thought of them in the early morning when I couldn't sleep and my head jackhammered pain.

Almost every day.

Sirens sounded close by as I pumped Linda Holland's chest. Vehicles screeched to a stop outside. I stopped the CPR. Linda was gone and wasn't coming back.

I got up and kicked the Glock 23 that Holland had tried to shoot me with fifteen feet away. I took three steps away from my Ruger, which was already lying on the floor. I stood, legs splayed and arms like goalposts next to my head.

"Police!" Footsteps down the hallway. "Get down on the floor! Arms out to your sides!"

CHAPTER FIFTY-SEVEN

I WASN'T HOME when Leah got back from Santa Barbara. Didn't make my appointment with Dr. Andrews, either. Or Leah's appointment for the sonagram the next day.

I was in the county jail. Initially charged with murder. Two counts. Bryson Basquez Jr. told the sheriff's deputies that I invaded Linda Holland's home and killed Robert Fuentes and Holland in cold blood. Some truth in that when you leave out other specifics. April Mathewson, the real name of the woman I'd locked in the trunk of the Volvo who liked needles, had her own story about me. Tack on a kidnapping charge and another murder charge for Michael Dillman, alias Dan Williams.

I still had Sheila Perkins, who told Detectives Hartunian and Shane everything the way it really happened in the warehouse and before, on my side. And I had the recording I made at the Holland death house on my phone. The recording wasn't admissible in court because of the two-person recording consent law in California. That didn't mean the police and prosecutors from the district attorney's office wouldn't listen to it.

Still, two days after my arrest, I remained in jail. But April Mathewson was in jail now, too. In the Los Colinas Detention and Reentry Facility. Also known as the women's jail.

Leah visited me in the long, narrow concrete bunker visitation room. I'd been on her side of the glass a couple times over the years. The stench of desperation and fear was much worse where I now sat.

She looked like she hadn't slept since I woke her up predawn Saturday morning in Santa Barbara with a phone call from jail. The kind of stress you shouldn't put on a pregnant woman who'd suffered two miscarriages in her past. But I made a vow to myself in the back of the sheriff's deputy SUV that I wouldn't keep any more secrets from Leah. In or out of jail, the remainder of my life would be counted down in years, not decades. Time was too precious to spend any of it in deceit.

"Rick, are you alright?" Leah held the phone receiver to her ear on the other side of the glass. Dark rings under her eyes. Her hair back in a haphazard ponytail. But she looked as beautiful to me as she did the day I fell in love with her. "Let me see your hand."

I held up my now properly bandaged hand. Sill missing a fingertip, but the wound had been sewn up, and I had access to jail-prescribed pain meds.

"I'm good." Not a lie. The painkillers had somewhat numbed the pain and I was staring at the woman I loved, who in a few months would give birth to our child. And the woman who threatened Leah's life was in jail. The two killers she worked with were dead. April Mathewson had other things to worry about now. Like murder and kidnapping charges and how to avoid spending the rest of her life in prison. "Don't worry about me. Just make sure you get plenty of rest and eat for two."

"You're good? You're in jail and have been charged with murder." Eyes wide and voice loud enough for the other visitors on her side of the glass to hear. And maybe a couple inmates on my side. I didn't care. Might help my jailhouse cred.

"It will work out. I have an eyewitness who was kidnapped by the same people who kidnapped and tortured me." More of an ear witness for the mutilation of my finger. But Sheila had held the severed tip in her hand and I had the stub as proof.

She could testify that killing Dan Williams was in self-defense. He and I both reached for his gun at the same time. Maybe I didn't have to shoot him, but I was still partially strapped to a chair with Mathewson racing at me with a hypodermic needle full of propofol. I didn't have a choice. Kill or be killed.

Robert Fuentes was more problematic. I'd illegally entered Linda Holland's house, assaulted Fuentes while doing so, and shot him dead as he pulled his gun on me. Bryson Basquez Jr. told SDSO detectives that I'd broken into Linda Holland's house and held him and Linda hostage before I shot and killed her. The tape I recorded on my phone, while incriminating to him, mostly backed up his statement except for the final face-off with Holland.

I didn't have any friends in the Sheriff's Department or in the D.A.'s office. But Moira did and my lawyer, Ellison "Elk" Fenton, thought he had a decent chance at getting most of the charges dropped and avoiding a trial. He was doing his best to help the sheriff's detectives put all the pieces together to complete the whole jigsaw puzzle of Linda Holland and Bryson Basquez's criminal enterprise. Scot Sandstrom's culpability was in question.

Moira and I had separately downloaded everything we knew to Elk and he told the detectives all of it.

And we had Luke, who came in from the cold the night he found out Gabby was dead. Despite the messy condition of his apartment, Luke took meticulous notes. With Gabby Dates' help, he'd gotten an inside look at Bryson Jr's fraudulent scheme and chronicled all of it. And that Friday night at Linda Holland's condo, he'd found an email on her computer when she used the bathroom that confirmed that she and Bryson Junior were working together. He told Jim Harkness later that night at the ConnectTech office.

When he drove by the office early Saturday morning on his way to run on the beach, he saw Harkness' car parked in the same spot it had been Friday night. He stopped to check in and found Harkness' body. Instead of calling the police, he ran. But not until he bought burner phones for himself and Gabby to use and after she gave him a wad of cash in an envelope.

He stayed alive. Because of him, Bryson Junior would have zero credibility, once law enforcement saw the whole picture. At least, that's what Elk kept telling me.

But I had other concerns than just my own freedom. The woman staring at me across the glass and the child growing inside her.

"I need you, Rick." Tears slipped out of Leah's eyes. A hole opened up in my chest. "And our baby needs a father who's present in its life. I love you. You've given me a second chance to live. To have a family. I can't do this without you."

She pressed the receiver hard against her ear and leaned her forehead against the glass. Her voice, softer. "I know there are things about you that you don't want me to know. I don't care what they are. I know your heart. You're the best man I've ever known."

"We'll have that life together." Tears welled in my eyes and I pressed my forehead against the glass opposite hers. "With our child."

*　*　*

I had another visitor later that day. Moira MacFarlane.

She grabbed the phone on the opposite side of the glass.

"How's Luke?" I asked.

"He's in a lot of pain. Just like when his father died. But he's alive and safe." She let out a long exhale. Her eyes were bloodshot, probably from lack of sleep. "I should have gone with you to Gabby's house. None of this would have happened."

"Yes, it would have. Only there'd be two people behind bars with stubby middle fingers." I smiled. She didn't. "You know how it works, Moira. I play by my own rules and live with the consequences. And Elk Fenton will find a way to get me out of here soon, anyway."

"You can't live by your own rules anymore. What about your condition? Have you told Leah about it yet?"

"Not until I get out." Moira had chosen to be my friend when I didn't have many and really didn't want any. She'd saved my life and broken the law because of me. She'd tried and failed to rein in my impulses and been put in danger because of them. She saw the darkness in me, but had faith in the light. Because I was her friend, she accepted the rest. "I don't want to upset her more than she already is. She's got a baby to worry about."

"What?" Moira's voiced vibrated the phone in my ear. Joy in her face. Past all the agony she felt about her son, and me injured in jail. Joy.

"Yeah, I'm going to be a dad." My voice caught in my throat and tears welled in my eyes. "And I'm going to need some help."

I looked across at Moira. She was already crying.

* * *

Luke visited me the next day. A surprise. He looked thinner and much more pale than when I'd seen him last. He had an olive complexion but it had turned ashen during his week in hiding. Losing a loved one can bleed the life out of your skin, too.

"Thanks for trying to help my mom." Luke kept his head down as he spoke quietly into the phone receiver. Nothing aloof or arrogant about his speech now. Just sadness. "Sorry you ended up in here."

I had to be careful what I said. All jail phone calls and visitations are recorded.

"I owe your mom more than anyone will ever know. But it's not your fault or hers that I'm in here." The kid had enough weight on his heart. He didn't need or deserve any of mine.

Killers had threatened the woman I loved. I couldn't let that stand.

"I shouldn't have gone into hiding." He looked up at me. Dark, hollow eyes. Patches of stubble on his jawline from not shaving during his hideout. "I shouldn't have left Gabby alone."

"You can't take that on, either. Linda Holland and Bryson Basquez and the evil they hired killed Gabby. If you'd been with her, they would have killed you, too."

"I should have protected her." The last bit of color faded from his face and tears filled his eyes and he looked away.

"Luke." I waited until he looked back at me. "You did what you thought was right. You did the best you could. Mourn Gabby. Remember her. Allow yourself time to grieve. But don't feel responsible for her death. She'll always be a part of you, but you can't let her death be the end of your life. You have to cut the guilt loose now. Your life has changed. You have to make the best of what's left."

"That's easy for you to say." Sadness, not anger.

"No. It's not." It took me fifteen years to figure it out.

* * *

Three days later, Elk Fenton, with the help of Moira and Sheila Perkins, worked some magic with the D.A.'s office. My charges were reduced to a misdemeanor offense for negligent discharge of a fire-arm. I got out of jail with time served, paid a fine of $1,000, and had my conceal carry license revoked.

I could live with all of it. I wouldn't need a gun sitting behind a computer all day, anyway.

EPILOQUE

THE SALE OF Sequence Corp to Johnson and Johnson was quashed.

Charlene Dewey had Phillip Dewey's body exhumed and an autopsy performed. Trace levels of cyanide were found in the blood cells of his liver and spleen. The county medical examiner changed the manner of death to homicide.

Bryson Basquez was convicted on three counts of solicitation of murder. Phillip Dewey, Jim Harkness, and Gabriela Dates. April Mathewson was convicted of the first-degree murder of Phillip Dewey as she was determined to have administered the cyanide into Dewey's system as there was a needle mark found in the back of his neck and cyanide was found in a storage unit that she rented. Both Basquez and Mathewson were sentenced to life in prison.

Michael Dillman, aka Dan Williams, and Robert Fuentes had already been sentenced to death. The sentence carried out by me.

* * *

I was in the delivery room with Leah to see the birth of our daughter, Krista Moira Cahill. The moment I held Krista in my arms, that first touch of her skin, my heart opened up. The cloud on my soul lifted and I knew unconditional love for the first time in my life.

And I felt a responsibility greater than any I'd ever known. Or ever would.

* * *

Leah and Moira were both by my side in the hospital after the small tumor that had been hiding in the temporal lobe of my brain that was responsible for the fugue states was removed. No more foggy lapses. The headaches have lessened, but the diagnosis of CTE remains.

The prognosis from the removal of the tumor is good. The CTE is wait and see. But there are more grains of sand in the hourglass now. I've taken up crossword puzzles to stimulate my brain. The *New York Times* Sunday Crossword is a challenge, but I can usually knock it out in a couple sittings. And I have a healthy daughter who keeps me very active. Mentally and physically.

* * *

I was still bald when Leah and I were married. With a nice pirate scar on my scalp. Moira was my best man.

* * *

Krista is fourteen months old now and a fast learner. She has some athlete in her, too. She says "Dada" to make sure I'm looking, then flips a small rubber ball underhand in the backyard. Midnight lopes after it and drops it at her feet.

Dada.

Krista sometimes falls asleep with her head on Midnight's chest. He sleeps. And wakes. And licks her face.

And protects her with his life.

PUBLISHER'S NOTE

We hope that you enjoyed *Last Redemption*, the eighth novel in Matt Coyle's Rick Cahill PI Crime Series.

While the other seven novels stand on their own and can be read in any order, the publication sequence is as follows:

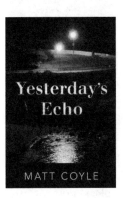

Yesterday's Echo
A dishonored ex-cop's
desperate chance for redemption

"Coyle knows the secret: digging into a crime means digging into the past. Sometimes it's messy, sometimes it's dangerous—always it's entertaining."

—Michael Connelly,
New York Times best-selling author

Night Tremors
Powerful forces on each side of the
law have Rick Cahill in the crosshairs

"Following an Anthony Award-winning debut isn't easy, but Matt Coyle slammed a homer. Hard, tough, humane— *Night Tremors* is outstanding" —Robert Crais,
New York Times best-selling and Anthony,
Macavity, and Shamus Award-winning author

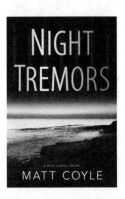

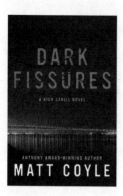

Dark Fissures

Hard-edged suspense with a heart
for fans of Robert Crais and Michael Connelly

"*Dark Fissures* is a roller coaster ride through the streets of San Diego. Tightly plotted with memorable characters. An outstanding read!"   —C. J. Box,
New York Times best-selling author

Blood Truth

Rick Cahill can't escape his past—or his father's

"Matt Coyle's protagonist, Rick Cahill, is haunted both by the sins of his father and by his own mistakes—but he's driven to find the truth, no matter where it takes him, and that's what makes this story so compelling. Coyle is the real deal, and [*Blood Truth*] is the best PI novel I've read in years, period."   —Steve Hamilton,
New York Times best-selling author

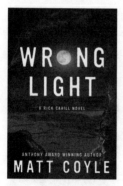

Wrong Light

Rick Cahill defies all limits in his quest for truth

"Coyle's fifth 'Rick Cahill' novel will please noir enthusiasts with its staccato prose, evocative descriptions, and hard-nosed protagonist. Readers new to the series can still enjoy this book as a compelling stand-alone mystery, and enticingly vague references to previous books make a strong case for checking out Rick's past adventures."
—*Library Journal*

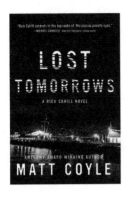

Lost Tomorrows

Perfect for hard-boiled PI fans who
like a tainted hero living by his own code

"Sharp, suspenseful, and poignant, *Lost Tomorrows* hits
like a breaking wave and pulls readers into its relentless
undertow. Matt Coyle is at the top of his game."

—Meg Gardiner,
Edgar Award-winning author

Blind Vigil

Every morning for the last nine months,
Rick Cahill has opened his eyes to total darkness

"Matt Coyle's seventh, and most intense novel to date, is a
visceral tour de force of the PI tradition. Emotionally
wrenching and haunting, the story got inside me and is yet
to go away. Bravo, Matt Coyle, for another wonderful
crime novel."   —T. Jefferson Parker,
New York Times best-selling author

We hope that you will read the entire Rick Cahill PI Crime Series
and will look forward to more to come.

For more information, please visit the author's website:
mattcoylebooks.com

Happy Reading,
Oceanview Publishing

M Coyle Matt
Coyle, Matt,
Last redemption /
22960002249455

2-22